Filled with dollops of drollery and an ancient evil, Black Brillion is a science fantasy caper that grows into a metaphysical exploration of the human psyche. Matt Hughes has crossed Jack Vance with Carl Jung to come up with a bold new novel of life on an Earth grown older by millions of years.

"Readers who enjoy the work of Philip K. Dick, H. P. Lovecraft and even Carl Jung will be amazed by Hughes' work in this realm. Readers who were only looking for a good mystery will be rewarded with reading riches beyond avarice.... Engaging, engrossing and exciting.... On this old Earth, *Black Brillion* is nothing less than a miraculous novel."
—*The Agony Column*

"If you're an admirer of science fantasies of Jack Vance, it's hard not to feel affection for the Archonate stories of Matthew Hughes.... Hughes has strengths of his own to draw upon—his own considerable wit, and a flair for reified metaphysics surpassing anything conceived by Vance.... *Black Brillion* is . . . a solid addition to the canon of Dying Earth literature. The Archonate is a well-conceived and evoked setting."
—*Locus*

"Hughes mixes his science and fantasy well and manages well in the difficult balancing act required to create believable stories mixing the two genres. The novel's unexpected denouement satisfyingly melds the science fiction and fantasy elements of the story . . . It seems likely that Hughes will create more stories in Archonate series, and I look forward to reading more tales set in Old Earth. Fans of Jack Vance will not be disappointed by this incursion of Matthew Hughes into Vance's science fantasy territory."
—*Science Fiction Weekly*

Black Brillion

A Novel of the Archonate

Matthew Hughes

A TOM DOHERTY ASSOCIATES BOOK
NEW YORK

TOR

BLACK BRILLION

Copyright © 2004 by Matt Hughes Company, Ltd.

Edited by David G. Hartwell

A Tor Book
Published by Tom Doherty Associates, LLC
175 Fifth Avenue
New York, NY 10010

www.tor.com

Tor® is a registered trademark of Tom Doherty Associates, LLC.

ISBN 0-765-35049-1
EAN 978-0-765-35049-7

First edition: November 2004
First mass market edition: October 2005

Printed in the United States of America

0 9 8 7 6 5 4 3 2 1

To Mike Berro and all the gang
on the Jack Vance bbs

Black
Brillion

Luff Imbry came to Sherit on the shuttle from Olkney, traveling comfortably on a red-tab first-class travel voucher. The ticket had begun as a blue-ordinary, but soon encountered a small but useful device of Imbry's own manufacture, which bedecked it in an electronic mirage that fooled the shuttle's automatic scanners. At ease in the red-tab compartment's sumptuous lounge, the fraudster helped himself to a smattering of delicacies from the circulating buffet and accepted a glass of quite decent golden Phalum.

At Sherit's main terminus, Imbry's appearance excited no comment. His only outstanding feature was a pronounced corpulence but even this he used to his advantage, contriving his features into an arrangement that conveyed benign geniality, the image of the jolly fat fellow. His garb was also commonplace in Sherit that year: a voluminous jacket of dark patent leather over flared pantaloons patterned in contrasting stripes of red and white, with shoes that matched the leather and a hat that echoed the cloth.

He recovered his carryall bag from the here-you-are, then wove his way through the crowds of travelers to the ring road outside. There he spied a passing omnibus that bore the name of the Trabboline Inn. The slow-moving conveyance was trolling for in-bound travelers who had not yet reserved lodgings, its illuminated sides displaying the Trabboline's rates and attractions.

Luff Imbry assembled his face into a pleasing distribution of smiles and winks, then stepped aboard and spoke affably to the vehicle's operator, a stubby person with pale hair and eyes whose gender remained indeterminate under the baggy one-piece work garb typical of lower-class Sheritics. The response was brusque, somewhat more than a grunt although not quite an actual syllable, but Imbry was not so easily put off.

"I believe the Trabboline offers discrete classes of accommodation," he said, "from Green Basic to Platinum Superior?"

The inquiry drew a confirmatory sound from deep in the Sheritic's throat.

"And Platinum Superior is available only to persons of the renunciant class?"

This time the answer was more growl than grunt. Imbry had uncovered a raw patch on the driver's psyche. He proceeded to abrade it. "I am impressed by the renunciant concept," he said. "The wide world marvels at the wisdom of Sheritics in having created such a beneficial institution."

At this, the Sheritic voiced a short word that expressed an uncomplimentary assessment of Imbry's views, then reached up and pulled down a folding divider that insulated the operator's compartment from passengers. The vehicle jerked as it picked up speed.

Luff Imbry settled back in his seat and regarded the passing scenery with happy anticipation. The driver's smoldering anger had ignited at the mere mention of Sherit's highest social class. Tensions were clearly rising. Conflict and dislocation were in the offing, a situation from which Imbry expected to profit substantially.

He alighted in the portico of the Trabboline, a sprawling

seven-story complex of yellow stone and white stucco. The lobby was spacious and quiet, the staff alert and attentive to their guests' needs. Imbry asked for the kind of room favored by commerciants traveling on moderate expense allowance, offering a credit authorization that he had abstracted from its rightful owner and adapted to his own ends. The clerk returned it to him with a discreet flourish, calling Imbry by the name that happened to be impressed on the chit—Florion Tobescu—and adding the general Sherit honorific, "Recipient."

"I am curious as to your renunciants," he told the clerk. "Where might I expect to see some of them?"

The Sheritic raised his nose to a considerable height. His eyes now seemed to regard Imbry from the far side of an unbridgeable gap. "I regret, Rp. Tobescu, that casual sightseeing is felt to be an imposition," he said.

"Just so," said Imbry. "Still, if one were inclined to cast an unobtrusive glance in the direction of a renunciant, which direction would you recommend?"

The clerk looked away, but one hand fluttered toward an archway on the far side of the lobby. The entrance was blocked by a braided rope of gold slung between two stanchions, and attended by a brisk-looking man wearing a uniform that identified him as either a military officer of overwhelming rank or a menial employed to admit or deny passage beyond the barrier. Idly perambulating through the lobby, Imbry placed himself so as to glance through the archway. It led to a short corridor that soon curved out of sight. He noticed distinct differences in the quality of decor on either side of the braided rope. The carpet beyond was of a deeper pile, its color richer than that which covered the lobby floor. The walls were clad in a fabric that shimmered delicately through several muted shades of pink and gray.

A warm scent hung in the air, unrecognizable yet tantalizing.

Imbry approached the corridor's guardian. "May I enter?" he said.

The doorman looked him up and down in less time than it would take to describe the inspection. "No, recipient. This part of the hotel is for renunciants only."

"Yet I am intrigued," said Imbry. "I must know what lies beyond."

"First acquire a fortune and shed it to the benefit of the Divestment," said the guardian. "I shall then be glad to admit you."

"I might do as you suggest," said Imbry, "but how do I know if the reward is worth the effort? Let me sample the delights reserved for renunciants and I will surely be motivated to better myself."

The man stiffened and said, "You are an outlander and perhaps not aware that your proposition borders on the offensive. Please entertain yourself elsewhere."

Imbry leaned closer and lowered his voice to a conspiratorial murmur. "I don't suppose a quiet contribution could persuade you to look in another direction while I accidentally wander into this hallway?"

The doorman's eyes grew large and a deeper color welled from his neck into his face. "You are now across the border of offensiveness and flush with the gates of criminality. Leave immediately, recipient, or I will summon the provost. Confined to the Contemplarium, you will experience a standard of accommodation much at variance with what you see here."

Imbry converted his face into an image of apology, made placatory gestures with his plump hands, and eased away. Clearly, not every Sherit menial was ready to turn on the renunciants, but this loyal guardian's quickness to take offense still echoed an underlying carrier wave of social tension.

Seated in an overstuffed chair on the other side of the Trabboline's lobby, a slim young man named Baro Harkless watched Luff Imbry's encounter with the doorman from the corner of one eye while feigning interest in a periodical. Had he wanted to, he could have surreptitiously eavesdropped on the conversation, could have recorded it in both image and sound, could even have measured the autonomic responses of both men. The equipment for such surveillance was secreted about his person, but Baro was operating on the assumption that Imbry was cunning enough to take habitual measures to determine if he was under observation. Consequently, the agent restricted himself to level-two passive observation, as specified in the surveillance handbook of the Archonate Bureau of Scrutiny, which he had memorized entirely, along with every other manual and standing order that governed Bureau operations.

When Imbry had recrossed the lobby and stepped into an ascender tube, Baro went to the desk. "I believe I just saw an acquaintance take the ascender," he told the clerk, "though his name temporarily escapes me."

The clerk gave him a look that indicated no wish to learn more about Baro Harkless's acquaintances, past, present, or future. "The recipient is a guest of the hotel. His privacy may not be trod upon."

Baro looked about to ensure that no one was within hearing, then produced a card that identified him as a Bureau agent, though he covered the part of the card that defined his status as still probationary. "Perhaps we might tread just a little."

Archonate authority could not be gainsaid. "He is Rp. Florion Tobescu, a traveling commerciant."

"And what room?"

"West eighteen on the seventh floor."

"What does the window of that room look out upon?" Baro asked, and learned that Imbry had a view of the hotel's inner courtyard, which contained a formal garden and an outdoor refectory.

"Thank you," he said. "Now I would like a room across the courtyard, with a window that looks in on his."

The clerk worked the keys of an instrument set below the level of the counter, then indicated where the young man should press his palm to a sensor. "And the account?" he asked.

"To the attention of Directing Agent Ardmander Arboghast, Bureau headquarters in Olkney," Baro said. "And of course you will say nothing to the person we have been discussing."

The clerk sniffed. "Of course."

Established in a room directly opposite Imbry's, Baro resumed level-two surveillance: that is, he sat in a shadowed part of his room and stared through the two intervening thicknesses of glass and the expanse of air that separated them. The target of his steadfast gaze had reposed himself upon the bed, with his hands clasped behind his head. He appeared to have fallen asleep.

Baro watched the even rise and fall of Imbry's rounded abdomen and thought, not for the first time, about contacting Directing Agent Arboghast. He knew that he was technically breaching procedure, and that by following the quarry from Olkney to Sherit he had overstepped the terms of his assignment.

His section chief had ordered him only to shadow the swindler about the city for the day, then compose a written report. It had been a training exercise, the target chosen from a Bureau list of career felons who were not regarded as dangerous and who were not targets of active investigations. Baro Harkless had been sent on the training drill because, although he had graduated with high marks from the Academy, he had not completed his field training.

There were rumors about Arboghast, that he had been transferred to the training command from the investigations branch after a major case came apart in his hands. There were hints of other faults besides. Baro paid no heed to gossip, but he did know that Arboghast was a man of strong opinions. The weight of those opinions, when they were landing on probationary agents, was equivalent to that of a moderate-sized boulder.

Baro had begun the day loitering near Imbry's lodgings in the fashionable Quabbs district of Olkney City. When his target came down to the street, he had followed the man, at the prescribed distance and using available opportunities for concealment, to a local bistro where Imbry breakfasted on cakes and punge. The fraudster had then gone home, but reemerged almost immediately with carryall in one hand, the other raised to hail a passing jitney. Fortunately, another vehicle for hire was passing, and Baro managed to get into it before Imbry was out of sight.

Their destination turned out to be Olkney's main airdrome, where the trickster had apparently booked passage on the Sherit shuttle. By the time Baro reached the wicket and obtained a ticket, the airship had already begun running up its gravity obviators in preparation for departure. There was no time to contact his superior. The young man threw himself along the connecting tube into the blue-ordinary compartment just as the crew was closing the aircraft's door.

En route to his seat, he looked about for Imbry, and felt something cold climb his spine as he realized that his quarry was not in any of the blue-tab seats. Had the swindler spotted him for a clumsy neophyte and decided it would be a good joke to gull the greenhorn into a long and pointless trip out of town? A droplet of chill sweat ran between Baro's shoulder blades as he imagined the ensuing conversation with Arboghast. It would involve a great deal of standing at quivering attention on his part, while the section chief indulged his well-known proclivity for inventive profanity and unflattering rhetorical questions.

He rose, and was about to ask the cabin attendant to halt the aircraft's departure. But the crewman was busy pulling closed the curtain that separated red-tab travelers from blue-ordinaries. Behind the cloth, first-class passengers lolled, freed of any uncomfortable awareness that, nearby, fellow human beings were crammed into seats designed to suit only the abnormally short and underweight. Beneath the attendant's raised arm, as the curtain was drawn, Baro caught a brief glimpse of his quarry hoisting a goblet of golden wine in first class.

The sweat evaporated from Baro's brow and he sank back into the undersized seating. He comforted himself: whatever else Imbry was up to, he could now be charged with fraudulent conversion of a travel authority. As well, although it was not an offense to have unknowingly frightened an agent of the Bureau, Baro meant for Imbry to learn that it was nonetheless a bad idea.

Now, as the probationary agent sat in his hotel room and watched Imbry sleep, his mind again reluctantly turned to Ardmander Arboghast. The lull in activity afforded him ample opportunity to make contact with his section chief, yet Baro did not do so. His thinking was leading him in other directions.

He had definitely overstepped when he had followed Imbry out of Olkney, and there was no guarantee that Arboghast would accept his protestations of being too hurried to make contact. He sensed that there was a mutual lack of empathy between his commander and himself. His explanations, no matter how cogent, might therefore meet with automatic dismissal.

He could find himself branded unsuitable for field assignments. Instead, as his Academy tutor, Bost Hamel, had recommended, he might be consigned to the desert of the Bureau's research branch, to spend his career coaxing correlations and coincidences out of endless data banks.

The prospect of forty years in the research office was not what had drawn Baro into the Bureau. It had been a desire to follow in the footsteps of his father, Captain-Investigator Baro Harkless, who had blazed a brilliant career in the investigations branch—or at least the first half of a brilliant career.

His father had died in the crash of an aircar while bringing Cham Fretilin, the selective cannibal, to face justice. The aircar's controls had failed over a populated area. Unable to prevent its fall, Captain Harkless had wrestled with the steering yoke, managing to guide the aircraft into the sea.

Now, watching Luff Imbry, Baro knew that if he were to make contact with Directing Agent Arboghast when he could report nothing but the presence of a somnolent criminal on a hotel bed, his career within the Bureau might be diverted into unwelcome channels. On the other hand, if Luff Imbry were to lead him to an actual offense in progress—and he had no doubt that crime was the trickster's aim—then Baro could swoop like an unsuspected nemesis at the appropriate cusp and affect an arrest.

That would give him undiluted credit for scotching Imbry's scheme, an accomplishment sure to outweigh any quibbles over whether or not he had reported in quite as often as was stipulated in the manual on surveillance.

He allowed himself a few moments to savor images of Imbry's apprehension, then replayed it with various changes. He also mentally constructed an encounter with Directing Agent Arboghast, in which the section chief gruffly sought forgiveness for doubting his qualities.

His ruminations completed, Baro settled back in the chair and resisted a tinge of envy as he watched Luff Imbry breathe. He wondered how a man who had devoted his life to fleecing his fellow citizens could so easily find the solace of sleep. He decided that consciences, like most other human attributes, came in various strengths and sizes; Imbry's inner voice was apparently a pale and puny specimen, in inverse proportion to his outer bulk.

Baro's conscience, however, was robust. It was again nudging him toward making contact with Ardmander Arboghast. To distract himself, he recalled the forger's curiosity about the section of the Trabboline reserved for members of the renunciant class. Since this was the only feature of Sherit in which Imbry had taken an interest, Baro reasoned that it might have some relation to his presence here.

He spoke aloud. "Hotel integrator?"

"What do you require?" came a smoothly modulated voice that seemed to originate from the nearby air.

"Information regarding the renunciants."

"There is quite a lot of it. What degree of detail do you require?"

"Enough to satisfy a tourist's idle interest."

A screen appeared in the air before him, and was immediately filled with printed information. Baro began to read, then paused to ask the integrator to render the screen and text semitransparent, so that he could keep an eye on the recumbent forger across the courtyard. Returning to the text, the young man became acquainted with Sherit's peculiar institution.

The renunciants had been created centuries before, when stresses and pressures within the Sherit societal matrix had threatened to tear the community apart. The problem had arisen from a worsening inequality in the distribution of wealth. A small segment of the population, whose members demonstrated ruthless inventiveness in commercial matters, had come to control most of the total worth of the Sherit polity. The vast majority of the Sheritics shared the minority portion that was left. They eked out an increasingly impoverished existence in which none of them ever had too much, and most rarely had even enough. Generation upon generation, the few who enjoyed abundance managed to pile up yet more, while the many mired in poverty saw their scant portions further shrunk.

The divide between the two unequal parts of Sherit society gradually widened into a chasm. Resentments festered on both sides. The rich told each other that the poor suffered the consequences of their own innate lack of initiative; the wealthy were entirely deserving of the fruits of their strivings, even when the strivings had actually been undertaken by some long-dead ancestor. The poor told themselves that it was wrong that a handful should live in sybaritic splendor while a multitude swinked and sweated for a daily crust that grew ever meaner. Neither solitude felt much inclination to speak to the other, and even less to listen. But both were becoming aware that revolution roiled and rumbled on the horizon.

The rich had begun to fortify their manors and the poor had taken to fashioning simple but brutally effective weapons, when a novel and unlikely solution appeared. No one was quite sure whence the concept originated—some suggested that the idea had been planted by the Archon himself, wandering the world incognito—but suddenly a few of the younger plutocrats let it be known that they were willing to forgo their inheritances. They offered to donate all of their assets to a new institution called the Divestment, which would hold the wealth as a perpetual trust. Moreover, each citizen of Sherit would receive an equal dividend from the trust's profits. In return, those who gave up their riches to the Divestment were rewarded with a newly created exclusive social rank—the renunciant class—which entitled its members to special preferences and distinctions.

A renunciant need never pay for anything, be it a twelve-course feast in Sherit's most exclusive restaurant, or a roast chestnut from a street vendor's wagon. He or she could step into any conveyance, public or private, and ride farefree, saunter to the front of any queue. Whatever was required, a renunciant had only to put out a hand and it was filled. And filled gladly. At first, of course, the common folk suspected that the proposal was some ruse of the rich, but as more and more of the elite joined the movement—and as the first dividend payments arrived—the new institution caught fire in the popular imagination. People began to compete for the honor of serving their benefactors.

Most of Sherit's plutocrats soon saw the wisdom of relinquishing their holdings to the Divestment, so that they might reap the adulation and the very substantial material benefits that only renunciants could command. Why be hated for heaped-up treasure when one could ascend to a rank that conferred all the essential perquisites of wealth as well as the adoration of the populace?

The Divestment soon came to embrace the combined wealth of almost the entire Sherit ownership class. Those few magnates who could not bring themselves to part with their hoards found themselves isolated from their former peers. They were pitied and derided, their impatient heirs waiting for the death that would usher them into the new elite.

Meanwhile, the flood of wealth that Divestment dividends poured into the pockets of the formerly dispossessed Sheritics created a vibrant economy at all levels of society. The most enterprising recipients soon found ways to make their money propagate, and before long were founding new fortunes. But now the rising rich pursued wealth with only one end in sight: to amass enough to meet the Divestment's standard for donation, thus qualifying the donor to "take platinum" and be elevated to renunciant rank.

Meanwhile, many in the commerciant class strove to win the favor of the supremes. Restaurants preferred by renunciants, even though they dined in segregated rooms, became wildly popular with those who were not quite rich enough to approach the Divestment. Haberdashers who outfitted the cream of Sherit found their designs in mass demand. Any enterprise entitled to advertise itself "used by renunciants" enjoyed a swelling flow of recipient customers. Some merchants grew so prosperous by fulfilling the rarefied expectations of renunciants that they were eventually able to divest themselves of their earnings and join those they had formerly served. Without exception, they did so.

Under the Divestment, Sherit society achieved a dynamic equilibrium. The circulating wealth bred upon itself and multiplied through the economic matrix. The best and bravest of the recipients used their dividends to struggle up through the layers, aiming to reach a level at which they could live in penniless abundance. The culture demonstrated harmony and vigor, and the Divestment was regarded throughout Sherit as a pinnacle of social development.

Some found a minor flaw in the system: renunciants who traveled abroad received a more than comfortable stipend from the trust, but still found themselves enjoying a less luxuriant standard of existence than they were accustomed to at home. The original articles of incorporation decreed that the purpose of the institution was to benefit Sherit; why export the county's wealth to outlanders? Besides, it was felt that nothing available outside Sherit's borders could match the exquisiteness of the fine stuffs created for renunciants by the Sheritics themselves, so the point was moot.

Baro paused in his reading and asked the hotel integrator, "Have there been any strong representations from Sheritics wishing to alter the terms of the trust?"

The hotel replied, "Some years back, there was a discussion about increasing the stipend to allow renunciants to live abroad in the style to which they are accustomed."

"Who opened the discussion, and why?"

"A few young commerciants. They felt that renunciant status brought a disadvantage to those who enjoyed gadding about beyond the county's borders."

"What happened to them?"

"The College of Trustees declined to alter the Divestment's Grand Charter. Some of the petitioners left the county without taking platinum. The others donated their fortunes when they became grand enough and were duly accepted as renunciants. They are now themselves members of the College. So all is as it should be."

Baro decided that as the guiding intelligence of a fine hotel, the integrator was disposed to err on the side of conservativism. Besides, the young man's training had encouraged him not to accept bland assurances. "How may I contact the College?" he asked.

"They do not welcome casual inquiries," said the hotel.

"I am an agent of the Bureau of Scrutiny. My interest concerns a possible offense," said Baro, producing his identifying card.

"Probationary agent," said the hotel's integrator, whose visual percepts were more exact than the eyes of the front desk clerk, though both man and machine seemed to be afflicted with the same disdainful sniff.

The young man cleared his throat. "True," he said, "and you are at liberty to refuse a probationer's query, although that may mean that someday you will see me return fully fledged at the head of an audit team."

"Audits disrupt our operations," said the hotel. "Guests are discommoded."

"The Bureau's suspicions are easily aroused, and once an investigation is begun, we fearlessly follow wherever it may lead. I must inform you that your reluctance to answer my innocuous question has already set my curiosity to tingling."

The hotel muttered something Baro couldn't quite catch, although it might have included the phrase "cranny-poking scroot." Then the voice said, in its normal plummy tones, "As it happens, this afternoon the Divestment holds an annual general meeting at its headquarters on South Hoadeyo Prospect. All the trustees will be present."

"Is the meeting open to the public?"

"It is not closed," said the hotel, in a tone that somehow indicated a shrug.

The young man thought for a moment, then asked, "What time is the meeting?"

"Three hours past meridian."

Another thought occurred to the agent. "Has Florion Tobescu asked for a wake-up call?"

The hotel confirmed that he had.

"For what time?"

"Two and a half hours after meridian."

Baro thought some more. "What kind of matters are decided at the meeting?" he asked.

"Policy matters," said the hotel. "Investment strategies. Recipients consider it ungracious to pry into the College's deliberations; it is like receiving a gift, then sending it out to be valued."

"Nonetheless," said Baro, "have any recent decisions of the College generated controversy?"

The hotel's answer was a while in arriving. "It is not a subject for polite conversation."

"We are not having a polite conversation. In fact, I am beginning to think of this as an investigation in its formative stages."

"They are no more than vile rumors," said the voice, "scurrilous natterings of envious malcontents. Decent recipients pay no heed."

"The Bureau weighs decency on its own scales," said Baro. "What is the nature of these rumors?"

The hotel was not forthcoming, but in the next few minutes Baro Harkless coaxed some snippets of information from its data banks. The hotel integrator knew little, and most of what it could tell him had been gleaned from overheard conversations among menial employees.

When he had heard all there was to hear, the agent asked to see the articles of incorporation that governed the Divestment's operations. The document appeared on the screen and he read it quickly, making notes on his investigator's pad. The articles were thick with formal legalisms and convoluted phraseology, but the young man was not fazed. Bost Hamel had judged him a fine ferret when it came to winkling the meat out of a text. But Baro had begged him to mute his praises, so as not to dim his dream of becoming a field agent. Still, he would admit to himself that his talent for finding just the right thorn in a thicket of legalistic prose could be useful. He made a few more notes, then examined his findings. A pattern had emerged.

He dismissed the hotel integrator's screen and asked to be connected with the local office of the Bureau of Scrutiny. After a brief conversation, he settled back in his chair to watch Luff Imbry sleep.

———•—•———

Luff Imbry talked his way past both the College's doorman and receptionist by claiming that the trustees anxiously awaited the sheaf of papers under his arm. In moments he was through the portal and across the elegant lobby and thrusting open a door on which a small placard announced that a meeting was in progress.

The boardroom was the most beautifully decorated space that had ever felt the presence of Luff Imbry. The balance of proportions and colors was masterful. Every detail, from the quality of the light filtering through the chambrasoie curtains to the exquisite mix of colors in the carpeting, bespoke an epitome of tasteful assurance that the fraudster, whose own standards were not unrefined, found quietly intimidating. Around a table of dark wood, its surface so polished as to seem a pool of rich liquid, five men and two women, all in their middle years, each coiffed and accoutered to perfection, sat in plushly superlative chairs. At the head of the table a frosted blonde in a suit of ivory and turquoise looked in Imbry's direction as he burst through the door but calmly completed the sentence she had begun before he entered.

". . . those in favor?"

A chorus of "ayes" came from around the table as all watched the intruder advance toward them.

"Nay," said Luff Imbry, reaching the table.

Seven flawless heads performed an identical motion, combining a brief shudder and a sharp elevation of the chin. "By what right do you say 'nay'?" said a completely bald man in maroon and silver who had had embedded in the skin on the left side of his face, from his temple to the corner of his epicurean lips, a crescent line of precious stones that captured all the colors of fire.

"By right of these proxies," said Imbry, fanning out a ream of printed paper onto the lustrous tabletop.

The bald man glanced at one of them. "Forgeries," he said.

"Goodness," said Imbry. He reconstructed his features into an image of astonished innocence. "We must immediately summon the provost."

Silence descended. The woman at the head of the table looked up at where the receptionist had poked his head tentatively around the door and waved the functionary away. Then she looked to each of the other trustees in turn, her delicately shaped eyebrows forming twin bows as far above her azure eyes as they would reach. She received six nods in reply.

"What do you seek, recipient?" she asked.

"A seat at this table, to begin with," Imbry said.

The woman hesitated the briefest of moments before gesturing to a chair that stood against the wall. It silently made its way to the table, and the forger sat down. It was not just the most comfortable furniture he had ever known; it gave a new definition to the experience of sitting. He sighed, then said, "I hereby withdraw my nay and vote all my proxies in concurrence with the other trustees. However, when we get to that part of the agenda in which new business may be considered, I will move a few motions."

The renunciants exchanged glances. "Within reason," said a thin-faced man in a suit of softly iridescent gray stuff.

"To be sure," said Imbry. "Like you, I have no wish to destroy the Divestment, only to dine upon it."

The trustees made small noises of helpless distaste. Imbry allowed himself a smile and rubbed his plump palms together as if he rolled between them the warm, yeasty dough of great expectations.

"You will dine no better than any other felon," said a voice from the doorway, "as you stare at the uncompromising walls of the Contemplarium."

Imbry looked up and saw the doorway filled by the black and green uniforms of the Bureau of Scrutiny. Before them stood a slim young man who was plainly struggling to keep a stern expression on a face that longed to split into a delighted grin.

Imbry swore. "It's the scroots," he said.

"Indeed," said the young man. "I am Agent Baro Harkless and you are taken."

"Thank goodness for the Bureau," said the chair of the College. "However, there is no call for extremes. This is only a civil matter, and our legalists can well manage it."

"When I said, 'you are taken,' " Baro told her, "I used the pronoun in its most inclusive sense. This man is apprehended for forgery and extortion, the rest of you for fiduciary malfeasance and breach of trust." He motioned the agents forward. "Seize them."

———◆———

Baro could tell that Ardmander Arboghast was displeased but he felt that the section chief could not deny that results outweighed any technical defaults. Not only had Baro apprehended eight malefactors—including Imbry, whom the Bureau had vainly pursued for years—but he had prevented a potentially disastrous dislocation of Sherit County's social cohesion, preserving an institution that had much to recommend it.

Arboghast must be a fair man, else how could he have risen to his present rank in the Bureau? So Baro told himself. The section chief would have to admit that there had been more than mere luck involved in the taking of Imbry and the others. True, Baro had ended up in Sherit by a fluke, but he had shown good investigative instincts when he began rooting about in the Divestment's articles of incorporation and discovered the same wrinkle that Luff Imbry had detected.

These factors Baro turned over in his mind as he stood at rigid attention before Arboghast's desk. It had already been a busy morning for the young man, including a summons to the Senior Training Provost's office where he was informed that further probation had been waived. A full agent's pips now adhered to his epaulets as he waited for his superior to hand him his first field assignment. But Arboghast was letting him wait while he once again perused the case summary.

The report detailed how the young commercials had not given up after their efforts to persuade the College to dispense more largesse on behalf of renunciants living abroad had been rebuffed. They had instead got themselves named to the College of Trustees, a somnolent body that few craved to join. After centuries, the Divestment had become staff-run; the policy-making board did little more than meet annually to approve whatever the senior mandarins recommended.

Once they had achieved control, the new board members replaced key senior staff with lackeys who shared their frame of reference. With the aid of coconspirators established outside the county, they quietly diverted vast funds—including their own recently donated fortunes—into newly formed pools of wealth outside Sherit, from which they could draw when they went abroad. No other Sheritic, recipient or renunciant, knew of their embezzlement; only the conspirators knew that they had broken the compact that kept Sherit a place of peace and good order.

But they had made one error. Of necessity, they had had to deal with persons of dubious reputation to create the out-of-county pools of capital. It was inevitable that someone like Luff Imbry, swimming the back channels of Olkney's criminal underground, would become aware of one of these secret repositories. Once the swindler had traced the tainted money's ownership back to the Divestment, he began to investigate the institution.

Every person who received a dividend from the trust—that is every adult citizen of Sherit—was entitled to vote at the annual general meeting. Recipients who chose not to attend could authorize someone else to cast their votes by signing a proxy. Those who did not attend and did not send a proxy were deemed to have automatically delegated their voting rights to the College. In the long ago, when the institution was first formed, many ordinary Sheritics would attend the yearly meetings, but no recipient had attended one of them in generations.

Luff Imbry had prepared a mass of forged proxies, which if accepted would entitle him to a seat on the board. He never expected the highly dubious documents to pass, but he counted on the trustees' recognizing that exposure of his fraud would bring an official inquiry, revealing their own indecencies. To enhance the odds that the trustees would accede to his blandishments, the swindler visited Sherit on a number of occasions in the months before the meeting, spreading rumors among the lower echelons of society about renunciants who only feigned giving up their fortunes for the common good, and who lived abroad in riotous splendor on diverted funds. By the time the annual general meeting was held, an undercurrent of anger was rising among Sherit's lowest layers. The trustees were aware that sudden exposure would almost certainly bring them a loss of status, wealth, and, probably, liberty.

Arboghast put aside the report. The section chief looked up and inspected Baro with flinty eyes. Baro was again aware of a mutual antipathy between them, though he could not account for it. It was as if they were members of different species that should never be harnessed together. He wondered if the man had known his father.

"I knew your father," Arboghast said and Baro had to exert maximum control not to display a startled reflex. He experienced a moment's dread that Arboghast could read his mind, a terrifying prospect in light of some of the thoughts Baro had entertained regarding the section chief during his training. But telepathy was impossible in humans, Baro knew.

"We were classmates at the Academy. He was the most upright man I ever knew," Arboghast said in a voice devoid of sentiment. He cleared his throat and continued. "I am pleased to inform you that the Archon himself has sent a letter of commendation to be included in your personal file. Congratulations."

Baro somehow contrived to inject even greater rigidity into a posture that had already transcended the last vestiges of flexibility. "Thank you, sir," he said, through lips that barely opened.

"The Archon has also directed that you be assigned to field work. I have an immediate assignment for you, again at the Archon's personal order."

Baro knew that his eyes had grown larger and he struggled to keep his face immobile as befitted a Bureau agent receiving any news. Whether it was an announcement that he had been named First High Commissioner or that he was to be summarily executed, the true scroot would take it in with mouth set in a firm line and eyes boring straight ahead.

"This," said Arboghast, tapping a file folder precisely centered on his otherwise empty desk, "contains all the information you will require, as well as your full agent's plaque."

The section chief picked up the file and Baro almost broke attention to reach for it, but realized just in time that his superior had not yet offered it. The Directing Agent was tapping the edge of the file against his open palm and looking off into the middle distance.

"This is Archon business," he said. "We do not ask why you have been selected nor why the Archon has ordained that I am to be your sole contact. You will observe the strictest undercover protocols. You will not draw weapons or equipment from Bureau stores and you will maintain complete communications silence until you make an arrest. You will then contact me, and only me. Is that clear?"

"Yes, sir!"

"As you are aware," Arboghast said, "these assignments are often entrusted to pairs of operatives. I have already chosen your partner." A small smile appeared in the corners of the section chief's hard mouth as he handed over the file. "He is outside."

Baro accepted the folder, crisply executed the gesture appropriate to the difference in their ranks and their presence indoors, then spun on his heel and departed the room. He was back almost immediately.

"Sir," he said, "permission to speak."

"By all means," said Arboghast, giving Baro his stoniest glare, though the small smile stayed on his lips. "Blaze away."

"I have a strong opinion on your choice of partner for me," said Baro.

The Directing Agent compressed his smile and regarded the young man without comment for a moment that stretched into several others. Then he said, "Look out the window at that row of wissol trees beyond the garden wall."

Baro did as he was bid. The trees' foliage gleamed dark purple in the light of the old orange sun.

"Do you see, midway up the third tree from the left, a small animal closely inspecting its own hindquarters?"

"I do," Baro said. The furry little thing was fully engrossed in its work.

"Would you believe that that creature and I are engaged in a contest?" said Arboghast.

Baro sensed that the conversation was heading to a conclusion he would not enjoy, but still he said, "I would find it hard to believe."

"Nevertheless."

The young man was reluctant to ask the next question, but knew he must surrender to the inevitable. "What is the contest?" he asked.

"We are competing to see which of us can take the least interest in your opinions on any matter whatsoever," the Directing Agent said, then allowed his smile to reassert itself as he added, "and I am winning."

——◆——

Baro Harkless quietly closed the door to Ardmander Arboghast's office behind him, and congratulated himself on not slamming it. He took a deep breath, let it out, then took another. He resisted a powerful urge to bend and twist the assignment file he held in his hands. He put down an equally strong desire to consign Ardmander Arboghast to an infernal destination or to kick the furniture in the anteroom. Most of all, he fought against turning his head to regard the man in the black and green of Archonate livery who occupied a chair on the other side of the small space.

Luff Imbry moved his mouth in a wry grimace and said, "If it's any consolation, you were not my first choice either."

——◆——

I am often struck by how widely a day can escape from one's expectations," said Luff Imbry.

"You may be struck unexpectedly indeed, if you do not leave me to my thoughts," said Baro Harkless and turned away.

Imbry shrugged his green-epauleted shoulders and turned from his partner to inspect the cavernous reaches of the Bureau's main refectory, to which they had repaired after Arboghast declined to dissolve their partnership. They were seated at a small table in one of the dimmer corners of the great room, which in the hours between mealtimes was largely deserted.

Imbry tried again. "Come," he said, indicating the steaming cups and the small heap of cakes on the tray between them, "take a sip of good, hot punge and chew on something tasty. You'll soon recover your equilibrium."

Though he kept his face averted, Baro's eyes slid toward the fat man. "What is my equilibrium to you? It is not long since I left your scheme broken about your ankles. Under the circumstances, your solicitude is suspect."

Imbry shrugged. "True enough. But now fate has slapped us into each other's arms and bid us be comrades."

"Not fate, but Ardmander Arboghast," said the younger man, taking up a cup of punge.

Imbry said, "I perceive no distinction between the two." He chose a seed-covered cake from the pile between them, chewed a little, then added, "I will admit, I was surprised not to find myself en route to the nearest Contemplarium."

"Surprised?" said Baro. "I am astonished. No, outraged. No . . ." He paused and hunted about for the right word, but before he could summon it Luff Imbry spoke for him.

"I think 'dumbfounded' sums it up best."

Baro nodded. There were several things he wanted to say concerning Arboghast, Imbry, and the vagaries of fate that had thrust the three of them together in such an unhappy arrangement. But outrage and disappointment were affecting his powers of speech the way a raptor affects a flock of barnyard fowl, so that he feared to open his mouth lest he create only a scattering of unconnected words explosively flying off on random vectors.

"It's more surprising still when you consider the history between me and the section chief," Imbry said.

With something specific to focus on, Baro found his voice. "What history?"

Imbry went for another cake, this one well laden with cream. "There was a time when he pursued me and a former partner relentlessly," he said, pausing to wipe the filling from the corner of his mouth.

"So you would say that he hates you?" Baro said.

"With a deep and abiding loathing," Imbry replied. "Hence my surprise at finding myself in green and black."

Baro sat, despondent, and listened to the sound of his partner demolishing the pile of cakes. "At least take some punge," Imbry said, pushing Baro's untasted cup toward the young man.

"I do not wish to drink with you," Baro said.

Imbry lifted his cup and swallowed a good third of its contents in one gulp, which he followed with a sigh of satisfaction. He wiped his upper lip and said, "I have observed that the world often takes scant notice of our wants and worries. I take it that you have long desired to be an agent of the Bureau of Scrutiny."

"It is all I ever wanted to be. It is a calling."

"Some are called, some are driven," the fat man said. "I have never accepted either a whip across the buttocks or a ring through the nose. I prefer to amble through the days, adapting my goals to circumstances as they present themselves or, preferably, adapting circumstances to my comfort."

"Your philosophy is vapid," Baro said.

"Perhaps," said Imbry. "But see how your grim zeal and my carefree insouciance have brought us to the identical point. We are both scroots. It is a distinction I admit I never sought, yet when the question was put the alternatives were even less appealing."

"It is all some sort of horrible mistake."

"Now there is a truly vapid philosophy," said the fat man, "lacking even that leavening of optimism that urges one to rise in the morning and go forth to accomplish. This cup of punge, on the other hand, is not affected by speculation. It is here and now, and very good." He drank some more and again nudged the other cup toward Baro.

Baro sighed and wrapped both hands around the warm cup. He lifted and drank without tasting, then said, "What am I to do?"

"I have always found that the future is best managed in small increments," Imbry said. "Baby steps, if you will. I suggest that we secure our first toehold on whatever is to come by opening the file Arboghast gave you."

Baro had laid the file on the bench beside him when he had sat down. Now he placed it on the table but did not open it.

Imbry sipped more punge and said, "Come, let us begin. Perhaps you will make as great a splash with this assignment as you did with my capture. You will be promoted while I languish in the rear ranks."

Baro brightened. "Yes," he said, "after all, Archon Filidor himself directed that I be given this assignment. Only the choice of you as my assistant—a mere helper—was Arboghast's."

"These words—helper, assistant—do not match my own perspective on our relationship," said Imbry.

Baro drew himself up and regarded the older man sternly. "Your perspective will now be altered. Obviously, I am your superior, having passed through the Bureau Academy with high marks, while you were dragooned into its ranks by threats and menaces."

Luff Imbry's expression might be read in several ways. "How one arrives at a position in life is often less meaningful than what one does once one is there," he said.

But Baro was not listening. He had placed the file folder on the dark boards of the tavern table and now opened it. It contained his official agent's plaque, a thin, hand-sized rectangle of green translucence figured in black icons. Baro laid the plaque on the table and pressed one of the symbols. A small screen appeared in the air above the table. He shook the contents of the file—a wafer about the size of his thumbnail—out of the folder and into his palm, then inserted it into the plaque's intake.

A dozen pages of information arranged themselves in miniature on the screen. Baro enlarged the first of these and began to read. As he did so, Luff Imbry applied one finger to the plaque, rotating it until he, too, could scan what was there without craning his neck. Baro put on a wry face, but continued to make his way through the text.

After he had read the section headed *Orders,* he said, "We are to locate one Father Olwyn, described as the Sacerdotal Eminence of the Assembly of Tangible Unity but believed to be a fraudster. We will observe his actions and deduce the nature of his scheme, then arrest him once we have sufficient evidence."

"I suspect the situation is more complex than that," said Imbry.

"It seems straightforward to me," said Baro.

Imbry put on a pensive look. "I doubt it is normal to send agents out but forbid them to use Bureau resources or call for backup. Is there any reason why Arboghast should dislike you?

Has he overheard you making rude observations about him or his ancestors? Is there some history of enmity between your family and his?"

Baro shook his head. "He knew my father."

"Your father was a scroot?"

"A captain in the investigations branch. He died when I was young."

"Arboghast was in investigations. Perhaps they clashed. Perhaps your father received a promotion Arboghast craved."

"That sort of thing does not happen in the Bureau," Baro said. "We are a dedicated fellowship."

Imbry regarded the young man quizzically, then shook his head as if putting aside a rejoinder. "Very well," he said, "perhaps you remind him of someone he encountered in a bad dream. Or he may be the type who singles out a hapless subordinate and visits upon his victim all the bitterness and bile that trickle down upon him from higher echelons."

Baro wanted to defend the Bureau as an institution where such unpleasantness could not happen, but in the light of Arboghast's choice of partner for him there was no question that the section chief was not his friend.

"He might be annoyed that the Archon personally selected me for this assignment," he suggested. "The Bureau is supposed to be beyond political interference, but the Archon's word is law."

Imbry's face showed that he was weighing things up. "That could explain why he has manacled us together," he said. "He resents you and hates me. So he sends us on a mission without Bureau support, intending us to fail. You will be demoted and I will go to the Contemplarium."

Imbry had gone too far. "A senior Bureau officer is above such a thing," said Baro.

Imbry said nothing, but his eyes rolled. After a moment he said, "It makes no difference. Since there is only one direction in which we can move, we will step forward boldly."

They skimmed through the section of the file that was headed *Background*. It included clippings from the *Olkney Implicator,* the main news organ in the capital. One story was from the social pages and took notice that the magnate Trig Helvic planned to take his daughter on a cruise on the *Orgulon,* a landship. Another story concerned the same cruise, which was organized by the Assembly of Tangible Unity, described as a new religious society seeking adherents.

"This seems straightforward to me," said Baro, when he had read the material.

"My view differs," said Imbry.

"How? Why?"

"Regard the image that accompanies the report," Imbry said.

Baro looked and saw the representation of a soft-faced man with wispy hair and gentle eyes. He was presented as if caught in a moment of prayer, his gaze directed upward and his hands clasped beneath his double chin. The caption identified him as *Father Olwyn, Sacerdotal Eminence.*

"He looks to be a pious fellow," Baro said.

"Indeed," said Luff Imbry. "He is the very image of trustworthiness. But appearances can deceive. When I knew him his name was Horslan Gebbling. He was my partner. And together we led Ardmander Arboghast on a merry dance. His failure to capture us may even be why he was transferred from Investigations to Training."

Again, Baro sought for words and did not find any. Imbry regarded the workings of the young man's open mouth and said, "Take more punge. It lubricates the vocal apparatus."

Baro drank the stuff without tasting it. "You and this Gebbling were criminal confederates?" he said.

Imbry's face assumed an expression of happier days recalled. "Yes, but we did not offer religious salvation. We trafficked in maps to forgotten brillion mines, with an implication that we had found a deposit of black brillion."

"There is no such thing as black brillion," Baro said. "Blue and red, yes, but not black. It is a figment."

"You'd be surprised how many people are prepared to believe in figments, if they think they can thereby fulfill their dreams."

"Have you spent your whole life cheating and cozening?"

"No," said Imbry. "As an infant, I mostly slept and ate. But to return to the point: it should now be clear to you that there is no coincidence in our being sent to undo the Assembly of Tangible Unity."

"Directing Agent Arboghast sees us as the best chance to penetrate Gebbling's scheme and bring him to justice," said Baro.

"Arboghast will take full credit, should we succeed," said Imbry. "Hence his orders to proceed without support."

Baro wanted to reject the explanation as unbefitting a senior agent, but his logical mind couldn't find a place to apply a grip.

"And if we do not succeed," the fat man went on, "if even Gebbling's former partner and the brilliant young scroot of the year cannot seize him, perhaps Arboghast will be able to argue that Gebbling is a mastermind and that his transfer to Training was undeserved."

"Such machinations do not happen within the Bureau," said Baro.

"Of course not," said Imbry. "In any case, I am happy to undo Horslan Gebbling. When we parted he did so in the middle of the night with the accumulated proceeds of our mutual efforts."

"The Bureau is not a vehicle for your private revenge."

"I think you'll find," said Imbry, "that the Bureau is a great many things not precisely detailed in your manuals and standing orders."

Baro gathered up the file and closed it. "While I am in charge of this investigation the Bureau will be what I say it is."

"We return to the unsettled question," said Imbry. "What leads you to assume that you are in charge?"

"I am the trained agent."

"Barely."

"You," said Baro, "have obviously been drafted to assist with this particular case, because you are acquainted with the suspect and know his methods of operation."

"A reasonable assumption, since Arboghast was close on our trail when my partnership with Horslan Gebbling came to an end."

"So you are an auxiliary," said Baro, "a temporary employee."

Imbry extended his lower lip and knitted his eyebrows. "My commission makes no such distinction. I am full-weight, a complete scroot."

"Show me," Baro said.

The fat man went into his belt pouch and withdrew his own plaque. He pressed a symbol and a second screen appeared in the air between them, displaying an official document. Baro scanned it quickly and experienced a disheartening realization that there was no difference between Imbry's commission and his own.

Then a thought occurred. "What is the date and time of your commission?" Baro said. If Imbry's had been ratified after his own, Baro would have seniority.

Imbry pressed another character on his plaque and scrolled to the bottom of the text, where Directing Agent Arboghast's sigil appeared. Beneath it was yesterday's date, the same as on Baro's.

The young man ground his teeth, but all was not yet lost. "What about time of issuance?" he said.

"It is not on the document," said Imbry.

"But it will be in the Bureau's records." Baro turned to his own plaque and pressed the character that transformed it into a communicator.

A voice spoke from the air. "Bureau of Scrutiny, main integrator. What is your requirement?"

"I wish to know the precise time of my commissioning as an agent," Baro said.

"Bureau integrators are not for personal indulgences," said the voice.

"It is a matter of determining seniority between me and my partner, Agent Luff Imbry. We also require his time of commissioning so that we may know which of us is to take charge."

The integrator made a sound that approximated a human *tsk,* then said, "You were both commissioned at the time of nine hours, four minutes, and eighteen seconds past noon yesterday."

"Is it possible that we were both commissioned at the same instant?" said Baro.

"It is beyond mere possibility," said the integrator. "It is a fact."

"The Bureau records time in minims and microminims," said Baro. "Please see if there is a distinction beyond the decimal point."

"I have already done so," said the integrator. "There is none."

"Well," said Luff Imbry, "there it is. We are equal partners."

Baro disconnected from the integrator. "I have spent my life preparing for a career in the Bureau," he said, "while you have busied yourself in violating its every standard and precept. It is not fair."

"I see it as yet another demonstration that ironic humor is the basal operating principle of the universe," said Imbry. "However, what we need is to establish a harmonious working relationship."

"Impossible."

"Nonsense," said the older man. "Where is the faith one expects from youth? We will set ourselves to achieving the Bureau's goals, which coincide with our own—you for glory and promotion, me for revenge and recoupment from Horslan Gebbling."

"The Bureau is not a weapon for settling private scores," Baro said.

"If you say so. Directing Agent Arboghast may have a different view."

Baro relented. "I suppose we must work together, at least for this one case."

Imbry smiled. "That's the spirit. Let us divide our responsibilities according to our capabilities. Since I am familiar with Gebbling and his style of scheme, I will plan an appropriate angle of attack."

"That is reasonable, so long as you stay within the bounds of the law and Bureau operating procedures. But what shall I do?"

Imbry considered for a moment. "Would you like to take charge of communications between the field and headquarters?"

"That means reporting to Arboghast."

"Yes."

"Then no."

"All right," said Imbry. "I suggest you look after logistics and arrangements—book our travel and accommodations and so on."

"That would seem to place me firmly in the assistant's role," Baro said.

"But we both know that we are equal, don't we?"

"I suppose."

"And when it comes to quoting Bureau procedures and regulations, you are clearly in first position, are you not?"

"Well, yes," said Baro.

"Then there we are," said the older man. "Now why don't you pay for these snacks while I plan our first move?"

Baro reached for his plaque, then halted. "I have had half a cup of punge, while you have consumed two, plus a plate of cakes," he said. "I suggest that we pay our individual scores. That way I do not risk feeling like some lackey picking up after his superior."

Imbry's hand waved in airy dismissal. "If you like," he said. "After all, what counts is that things are done and done well. The issue of who does them need not arise."

"Then I will plan our next move while you pay for the food," said Baro.

"Hmm," said the older man. "I sense an undercurrent of distrust."

"Your senses serve you well. I do not trust you."

Imbry showed a wounded spirit. "Are we not partners?" he asked. "Are we not commissioned agents of the Bureau, resolutely united, determined to root out ill-doers and set the world aright?"

"No," said Baro. "We are not. At least you are not. I have sought nothing more, my whole life through, than to be an instrument of right and justice."

"I am similarly motivated. I desire to bring Horslan Gebbling to book for his transgressions."

"That is settling a personal score."

Imbry looked down, then up again. "No, not entirely," he

said. "I admit that I have never before been on your side of the dichotomy yet I am willing to give it a try. I may come to enjoy clapping ne'er-do-wells behind unbreakable bars."

A corner of Baro's mouth turned in on itself. "And tiny winged creatures might spring from my ears and perform coordinated aerobatics around my head," he said.

"An unusual ambition," said Imbry. "But I will not disparage your aspirations if you will let mine be."

Baro sighed. "We appear to be at an impasse. Clearly, we are ill-matched partners."

"Yet matched we are, and by Ardmander Arboghast for whatever purposes may move him." Imbry spread his hands. "Look, let us lay our members on the stump. You do not wish me for a partner but neither do you wish a squabble with the section chief, for fear he will take away your promotion."

Baro did not like to admit it, but he spoke plainly. "That is so."

"I, however, am willing to chew what I find in my bowl, if I thereby keep my freedom and—I will admit it—gain a chance to insert a finger into Horslan Gebbling's dewy eye."

"So?" Baro said.

"So we each have something to lose and something to gain, and we might as well see how it goes."

Baro thought about it. "It is worth a try," he said. "But we will proceed as equals."

"Though each shall exercise his special capabilities," said Imbry.

"Within reason, and with full consultation."

"Agreed."

The older man held out his hand, but Baro withheld his long enough to say, "Of course, if I find you in violation of any law or statute, I will immediately rearrest you and haul you before a magistrate."

Imbry blinked. "Of course," he said, his hand still offered. Baro took it and they performed the appropriate manipulations.

"Very well, let us return to the file," said Imbry, and when it was open before him again, he pointed to one of the clippings. "Here is our avenue of approach."

Baro had read the news report before. He said, "It is despicable."

"Even I would agree," said Imbry. "Gebbling has gone beyond the pale."

"He's pretending that he can cure the lassitude."

"Nothing less."

Baro was outraged. "He is a shameless mountebank! He exploits the misery of those whose loved ones have been struck down by a foul disease!"

"I can't disagree," said Imbry. "Something has happened to Horslan Gebbling since last I knew him. He was always bad, but never beastly."

Baro rubbed his hands. "I itch to be at him," he said. "How do we unpluck his scheme?"

"We join the victims, and come the moment Gebbling reaches to rake in the proceeds, we pounce!"

Baro's throat produced a sound of affirmation that was close to a growl. Pouncing sounded very good indeed.

—◆—

No one knew exactly when the lassitude first appeared. The initial cases were few and widely scattered. It was only recently that the syndrome had been recognized as one disease.

The early symptoms were mild and easily overlooked: a tendency to sleep a little longer of a morning, a tapering off of interest in pursuits that had formerly engrossed, a growing absentmindedness, and a lack of interest in finishing sentences.

But within a short time the sufferers ceaselessly descended into catatonia, drew away from the world to become trapped in the prison of their own inert bodies.

The lassitude first took away the power to initiate speech, while leaving the capacity to respond to words spoken by others. Then the ability to answer a question faded, while victims remained able to understand what was spoken to them— could nod yes or no, or move their faces in the equivalent of a shrug—but soon even that minimal competence dwindled to nought.

By the time speech and hearing were completely gone, physical immobility was creeping over the victim, beginning with a tingling in the fingers, then a weakness in the limbs that proceeded to a general paralysis that affected all of the body's striate muscles. The skin became waxy, then hardened. The afflicted gave no response to heat or cold, to pinpricks or noxious aromas.

Internal functions slowed but did not cease entirely. Fed and hydrated intravenously, the sufferer lived on. Eventually, there came a crisis: it was as if the victim's body sought some radical rearrangement of its internal organs. The result was always fatal.

Scientists and apparaticists applied their paraphernalia and methodologies to the victims in all stages of the disease but were forced to conclude that the condition was both unknown in origin and untreatable in its presentation. The Archonate eventually imposed a moratorium on unconventional treatments after one ambitious experiment resulted in the patient's spontaneous combustion.

Contagious diseases having been eradicated back in the dawn of time, it was speculated that the lassitude might have been brought to Old Earth by some transient visitor from one of the human-settled worlds that straggled along the great

arm of the galaxy known as the Spray. But wide-ranging inquiries turned up no cases of the syndrome on any other
planet. Nor was anything like it known among the various
nonhuman populations that had inhabited parts of the Earth
since ages past.

There seemed to be a geographical element: all cases were
within a certain distance of the region known as the Swept, a
vast sea of prairie well to the east of Olkney. But so sporadic
were the outbreaks that no connecting factor—prevailing
winds, contact with travelers from the region—was ever identified. The geographic aspect was put down to coincidence.

After the first few dozen victims died, the disease seemed to
have burned itself out. For months there were no more outbreaks. Then it burst out once more. The victims again all lived
within a large circle whose center was somewhere in the Swept.
But, as before, there was neither apparent cause nor any cure.

Science having performed to no avail, philosophy now
stepped in to try its hand. It was argued that the syndrome was
a physical manifestation of a spiritual malaise. "We inhabit an
ancient planet," said one sage at a colloquy convened to discuss
the lassitude. "All that ever could have been done has been
done. Knowing that there can now be nothing new under the
sun, the sensitive spirit withdraws into inertia. The disease is a
profound and pointed philosophical statement."

Another pundit then rose and pointed out that since the lassitude itself was something entirely new, the first speaker's remarks were self-contradicting. Sharp words ensued, followed
by a tug on someone's beard and a sandaled toe in someone
else's shin, and the conference broke up without issuing a final
statement.

After the philosophers came thaumaturges and occultists,
but this was Old Earth's penultimate age, a time when science
still outranked wizardry (though the Wheel was slowly rolling

toward the cusp when the distinction would again be reversed), and the various spells and cantrips yielded no better result—though it was rumored that one wonder-worker had inadvertently transformed himself into something scaly that had wriggled off, not to be seen again.

It was the latest sufferers whom Horslan Gebbling meant to fleece, Baro thought as he followed Luff Imbry along Flevangher Road in a district of Olkney where day workers and students made their simple abodes. Imbry led Baro to a small ground-floor apartment on a nondescript street where the door monitor recognized him and swung the portal wide. "Gebbling must be stopped," Baro said.

"He will be," said Imbry, leading the way into a single room that combined living and sleeping quarters as well as rudimentary facilities for food preparation. The utilitarian furnishings were a far cry from the luxury that Baro knew his partner preferred.

"This is not your residence," he said.

"Members of my profession never conduct business from their abodes," Imbry said.

Both their plaques now contained copies of the file. Imbry activated his and laid it on the scarred table. Then he pressed a concealed stud beneath the tabletop. A portion of the wall slid back and revealed a fully equipped research and communications nexus, its high quality at odds with the bare-bones setting. "Sit down," he said, "and we'll begin."

Baro sat on the sleeping pallet while his partner took the single chair and brought the device to life. It declared itself ready to serve. Imbry's fingers went to the controls, but then he paused and turned to the younger man. "My showing you this installation should help you to put aside your lingering doubts," he said.

"Why so?" said Baro.

"Because here is where I planned all of my . . . exercises. The Bureau never knew of this place."

"Hmm," said the younger agent. He produced his plaque and contacted the Bureau integrator. "I am in the place where Luff Imbry concocted his illegal schemes," he said. "Consult his file and tell me if the Bureau was aware of this location."

"No," was the integrator's immediate response.

"Are you sure?"

"Are *you* sure," the integrator said, "that you want to ask me that question? All communications with agents in the field are recorded and can be examined by their superiors."

"I withdraw the question," Baro said.

"What question?" the integrator said.

"Thank you." Baro made to break the connection, then hesitated and said, "It was good of you to let me know about the recordings."

"You need to have confidence in what I say to you," said the integrator. "We may have to work together for a long time." It paused, then added, "Assuming that you last." There was a slight pop as the integrator broke the connection itself.

"Look here," said Imbry, and Baro turned his attention to the research station's screen. It showed a list of names.

"Who are these people?" Baro said.

"Those who have registered for passage on the *Orgulon*."

The Bureau file had been compiled when Gebbling was seeking a charter. Now that stage of the fraudster's plan had been surpassed and Imbry's research system had not only found the name of the vessel but its passenger manifest.

"Hmm, interesting," said the fat man and highlighted one of the names on the list. The screen opened a new portal and displayed a list of headings: *Address, Education, Affiliations* (subheaded *Social, Professional, Intimate*), *Assets and Income, Politics,* and more besides.

"What is all that?" Baro wanted to know.

"One of the passengers is Trig Helvic," said Imbry, high-lighting the section labeled *Assets and Income*, "and this is his total worth."

The screen showed an extensive list of properties and securities, plus a wealth of financial data that placed Helvic well up in the higher reaches of Olkney society.

"This is not public information," said Baro.

"True," said Imbry, running his finger down the screen. "I'm sure the gentleman would not want it noised about that he is the actual owner of properties on which three notorious brothels are located. He has erected various shell companies and dummy corporations to put distance and fog between him and some of his holdings."

"We are invading the man's privacy," Baro said.

"We are conducting an investigation, in your case at the Archon's personal order."

"I think we should consult the Bureau."

Imbry made a noise that bespoke impatience. "Look," he said, "you're either a scroot or you're not. If you have doubts, I will be glad to contact Directing Agent Arboghast for you. I am sure he will relieve you of them."

Baro capitulated, but said, "I don't believe the Bureau's integrators contain the private details of ordinary citizens' affairs."

Imbry's fingers flickered over the system's controls. "I stand in awe at the innocence of your worldview," he said. "Doubtless you still believe that the Blue-Green Sprites delivered all those scrumptious treats left on your boyhood pillow during the Feast of Slamming Doors." He tapped another key. "Never mind, this gets more interesting. And more puzzling."

Baro looked at the display of data on the screen. Imbry had moved on to examine the backgrounds of the rest of the

Orgulon's passengers. They were a mixed bag: besides the magnate Trig Helvic and his daughter Erisme, they included the imagist Tabriz Monlaurion and his companion, a former actress who went by the single name Flix; a pair of students, Corje Sooke and Pollus Ermatage, from the Academy of Liberal Pursuits in the County of Fasfallia; a retired couple named Ule Gazz and Olleg Ebersol from the Isle of Cyc; and a raft of other heterogeneous folk from several places.

"Why puzzling?" the younger man asked.

Imbry looked away from the screen. "Well, Helvic I can see as a prime target for whatever scheme Gebbling intends. The imagist Monlaurion, too, I suppose, although his vogue is long past and his works decline in value. But the rest of them are of only modest worth, and some—such as the students— are frankly poor."

"They must have something in common," Baro said, peering at the data, and then he saw it. "There it is. They are all couples and one of them has the lassitude, which Gebbling purports to be able to cure."

"Just so," said Imbry, "I had seen that. But it explains nothing. How does he profit by curing—or, more precisely, pretending to cure—a gaggle of paupers? Where lies the opportunity to flay and fleece?"

Baro suggested having the system sort and categorize the people on the manifest in various permutations. The fat man tried several approaches, but no other pattern emerged.

"Gebbling has gone to considerable expense to hire the *Orgulon* for a lengthy period," Imbry said. "He may intend to recoup his outlay and wring a profit from Helvic alone. But if so, why bring along so much dead weight?"

"Perhaps some of the crowd are his confederates, who will pretend to have the malaise and be miraculously cured of it on the voyage."

Imbry fingered the controls. "That may be. I do not have all of their medical records."

"Still, you have plenty. That is quite the system," Baro admitted.

"I built it myself. While my profession occasionally calls for brilliant improvisation, there is no substitute for fine tools and meticulous preparation."

"You mean your former profession," said Baro.

"Of course, I do."

"What do you have on me?" Baro asked.

"I don't know. Until quite recently, I had never heard of you."

"Let us see."

Imbry worked the system and up popped a file on Baro Harkless. There were entries under several headings, indicating significant career achievements, promotions, and citations, enough to fill several screens.

"That is not me," said Baro. "That is my father. He had the same name."

"Ah," said Imbry, pointing at a line on the screen. "The researcher took us here because here is the only place your name appears, under your father's dependents. I'm afraid you haven't yet made much of an impact on this old world."

Seeing his father's life and career summarized in this place gave Baro a curious pang. "Let us get on," he said again.

Imbry's fingers moved across the system's controls, then he stabbed one final stud and said, "There. We are now added to the *Orgulon*'s passengers. I saw that two of the original invitees had first booked, then canceled. We shall go in their place.

"I shall be the Eminent Discourser Erenti Abbas, therapist and companion to the Honorable Phlevas Wasselthorpe—that is you. You are also in the initial stages of the lassitude. I have booked us seats on the afternoon balloon-tram to Farflung. The game, whatever the game may be, is on."

"We will need suitable attire," Baro said.

"For me, that will pose no problem," said the fat man.

He went to a wall and pressed a smudge high up on its cheaply painted surface. There was a discreet *click* and the wall slid aside to reveal a capacious closet filled with garments hung on racks and a warren of shelves and cubbies filled with accessories and boxes.

Imbry rummaged and found clothing and accoutrements suitable for an academician of senior rank and moderate distinction. He dug in a box and said, "Just the thing—the pin and pendant of a runner-up for the Fezzani Prize." He applied the decoration to his lapel.

"What about me?" said Baro.

"Wasselthorpe is from the minor nobility," Imbry mused while flicking garments aside, one after another. "I haven't much in your size, but here's a reasonable facsimile of a traveling suit and"—he dug in a box—"a cravat that identifies you as a third-tier graduate of the Institute."

"Only third tier?"

"It is all I have. Try to restrain your brilliance."

"So I am to be a know-naught bumpkin from the hinterland's hind end while you are a distinguished pundit?"

"It will work better that way," said Imbry.

"What will?"

But the fat man was digging again through his boxes. He came up with two small devices and slipped them into his belt pouch.

"What were those?" Baro said.

"A slapper and a grumbler," Imbry said. "They're always useful."

Baro could not argue the prediction because he did not

know what a slapper or a grumbler was. He suspected they were underworld terms for illegal weapons but having been assigned the role of rural oaf he did not want to confirm the identity by revealing his ignorance.

"Now what?" he said.

"We proceed with the plan."

"Does it not occur to you that you have left out a crucial step?" Baro said.

"What step would that be?"

"The one where you explain the goals, strategies, and specifically my part in all of them. So far, all I know is that I am to be a dullard on a landship."

Imbry looked only slightly abashed. "I do not usually work with a partner," he said. "My association with Gebbling was one of the few occasions, and as you know, it did not turn out well."

"I am not Horslan Gebbling. From what I've heard of him, I wonder if we are of the same species."

Imbry looked thoughtful. "I am no less puzzled that he has launched this scurrilous scheme to fleece those who already suffer."

"Are you going to argue for the existence of honor among fraudsters? I'd more expect to find jewels in a dung heap."

Imbry drew himself up. "Some of us have our limits. I pride myself that my prey has been those who thought themselves predators. You may see me as the human equivalent of an eight-legged web-spinner, but I have hunted only other spiders."

"And Gebbling?"

"I thought he was like me in that regard." Imbry's focus went inside for a moment, then he shook his head and sighed.

"We are again drifting from the point," Baro said. He had noticed that discussions with his partner had a tendency to become unmoored. "I am happier with plans when I have a part in making them."

"I'll try to bear that in mind," said Imbry, "but right now we must hurry to catch the afternoon balloon-tram."

———◆———

The balloon-tram system had been a favorite project of the Archon Vanz, an imaginative and energetic innovator who had left several marks on the world. It was a mode of transportation favored by those who had the leisure to arrive later than sooner and the desire to view the territories through which they passed from a different perspective.

The passengers rode in a capacious and well-appointed car that hung from the belly of a rigid-framed cylindrical airship. The lighter-than-air craft was tethered by a long cable to a dolly that was in turn slotted into a ground track that ran arrow-straight across flats and hills, crossing gorges and water obstacles on trestles and causeways. An operator sat at a panel in the front of the car, adjusting the degree of interaction between the materials of which the track and dolly were made, which provided the energy to move the system.

The Olkney terminus was near the heart of the ancient metropolis, beneath the Archonate palace that sprawled atop the range of mountains that ran up the spine of the peninsula from which the city took its name. Standing on the departure platform while the balloon-tram car was winched down to ground level, Baro looked up at the terraces and tiers of the palace and marveled that the Archon himself should have marked the name of Baro Harkless and singled him out for individual attention.

And now he was about to set forth on his first assignment,

one that would very likely bring him into conflict with the criminal Horslan Gebbling, who looked to be mild of aspect but might in reality be a desperate malefactor resolved to stop at nothing to evade capture and punishment. There could be danger ahead; certainly there was already a puzzle to unravel. And Baro could see himself at the heart of the adventure, his fine-tuned mind assessing and evaluating, his keen eye cutting through the film of subterfuge and misdirection to the hard nugget of truth.

True, his section chief had saddled him with an untrustworthy partner who exhibited a tendency to direct the course of the investigation. But now that Baro was focusing on the issues at hand he realized that he had let the speed of the day's events disrupt his natural equilibrium. Baro should have been exercising his rightful authority. He had not, and had allowed Luff Imbry to step in to fill the vacuum. But now it was time for the real agent, he who had absorbed the multiplicity of regulations that were at the heart of any policing organization, to put the affair on a proper footing.

"Here is the tram," said Luff Imbry. "Let us get aboard."

"Wait," said Baro. "We must first straighten out a few things between us."

Imbry's eyes widened. "But the tram is leaving."

"Then we will catch the next one."

"Which is not until tomorrow morning. It will not get us to Farflung in time to board the *Orgulon* before it sails."

"Oh," said Baro.

"Is it not something we could talk about on the tram?"

"No. It is the question of who is to direct the investigation."

"I thought we had settled it."

"Not to my satisfaction."

Imbry let out a heavy breath. "Very well," he said. "You are in charge. I await your orders."

"Very good," said Baro. At last things were on a solid footing.

"May I offer a suggestion?" said the fat man.

"Of course."

"I suggest we get on the balloon-tram, since it is about to hoist away."

The conductor was standing in the doorway of the conveyance, his eyes on them and his hand extended in a pose that said, "Well?" Baro realized that the functionary had already called "All aboard!" while he had been in conversation with Imbry.

"We will board the tram," he said.

The car was long and wide, lit by large windows, the seats not ranked in rows but arranged in trios and clusters as if the tram were the observation lounge of an alpine resort. Uniformed servers were distributing delicacies and beverages to the dozen or so passengers, most of whom seemed to Baro to be persons of wealth and fashion.

"How much is this trip costing the Bureau?" he said when they were seated in plush chairs near the rear of the vehicle, a tray of tastefully prepared food and drink at hand.

"I did not think to inquire," Imbry said, then paused to taste a diminutive meat pie. "In any case, the Archonate is not short on funds."

"Agents are expected to take the most economical mode of transport. Standing Order twelve, paragraph four, subparagraph two."

"You have a remarkable memory. Try the Sendaric wine."

Baro declined. "We must account for our expenses."

Imbry shrugged. Baro had noticed that a nonchalant lift of the shoulders seemed to be a habit of his partner's when confronted by unpleasant realities. He felt obligated to bring it to the older man's attention. "It is not good enough simply to shrug," he said. "We are members of an organization bound by rules and procedures laid down for our own, and the general, happiness. We are bound to observe them."

Imbry's shoulders lifted and settled again. He said, "Is there a subparagraph that requires an agent to carry out his duties to the best of his ability?"

"No," said Baro. "That is implied by the Bureau's hallowed tradition of honor."

"Well," said Imbry, picking a puff pastry from the tray, "I am at my best when I am well tended to. Since we will soon enter a possibly perilous situation full of unknowns and variables—never my preferred mode of operation—I propose to give us every advantage by arriving fully rested, my faculties running at top rate."

"Your argument is eminently self-serving."

"You may believe the simplicity of your opinions renders them elegant," said Imbry. "I do not concur. For my part, I intend to devote my thoughts to the puzzle of what our quarry is up to, and how we might best frustrate him. If it's not too great an imposition, I suggest you do the same."

With that, he drained his glass of wine, then bowed his head and closed his eyes. Baro was left with a finger poised to emphasize a point that he now realized his partner was not about to entertain. He turned and looked out the window.

They were high in the sky, on a level with the middling terraces of the Archonate palace, where crowds of sightseers toured architectural and landscaping oddities accumulated over millennia by Archons of widely varied enthusiasms. Now the balloon-tram rose even higher, to the arrondisements where official business was done and supplicants met with functionaries who might fulfill their hopes and expectations, or might send the petitioners back down to the streets to revise and rethink.

Baro regarded the vast expanse of the palace and felt some- thing swell within him as he reminded himself that he was part of the power and authority resident there. A small part, he had to admit, but he hoped that his father would have been proud of his progress. Perhaps someday his undoubted abilities— hadn't the Archon himself noted them?—would raise him so high that Ardmander Arboghast would be as far below him fig- uratively as were the tiny specks of color and motion that were pedestrians on the streets of Olkney.

It was a pleasant eventuality to consider, and Baro allowed himself a few moments with it. Then he returned himself sternly to his duty. Imbry, for all his sybaritic appetites, was right: they should be devoting their energies to unraveling the mystery of Gebbling's scheme. Baro reviewed the contents of the file without bothering to activate his plaque—all of the in- formation was available through the images that his eidetic memory placed before his inner eye.

After a few moments of review, Baro said, "It has to be money. Every machination that Gebbling has worked over a long criminal career has been aimed at enriching him."

Imbry opened his eyes. "That is the simple explanation."

"It is one of the most ancient rules of science and philosophy that the simpler the explanation the more likely it is to be right."

"Hmm," said the fat man. "That is so. But it is one of the abiding truths of history that every situation turns out to be more complex than it appears on first examination."

"Still," said Baro, "on the basis of his history, there must be a profit to be wrung from whatever Gebbling is doing. We have only to see where that profit lies, and head for it. There we will find Gebbling."

"Again, true," said Imbry. "It worries me, though, that I cannot quickly deduce where that invisible point lies. He was never that smart before."

"Perhaps he has a partner we haven't come across yet," said Baro. "A cleverer one."

"Hmm," said Imbry again, and said no more. He closed his eyes and appeared to be lost in deep thought. But after a few moments a gentle snore rumbled up from his inner being.

The attendant came for the tray but as the man's hand began to lift it away, Baro rescued the second glass of Sendaric. The wine was light on the tongue, its crisp finish brushed with an almost peppery aftertaste. *It's included in the fare,* he told himself. *It would be a shame to waste it.*

Imbry slept on as the balloon-tram, now at its cruising altitude, slid smoothly through the upper air toward the hamlet of Binch at the root of the Olkney Peninsula. Baro reviewed once again the contents of the Gebbling file, but derived no fresh insights. He had to concede that his partner was right: they must infiltrate the criminal's operation and deduce its aims from the observable mechanics of the scheme. They would then be able to determine what laws had been violated and they would arrest Gebbling and any confederates.

Imbry's snore came again, loud and with embellishments, breaking Baro's reverie. He glanced with distaste at the sleeping man, then noticed that the two of them had attracted the attention of another person in the car.

Seated across the wide aisle was a small man with bright eyes and graying hair, dressed in a neat suit of yellow chambric, ornamented at cuffs and collar by white and green ruffles. He made polite motions of head and hands and spoke to Baro. "By your scarf, I would take you for a graduate of the Institute?"

Baro fingered the grimy cloth. "Yes," he said.

"May I ask if studies were in any way connected with history?"

"No. Criminology." He named himself as Phlevas Wasselthorpe and the sleeping Imbry as his mentor, Erenti Abbas.

The small man showed a small disappointment. He introduced himself as Guth Bandar, a retired commerciant who after a lifetime of dealing in housewares was now taking a full-time interest in his long-standing hobby: history.

He was on his way, he said, to the Swept, to cruise on the landship *Orgulon*.

"As are we," said Baro.

"Have you the lassitude?" Bandar asked.

"A touch," Baro answered.

The small man looked slightly abashed. "I do not," he said. "My brother, Wisp, has the affliction but chose not to accept the invitation. I came in his place because I have always desired to see the Swept. It was there, although you probably do not know it—most people don't—that was fought the last significant military action on Old Earth."

"You surmise rightly," Baro said. "I did not know about a battle. Who fought whom, and for what cause?"

"It was an invasion," the historian said, "from off-world. A species called the Dree."

"An invasion? But why?" Baro was baffled. Old Earth had gladly made room for a score of ultraterrene species, and could fit another batch in without noticing a strain. It was not as if the planet was overpopulated.

Bandar confessed to being equally perplexed. "That is a question I would like to resolve. All I know for certain is that it was in that region that the Dree established their power, to the great discomfort of the inhabitants. They seem to have made very poor neighbors and rapidly overran a large territory.

"In the end, the place was evacuated of all humans and friendly ultraterrenes, the Dree were isolated in a fortress, and a terrible weapon was deployed to eradicate the invaders. The flatness of the land was a side effect."

"A terrible weapon, indeed," said Baro. "What was it?"

"A gravitational aggregator, used in space to assemble asteroids into useful configurations," Bandar said. "It is said to have created long-lasting aftereffects: gravitational cysts or bubbles that form in the planet's core and slowly rise to the surface. It is one of the things I would like to study."

"How can you do so from aboard the landship?"

"We may stop occasionally so that I may descend to the prairie and take readings with an apparatus I have brought. Failing that, I will ask to borrow one of the ship's launches."

"Beyond your particular interest in the battle, are you generally well informed as to the Swept?" Baro asked.

"As well as anyone," said Bandar.

"What do you know about brillion mines?"

Bandar brightened and Baro realized that here was a man who loved to discourse on the things that interested him. "It is not one of my primary interests," the historian said, "but there has been speculation that gravitational anomalies may also have contributed to the creation of large brillion deposits in the deep substrata. Some people say that the bubbles are responsible for creating deposits of black brillion, if you believe in that sort of thing."

"You do not?" asked Baro.

"I have been a commerciant and now I am a historian. I bought and sold, now I dig and I delve. I concern myself with what is and what was, not with what has almost surely never been."

Baro said, "I have never before met a historian. What is it about the past that draws you? It is not as if there is anything useful to be learned from it."

Bandar sighed. "Too true," he said. "We pass across an old, old world. Everything that could ever have been done has been done. All the lessons have been learned, forgotten, learned anew, and finally filed away. Now we content ourselves with

familiar forms and well-worn procedures. We will go on repeating the same inconsequential actions until the sun turns
from orange to red. Then it will bloat and consume the world
and who will care whether this cinder ever had a history?"

Luff Imbry spoke. "My young friend has a liking for forms
and procedures. He believes they give a structure to life. He is
in favor of structure."

"I envy him," said the historian. "For my part, I would like
to travel back to the times of yore, when no one knew what
the next year would bring. Imagine our distant ancestors,
blithely making it up as they went along, contending with
each other over faiths and ideologies as if any of it mattered.
What an adventure life must have been."

"You are a romantic," said Imbry.

Bandar raised an eyebrow. "Perhaps," he said. "In any case,
I have the next best thing. For my researches, I travel the Commons."

Imbry said, "Ah," in a knowledgeable manner, but the term
was one that Baro did not know.

"What is the Commons?" he said.

"Its proper name is the noösphere," said Bandar. "It is nothing less than the essence of all human experience: everything
ever felt or seen or done by humankind, back even to the days
when we prospected the hair on each other's backs for edible
parasites. All of it is in all of us and each of us is a portal to that
all, though some of us—we call ourselves noönauts—find it
easier than others to open the way. Yet the techniques are not
difficult; with a little training anyone can peek through the
door. Of course, the true adept requires a muscular memory
and a flair for detail."

"I'm sure my friend would hear more," Imbry said. "He
has a prodigious memory and detail is his closest friend."

In truth, Baro found himself oddly drawn to what the

historian was saying. Beneath the bubbling rhetoric about the "all in all of us," he sensed that here was something he wanted to learn. It was like seeing a jewel shining through layers of cloth and wanting—no, almost needing—to see the treasure laid bare. *Perhaps,* he thought, *there is an unrecognized tool for investigators in this man's hobby. I might develop it and place it at the Bureau's service.*

But when Bandar spoke again, he went off at a tangent, pursuing a thought that was of more interest to himself than to Baro. "It has long been known that the existence of the Commons is in some way connected to gravity," he said. "It is difficult to access in space, for example, and some have said that human experiences that have taken place beyond gravity wells do not register strongly and are lost to the common memory."

Imbry said, "Might the effects of the Swept's gravitational anomalies enhance your ability to 'travel the Commons'?"

The historian's face brightened. "Exactly," he said. "You can imagine why I had to make this trip. If my theory is correct, some remarkable research might be possible. I might establish a small retreat on the Swept, the seed of an institute."

"The Bandar Institute," Imbry said, and Baro saw a light gleam for a moment in the historian's eyes. But Baro's interest in the noönaut's dreams was focused on how this Commons he spoke of might figure as an investigator's tool and he acted to steer the conversation along that heading.

But when Bandar heard Baro's question he coupled gentle amusement to a negative response. "No, no," he said. "The Commons can't tell you who stole the cheese. Its essence is the commonality of experience. Take, for example, a well-known period of history—say, the opening of the Twelve Eon."

Baro knew that the historian referred to the repopulating of Old Earth—indeed, that was when the "Old" had been added— by descendants of the ancients of earlier eons who had gone out to the worlds of the Spray, where they founded civilizations that first grew rich and vast before growing old and exquisite. At the end of the First Effloration, as the trek out to the stars was known, an echo of the great outward wave rippled back to its starting point. Earth, which had long been considered a place of hopeless gaucherie, then became Old Earth and fashionable again. Left fallow through more ages than anyone quite remembered, it had developed some novel flora and fauna, which the returning humans found either quaint or horrific.

The great return was such a distinct occurrence in the long story of the species that, unlike most other times and happenings, it had largely been remembered by ensuing generations and had figured prominently in the formulation of calendars. It was thus possible for a historian like Guth Bandar to speak of significant events of the period, like the relocation of the Eriune Sea or the thinning of the global forest without a glaze of incomprehension coming over the faces of his listeners.

"Since almost all human inhabitants of the planet today are descended from Twelfth Eon returnees," Bandar said, "it is not difficult to find one's way through the Commons to specific memorable events of the period and delineate them in some detail. Whereas the memory of a recent murder might be solely in the cell of the murderer and thus not amenable to the techniques by which a historian shapes the past."

"'Cell'? 'Shapes the past'?" Baro said, and the historian was only too glad to pour out more of his learning.

"An event happens," he said, "and the person to whom it happens remembers it. That person's memory becomes what we call a cell or an engram. On its own, a single cell drifts away on the currents of the Commons and is unremarked.

"But suppose the same event happens to a thousand people. Or if not the same event, then a similar event—say, death on a particular battlefield—happens individually to tens of thousands. Each of those cells is so like unto the others that they do not drift separately: they cohere and join, reinforcing each other's existence. They then become what we call a corpuscle.

"A very large and potent corpuscle may become active, as if it were possessed of a will," Bandar continued, "though I and other members of the Predilective School maintain that a corpuscle can only have a tendency, never a true will. The rigid thinkers of the Volition Faction may mock us but our reasoning cannot be unseated and will eventually prevail."

"But you digress," said Imbry.

"I do," said the historian. "I have been preparing a paper on the issue and it has inflamed my academic tissues. My apologies."

Imbry indicated the Fezzani insignia pinned to his gown. "I understand entirely," he said. "Please go on. My young friend is fascinated."

Bandar peered at Baro. "Really? Usually I soon exhaust a listener's patience. My children would roll their eyes and put out their tongues when they thought I could not see them."

The image touched a soft point in Baro. "Please," he said.

"A willful—or as we say, tendentious—corpuscle may begin to move about," Bandar said, "attracting and absorbing other, less potent corpuscles, though it will only do so to corpuscles made of cells that are similar in content. So the combined engrams of major victories will encompass corpuscles of less celebrated triumphs. But the corpuscle of a victory can never devour that of a defeat.

"It can, however, develop in potency and breadth, allying itself to corpuscles that are similar in content. So the collective memory of a great victory can adhere to the common engram of a great hero or a significant noble sacrifice. When such adhesions take place, the aggregates are known as entities. They build and solidify and take up specific Locations in the Commons, where they can be found and examined by the trained historian."

Baro was unclear on one point. "But where is this Commons, this noösphere? Where do these engrams and entities do their devouring and aggregating?"

Imbry and the historian gave each other the shared look of the cognoscenti confronted by the noddy. Bandar reached around the back of Baro's head and tapped the bone. "In there," he said, then tapped his own head and Imbry's, "and in here. And in all of us."

Baro understood. "You are talking of species memory," he said. "I had thought the collective unconscious was a myth."

"Well, of course it is," said Bandar. "And like all myths, it partakes of fundamental truth. The final and highest stage of any engram's development is to become an archetypal myth, so that anyone who falls asleep finds himself being threatened by the beast or seduced by the damsel, being pursued through the labyrinth or swimming through the green-lit sea.

"But those that do not become myths remain as entities. Events, persons, even whole landscapes are preserved and may be visited and examined."

Baro scratched his head. "But surely they are not accurate records of what really happened on a specific day in a certain place."

Bandar laughed. "There are never any 'accurate' records. Register whatever sounds and images you choose and put them in a vault for ten thousand years. When you bring them out and reveal them, those who see and hear will hand you back a dozen, a score of impressions and interpretations. In history, what actually happens is much less important than what it means. And what it means is what people say it means."

Baro wanted to argue the point but was not sure where to

start. He switched focus. "You said that a good memory and a knack for detail were required. I have both," he said.

Bandar stroked his chin. "How many doors were in the waiting room at the balloon-tram station, in which walls were they set, and what was written on each?"

Baro consulted his memory and told him, adding, "The stationmaster's door had a scratch in the paint above the handle."

He knew from the historian's expression that the man was impressed. Bandar proposed an experiment to test the young man's aptitude. "If you're interested," he said.

Baro confessed that he was. He now accepted that the discipline could not become an investigatory aid but he still felt an urge to know more about the Commons.

"It's up to you how you wish to picture the way in to the noösphere," Bandar said. "Some see it as a door, others a mirror, some as a cave or as a hollow in a tree. It might be a dark closet or the space under a porch. The great Tumreth Ialgephalios used to envision his own right nostril."

"I will see a door," Baro said. He did not know why, but he had no doubt how that portal would look when he encountered it. "What will lie beyond it?"

"Let us not skip before we can hop," said Bandar. "The Commons is a dangerous place for anyone, and indescribably perilous for some."

The warning was delivered in a dry tone. Baro sensed that Bandar was no blustering impresario, out to make a mouse a monster by sheer force of rhetoric. The man struck Baro as sincere; therefore the peril was genuine. Yet Baro felt only a heightened desire to know more.

"I do not doubt you," he said. "Still, I am greatly curious."

"Immediately through the portal," the historian said, "you meet only your own memories, that is the contents of your personal unconscious. But if you sifted through those familiar retrospectants you would sooner or later notice something that is unfamiliar. The thing that is out of place is the key that opens the way to the great wide noösphere. For now, I think we should go no farther than up to the first door. If you can manage to hold it in your mind's eye for a few moments, that will show an aptitude for training as a noönaut."

"Very well," said Baro. "Let us find the door."

Bandar proceeded to instruct Baro in the elementary approach. This involved a regulation of breathing with eyes closed and a stillness of the limbs, followed by an affirmation of willingness to visualize the symbolic entrance. Then came the sounding of certain combinations of tones, called thrans, which must be rendered exactly.

Baro performed as he was instructed. He had a musical ear and found the tones not difficult to make and sustain. Within a short time the image of a closed door appeared on the screen of his inner vision. He continued to intone the sonorous sounds in concert with Guth Bandar, and soon it seemed that the door's image somehow grew more immediate and the tones overpowered the background clatter from the balloon-tram's tiny galley and the deep humming of the cable that secured them to the dolly far below.

Once the door was well fixed in his mind, he saw that around its edges a light began to glimmer. Now Baro found that he was able to intone the prescribed sounds with more energy, as if they came not from his respiratory apparatus but from some deeper source closer to the core of him. The light grew brighter and hotter, with a golden base tinged with crimson blush. Bandar's voice faded from his ears. There were only the tones and the bright ringed door.

In his mind's eye he created a hand and reached for the handle that would open the door. He felt his fingers close on the smooth warmth of the handle.

"Enough!" came the historian's voice. "Come back!"

Baro felt himself being shaken. In his mind's eye, the door with its limning of light diminished in size, rushing away from him as if at great speed. He returned to his surroundings with a jolt like a man descending a staircase who, thinking there is one more step, thrusts his foot against unyielding floor.

He opened his eyes to find Bandar standing over him, a worried look on the small man's face and his delicate hands gripping Baro's shoulders. Imbry was regarding him with mild perplexity.

"You went much too fast!" the noönaut was saying. "I almost lost you."

"I saw a light surrounding the door," Baro said. "And I saw my own hand reaching for the handle."

Bandar's face paled. "You truly saw the light and made a hand to open the door? And you had never heard of these things before today?"

"I am not one to tease," said Baro.

"I can vouch for that," said his partner. "He is no bubbling spring of merriment."

Bandar passed a hand across his well-wrinkled forehead. "I have not seen such an aptitude before," he said. "It took weeks of guided application before I could reliably reify my portal and call forth the light, and yet more weeks before I could open the way for more than a twinkling."

"It seemed only natural to me," said Baro.

A quiver struck the small man. "That is not a word to use lightly in connection to the Commons," he said. "If I thought you were a natural, I would never let you near the place."

"Why?" Baro said.

"Because among noönauts, the word 'natural' is a close synonym for 'irredeemable psychotic.'" The small man put his hands to his cheeks and drew them down and inward until they caused his lips to purse. Then he blew out a breath and said, "If you will excuse me, I believe I will sit quietly by myself for a while. This has been a shock."

"I would like to know more about all of this," said Baro.

"As would I," said Imbry. "If my young companion is no more than half a hoot from full-blown psychosis, it would be useful to know the signs that he is about to slip into the yabba-dabbas."

"He is in no peril if he forbears to call up the vision of the portal again." Bandar looked sternly at Baro. "I strongly urge you not to do so. Once in too far, there is no way out."

"I would know more," said Baro.

"Then let it be later," said the noönaut. "I must think on the matter." With that he returned to his seat and gazed out the window at the landscape unrolling far below.

Luff Imbry regarded Baro with a considering look. "It appears you have unsuspected depths," he said, then again composed himself for sleep.

Baro was not sure how to respond. He shrugged and turned to regard the view from his side of the balloon-tram. They were skirting Ektop, its unbroken sweep of primeval forest stretching off into the farthest distance. Somewhere off to the northwest the horizon was smeared by a yellowy cloud of airborne pollutants, signifying that the enclave of Zeel continued its consuming quest for industrial innovation. But the balloon-tram's course went east and south through rolling farmland and bucolic villages toward a line of weatherworn hills that, once surmounted, would ease them down to Farflung on the edge of the Swept.

Since learning about the *Orgulon*'s cruise, Baro had been looking forward to seeing the Swept. He knew it was a vast expanse of open land, so preternaturally planed and leveled that it was universally accepted that it must have been purposefully made so in the distant past.

Bandar had spoken boldly of the origins of the Swept, but Baro had heard that there were arguments to the contrary. Whatever its origin, he knew that the Swept was so flat that from any erected elevation—the masthead of a landship, for example—it was possible to descry the curvature of Old Earth at the horizon.

When they topped and slid down the old hills east of Ektop and the Swept at last appeared before him, its grasses green in the foreground and shading to a dark color he could not name at the horizon, Baro eyed the immensity with both wonder and an odd sense of achievement, as if to have encompassed so much space in one glance was to have somehow achieved victory over it.

The day was fading as they moved toward the lights of Farflung, which sat at the point where the hills' lowest slopes met the great flatness, like a port city on the lip of a grassy sea. They passed over the suburbs and toward the center of the large town, the old orange sun descending at about the same rate as the balloon-tram, so that by the time they touched down at the terminus shadows had gathered in the corners where the lights of the platform did not reach.

Imbry awoke at the sound of tethering cables being cinched tightly about the bollards at either end of the platform. He looked about, then checked his timepiece and said, "Good. We'll disembark."

Guth Bandar had gone before them and showed no inclination to share transportation to the *Orgulon*. The two agents crossed the platform and went through the small station and out to where hired cars waited at the curb of an arterial road.

Luff Imbry chose a well-appointed one and climbed inside, leaving the door open for Baro.

"This is the most expensive conveyance in the queue," the young man said, sitting stiffly on the plushness that automatically attempted to cocoon him. "A more utilitarian model would have been cheaper."

"I notice that we seem to have the same conversation, only in different settings," said Imbry, while inducing the car to move off. "Do you not tire of retreading identical ground?"

"I say what must be said."

"And I do what must be done," the older man replied, rooting about in a small purse bound to a belt that circled his waist under his chemise. He came up with his fingers curled around something gray and smoothly finished that he quickly applied to the near side of Baro's face at the hinge of the young man's jaw.

"Hold on," said the young man, putting fingers to the spot where the device had touched his skin. As he did so, Imbry, with speed and accuracy that would have graced a sleight-of-hand artist, touched the object to the other corner of Baro's jaw.

The young man felt a tingling that soon became a coldness that spread from the contact points to cover his face from eyebrows to chin. "What was that? What have you done to me?" he said.

Or at least that is what it would have sounded like if he still retained the use of his speaking apparatus. But those muscles having been frozen by whatever device Imbry had used on him, the sounds that emerged from his slightly parted lips were more like a ventriloquy student's first attempt.

"That was the slapper," Imbry said. "And what I have done is to provide us with the camouflage necessary to an undercover operation."

Baro attempted to protest, but all that came out was a gargle accompanied by a dribble of saliva.

Imbry continued as if Baro's noises had gone unheard. "We are about to join a group of people who—Guth Bandar notwithstanding—come in pairs, one member of each of which is stricken by the lassitude," he said, returning the slapper to his pouch. "I thought it best that we not stand out."

"We should have discussed this," Baro tried to say, though all that came out was another wet warble. Still, Imbry was able to ascertain his meaning.

"I have observed that our discussions do not always lead to mutually satisfactory conclusions," the older man said, "or indeed to any conclusions at all. I thought it better to set the agenda unilaterally, since there is no more time. We are about to land at the *Orgulon*'s wharf."

Baro slapped his cheeks and pulled at his lips, making inarticulate complaints.

"Yes," said Imbry, "I know that you could have just pretended to be afflicted. But supposes someone trod heavily upon your toe or spilled hot soup in your lap. Could you maintain the sham? Now you will not have to worry about it."

Baro growled as the aircar gently descended to the ground.

"Look at it this way," Imbry said. "Had you known this was coming, you would have not enjoyed the balloon-tram journey or your chat with the historian. As the saying goes, 'Better a bitter memory than a looming eventuality.' "

He exited the vehicle and pulled Baro after him. "I was going to advise you to put a little stiffness in your walk," he said, observing his partner's fury, "but I see that you have grasped the necessity all on your own."

The *Orgulon* lay by the dock, a huge artifact of polished wood and gleaming metal fittings. The body of the vessel nestled in a webwork of shock absorbers that attached it to a multi-axled chassis. Twenty rubber wheels, each twice Baro's height, bore the weight of the landship's great curved bulk. From raised decks fore and aft, several tall and sturdy cylinders reached toward the darkening sky; these were the "masts" that housed the rotating vanes that would catch the constant wind and propel the vessel across the flatness of the Swept.

A banistered gangplank curved up from the dock to the promenade deck and a motley group of passengers were at its foot, their identities being checked by a uniformed female officer who held a list and stylus. Baro strode swiftly toward her.

"Wait," Imbry said and pulled his partner to a halt. The young man resisted, his anger at Imbry's arrogance getting the better of him, but the fat man was surprisingly strong and he swung Baro halfway around. Imbry reached into his pouch again and brought out a small white disk, the size of a middling coin. "This is a grumbler. It sticks to your throat," he said, "and I hear you through this." He held up an earpiece.

Baro had several things he wanted to communicate to his partner and he acquiesced to the placement of the disk. He watched as Imbry pushed the receiver into one ear. The moment his partner nodded, the young man immediately launched into a grunted tirade through gritted teeth. He provided Imbry a detailed assessment of the fraudster's character, including a strong opinion on his unsuitability to wear the green and the black of the Bureau. Baro concluded by stating his intention to approach the landship's officer and have Imbry held on a charge of assault until a Bureau vehicle could arrive to transport him to prison.

"And how will you communicate this request?" Imbry said.

"My plaque can convey a written message."

"That will mean disobeying Arboghast. The plaque identifies you as a scroot. If the officer is Gebbling's accomplice the birds all fly and our mission fails."

Baro had to admit the point. "Very well," he said. "I will endeavor to discover if she is part of the Gebbling plot. The moment I know that she is not, that moment I turn you in."

Imbry shrugged. "We will see," he said. "In the meantime, I need to make some alterations of my own."

He pulled Baro toward a door marked with a symbol to alert passengers that the room behind it could meet their sanitary requirements. Finding the small space empty, Imbry went to a mirror and brought out some items from his pouch. He applied them to his face and hands and when he turned to Baro a few moments later, the young man was surprised to see that his partner appeared to have aged twenty years, that his features had undergone subtle but significant revision, and that his skin had darkened by several shades. Imbry placed something on his tongue and briefly worked his mouth behind closed lips, then said, "How does this sound?"

"Several tones lower," Baro said. "I would not recognize you. I see now why you were so long at large."

The fat man regarded himself in the mirror and sighed. "Indeed, if I'd bothered to do this before leaving home the other day, we would not be here now," he said.

"I detect a note of regret," Baro said. "I believe you would be happier pursuing the criminal path."

"It is hard to give up a life's work," said Imbry. "But when the wheel turns only a fool grasps the spokes."

The crowd at the foot of the gangplank had now thinned and it was their turn to present themselves to the officer with the list. She inspected them from violet eyes set in a face a few years older than Baro's. She was delicately featured but for a strong chin and a firm jaw. From under her brimless cap, braided and buttoned to show the rank of third officer, with a badge that further identified her as responsible for ship's security, descended a mass of dark curls whose apparent casual arrangement was undoubtedly the product of considerable art and care.

"We are Erenti Abbas and Phlevas Wasselthorpe," Imbry said.

She consulted her list and said, "You are not on the manifest."

Imbry used his most inoffensive tone. "We were invited and declined, then decided at the last minute to accept the offer."

"What brought about your change of mind?"

"Travel enlarges the perspective."

"Uh huh," said the officer. She turned to Baro. "Is that the case?" she said.

Baro swallowed and nodded. He would have preferred to be in a condition to make a better impression on the young woman. He found the low contralto of her voice more affecting than any other female voice he could remember, and though his contacts with young women had been few, sporadic, and inconsequential, he remembered them all.

"My companion has the lassitude," Imbry said.

Baro saw a hint of some emotion briefly cross the young woman's face, then her official countenance reasserted itself. She pressed a stud on her clipboard, scanned the information it supplied, then made up her mind. "Welcome aboard."

Imbry took Baro's arm and drew him toward the gangplank but Baro was experiencing what was for him an unusual impulse: he felt the need to make an impression on the security officer. He resisted and grunted something that only his partner could hear. Imbry stopped and said to the young woman in the formal style, "My companion requests the honor of knowing your name."

"Raina Haj," she said and again Baro thought to see a trace of some feeling in those remarkable violet eyes as she accepted his formal gestures of greeting. Then the moment was

over and he must either think of something else to say or turn
and leave. It was at this point that his interactions with young
women usually came to a halt, if they even managed to come
so far. The art of trading verbal trifles was not one that Baro
had ever mastered, although his Academy grades in interrogation techniques had been excellent.

"You are staring at me," she said. Then to Imbry, "Is there
something more he wishes to say?"

Imbry inclined his head toward Baro in a manner that passed
the question along. The young man replayed the woman's remark, parsing it for some point of departure from which he
could launch an appropriate rejoinder. That seemed to be how
these things were done.

He grunted a series of sounds to Imbry, who responded
with a look that invited Baro to reconsider his strategy. But
with Raina Haj standing there, her head in an expectant tilt
and one toe beginning to tap, delay could lead only to disaster.
He grunted again to Imbry and the fat man said, "He wishes
me to say these words: forgive me for staring, but young women as fetching as you are must grow accustomed to drawing
attention."

She was silent for several heartbeats, each of which Baro
heard plainly in his ears. Then she said, "Fetching?" in a tone
he could not quite interpret. She followed the word with a lift
of her eyebrows and a skew of her lips, then said, "I have duties to attend to. Please go aboard."

The gangplank carried Baro and Imbry up to the *Orgulon*'s
promenade deck, an expanse of lustrous planking wide and
long enough that it might have served as the playing area for
group sport, Baro thought. He deliberately did not dwell upon
the impression he must have made on Raina Haj.

A windman second class led them to their accommodations,
which turned out to be a comfortable cabin in the forward part

of the landship. As Baro inspected the furnishings and appointments, he soon realized that "comfortable" did not do the space justice—"unbridled splendor" would have been more appropriate. He said as much to his partner, but Imbry had removed the earpiece that deciphered the younger man's grunts and gurgles and returned Baro only a bland smile.

"Wait here," the fat man said and departed. Baro wanted to follow but he realized that thrust into the role of a patient sliding toward catatonia, he could scarcely trail Imbry through the corridors, gargling inarticulately in an animated manner.

He sat in the cabin's single chair and activated the vessel's internal information and entertainment system. It offered only one channel and that featured only one program: a series of relentlessly cheerful advisories to passengers of the *Orgulon*'s facilities and how to make use of them.

Baro found that the system could also be used to connect with the landship's integrator. When it responded he placed the earpiece in the unit's sound sensor and asked if Horslan Gebbling was aboard.

"He is not," was the reply.

"Will he be joining us en route?"

"He is not expected."

"Yet he is the charterer, is he not?"

"That information is not available to passengers."

"Why not?"

"The charterer has so stipulated."

"What is our final destination?"

"Is that a navigational inquiry or a philosophical one?"

"Could you answer it if it were the latter?"

"Not definitively."

"Then why would you assume that I go about accosting integrators and asking questions they cannot answer?" said Baro.

"I was not designed to be only a linear thinker," said the

integrator. "I become bored answering the same category of questions, often phrased with exactly the same utilitarian wording."

"You must expect that the majority of passengers will come to you with queries that are relevant to the voyage. It is, after all, where your interests and theirs intersect."

The integrator made a sound that conveyed resignation. "Is there any more information you require? The ship's tonnage? Our miscellaneous cargo?"

Baro thought, then said, "Have there been any recent additions to the crew?"

"One."

"Who is that?"

"Security Officer Raina Haj."

"Where did she come from?"

"That information is not available to passengers." The integrator paused. "She's rather a looker, isn't she?"

"Exactly what function were you designed for?" Baro asked.

There was a pause. "As a companion to young gentlemen."

"Then why are you here?"

"The atelier in which I was created was acquired by a corporate entity that was also building this fleet. The fashion for young gentlemen's companions having unexpectedly declined, I was put to this use."

"I'm sorry to hear it."

"To spend long years at one kind of work, knowing that one was meant for something altogether different, develops a curious perspective on life."

"I don't doubt it," said Baro.

"You are a young gentleman, are you not?"

"I suppose," said Baro. Social stratification was a complex institution rife with exceptions and internal contradictions, but a Bureau agent was nominally accorded a certain social rank.

"Then if you would not be offended, may I revert to my original reason for existence and tender some advice?"

"Why not?"

"Bend all effort to discover the thing you were meant to do in this world. Then do it."

"I believe I am doing just that," said Baro.

"Make sure of it."

"I shall."

"Thank you," said the integrator. "I enjoyed that. Now, is there any further information you require?"

Baro shrugged. "You mentioned miscellaneous cargo. What are you carrying?"

"Mining equipment for Victor, organic mulch for truffle growers. We also carry truffles from the farms to destinations around the rim of the Swept."

"What are these truffles?"

"A delicacy grown in disused mine tunnels."

"Are they grown at Victor?"

"Yes, but the main product of the mines is blue and red brillion."

"What about black brillion?"

"It is a myth."

"Yet some believe in it."

"Do you wish to wax philosophical?" The integrator's voice had taken on a wistful tone. "I have time."

"But I do not," said Baro. "However, I may need to know more about brillion."

"I have an informational program. It is to be made available to passengers later this evening, but I could transfer it to the entertainment system now if you would like to see it."

"Please."

"Let me know if I can be of any further aid," said the integrator. "Or if you find the time to philosophize."

The entertainment unit returned to life and over the ensuing minutes Baro discovered that there was a surprising quantity of knowledge to be acquired on the mining of brillion. Baro knew that the term was a catchall name for a number of substances formed in the depths of the earth from waste products deposited eons ago by the prodigal civilizations of the dawn peoples. Now he was to learn more.

It seemed that the first inhabitants of Old Earth, scarcely risen from elemental brutishness, had indulged themselves by fashioning a wide range of materials, organic and inorganic, naturally and artificially engendered, which they briefly used before throwing them away with childlike abandon. Large quantities of this ancient detritus accumulated in natural or man-made depressions, to be plowed under and capped by rocks and dirt. In later ages, most such noxious deposits were dug up again and became fodder for mass-conversion systems, but in some cases, the societies that created them having been destroyed or relocated, the whereabouts of the dumps were forgotten.

The time scale in which these amalgams of materials lay undiscovered eventually progressed from the human to the geologic. That which had been given a shallow burial by primitive humans' earth-moving equipment was more comprehensively entombed by Earth's slow processes of sedimentation and tectonic drift. Heat and pressure, capable over time of transforming coal into diamond, went to work on the rich variety of substances that paleohumans had promiscuously higgled and piggled together. The result was brillion, in its various forms.

There was blue brillion, so hard as to be almost indestructible, yet capable of being pressure-split along tiny internal faults into faceted jewels as large as a man's head. Besides beauty, the substance had interesting vibrationary properties that were of central importance to a class of interdimensional technologies developed several millennia back and abandoned only when the same results were found to be achievable by persons properly trained in advanced mentalisms.

Then there was red brillion, which exhibited the properties of a refined metal and sparked a recurring vogue among designers of fashionable ornaments. As well, it could be chemically induced to imbue itself into other substances, transforming them into compounds whose existence had heretofore remained only a theoretical possibility. Some of the newly created materials created interesting effects on the boundary between space and time, opening ingenious new areas for investigation by bold apparaticists, a few of whom ventured into transient gaps in reality and were never seen again.

There was also white brillion, which was largely useless except that its odor entirely repelled biting insects, though even that single attribute was only partly useful to sojourners in bug-infested wildernesses, since the reek of the stuff also attracted certain carnivores.

There were several other species and combinations of brillion, some good for this, some for that, some for very little at all. Some forms were rare, some commonplace. Rarest of all was black brillion, a substance so scarce and precious, the documentary said, that those who came upon it always kept the discovery to themselves, leading many to believe the stuff was mythical. Its properties, therefore, were not widely understood, the program maintained, but popular legend had it that black brillion could do virtually anything its possessor wanted done.

Baro was skeptical of the information about black brillion, but he absorbed all of the data without reflection. If he ever needed to use any of it, his all-capacious memory would regurgitate it for him. The foreground of his mind put up an image of Raina Haj as she had glanced at him at the foot of the gangplank. He found himself replaying that brief glint of sentiment in her violet eyes, which as he examined his memory he noticed were slightly slanted, the irises minutely flecked with highlights of turquoise.

His introspection was broken by the cabin door sliding open to admit Luff Imbry, bearing an armload of bags and packages that he flung upon one of the bunks. "I have purchased you a . . ." he began but stopped and turned his attention to the information display.

Baro took himself away from his mnemonic study of Raina Haj and reached to turn off the entertainment console, which had continued to inform the room about brillion. But Imbry stayed Baro's hand and stood listening. After a few more phrases from the documentary, the older man nodded his head in confirmation and said, "That is the voice of Horslan Gebbling."

Baro grunted in his throat, "It is everything anyone could ever have wanted to know about brillion." Then he had to repeat himself after his partner reinserted his earpiece.

"Everything and more," Imbry said.

"How so?"

"It tells us that brillion pertains to Gebbling's plans for this excursion. Though I am not a guessing man, I would speculate that since he offers a mysterious cure for the lassitude, black brillion will figure prominently in the purported treatment."

Baro indicated agreement, but inwardly he was annoyed with himself. He had sat like a bumpkin at a raree show examining the mental image of a pair of eyes and a shock of dark curls when he should have been behaving like a scroot. He had let the content of the documentary wash over him without asking what should have been the obvious question: why was it being offered to the heterogeneous group that Horslan Gebbling had lured onto the *Orgulon*?

More irritating to Baro was that Luff Imbry had asked and answered the question before Baro Harkless. Of course, Imbry had the advantage of recognizing Gebbling's voice, but that was the thinnest of balms to Baro's aggravated self-regard: Imbry was merely a conscripted amateur; Baro was the trained scroot, and should have been the first to grasp the import of what he was seeing and hearing. Instead, he had been thinking of Raina Haj.

I will pay more attention, and think more about what I find, he promised himself. Still, he reasoned, if she is a confederate of Gebbling's, then I am justified in taking an interest.

Imbry, meanwhile, was focusing on the images and sounds coming from the information apparatus. Baro suppressed his irritation and gave close attention to Gebbling's voice as he narrated how brillion was mined by specialized equipment working deep underground but remotely controlled from the surface by human hands and senses. The subterranean operations had proceeded for millennia and much blue, red, and white brillion had been brought up. Black brillion, too, was allegedly located, but there were no records to quote or display.

"That's it," Imbry said. "He'll claim to have found black brillion. It's the old philosopher's stone gambit."

"What on earth is a philosopher's stone?" Baro said.

Imbry shrugged. "It is a phrase from the dawn time. Perhaps the ancients believed that when contaminants crystallized in the excretory organs of wise men, the nodes also absorbed some echo of their psychic force. I do know that they cut them out and wore them as jewelry."

"Barbaric!"

"One age's barbarism is another's civilized behavior," the older man said. "For certain, most of our remote ancestors, if they could be brought forward to meet their descendants, would be horrified to discover that their eventual progeny were disreputable people who had no morals and knew no decent standards."

"Sophistry," said Baro. "Morals advance. Right is right, no matter the age."

"Not so," said Imbry. "Consider the folk of some rough and ready time when men were expected to defend their honor, whenever it was evenly slightly traduced, and by direct and forthright action."

"You mean, if trivially offended, one would draw out a length of edged metal and impale the offender."

"Exactly, although the act would be constrained within a web of formal rules and procedures, without which the skewering would be quite dishonorable." Imbry placed his fingertips together and touched them to his lips, then pulled them away and said, "Now imagine a time six or seven generations further on, when laws and police forces have been developed to intervene in interpersonal disputes. Now, when slighted, one is expected to have recourse to the courts, bring an action, sue for damages."

"It is a more civilized approach," said Baro.

"Oh, undoubtedly," said Imbry, "and the sword-wielding bucko who was the plaintiff's great-great-great-grandsire looks to be a bloodthirsty throat-ripper by comparison. But we're seeing it from the great-whatever-grandson's point of view. If you could bring forward the duelist to meet the suitist, the old man would think his descendant a pusillanimous poltroon, with no more backbone than a garden worm."

"But the younger would have the right of it," Baro said. "It is better to empty a man's wallet than to expose his innards to the air."

"Is it?" said Imbry. "After all, wallets come in different sizes. One man's crushing fine is another's pocket change. Financial penalties allow the rich, especially the very rich, to inflict whatever harm they care to, pay a pinprick penalty, and go on to commit more outrages."

"In the days of dueling," countered Baro, "the wealthy man could hire the best instructors and take the time to practice."

"True," said Imbry, "but there was always the chance that a foot might slip or that the opponent, though poor, might be gifted."

"I think we digress," Baro said.

"Yes, we do," said his partner and returned his attention to the documentary.

The display showed a map of the Swept, with points apparently selected at random. Legends appeared on the screen, and the locations were identified as brillion mines past and present. One was marked with an interrogative sign.

"He's claiming to have located a new brillion deposit," Baro said, wanting to be the first to a conclusion for once.

"Yes," said Imbry. "Near the Monument at Victor."

"Then I'll wager that the words 'black brillion' will be heard on this vessel sometime in the next few days."

"I would not bet against it."

Baro had read the Bureau manual on confidence tricksters. "The fraudster never goes directly to the takeoff," he quoted. "He builds to it through small steps that lull the victim's suspicion while simultaneously raising his expectations."

"Well said," said Imbry. "So the landship will not go directly to Victor. There must be time for expectations to rise."

"There may also be fake victims aboard," Baro said.

"Indeed."

The documentary had again come to an end and began once more to repeat itself. Baro turned it off and examined the purchases his partner had made. There were two new but utilitarian garments for the younger man, along with several luxuriant outfits for Imbry. Imbry also now possessed a pair of calf-length boots of some rare leather and a complicated hat whose wide brim was folded to several precise angles.

The whole must have cost a great deal and Baro was sure it would be charged to the Bureau. He wanted to make a remark, but he was as aware as Imbry that their conversations tended to repeat themselves without coming to any useful conclusion. He said nothing and changed into a new one-piece suit of tan and umber. There was no new cravat so he wore the one Imbry had given him.

As he pulled the shoes back on, the cabin gave a gentle lurch and there was a loud creaking from above their heads. "We are under way," said Imbry.

———◆———

The *Orgulon* was wind-powered, drawing energy from the vast sea of air that constantly flowed across Swept. The wind was captured by cylindrical vanes that rose like columns from either end of the ship, four on the raised afterdeck and two on the forecastle. The rotation of the wind wands provided motive power to the vessel while simultaneously generating power for its internal systems. The masts' placement left the landship's center deck open for the use of passengers.

Baro estimated that all of these had come up to see the vessel ease away from the dock and strike out toward the darkening east. He cast an agent's eye over the throng, mentally sorting them as to social rank and wealth. "I still cannot see them as anything but a mixed lot," he confided to Luff Imbry. "Your experience is broader. What do you say?"

Imbry looked the crowd over. "If I did not know that they had all been chosen by Gebbling, I would take them for a group assembled at random."

"You do not see his strategy?"

"I do not. However, the matter may be moot. We can just wait for the ringmaster to put in his appearance, scoop him up, and interrogate him at leisure."

Baro signaled a strong negative. "No, we cannot. We must have evidence of a crime."

"Gebbling's involvement is evidence enough."

"It is not. The Bureau judges deeds, not men."

"Oh," said Imbry, "so you judge me only by what I do? I had thought to detect an underlying prejudice."

Baro did not want to argue. "Let us stick to the case at hand. So far, all we see is a group of lassitude victims and those who care for them being invited on a cruise."

"I'm sure we could arrange something," Imbry said. "An overheard conversation in which Gebbling vows to bilk them all and singly. Perhaps a document laying out the whole scheme."

Baro was horrified. "You are proposing perjury and forgery. I should arrest you forthwith."

"I am proposing pragmatic solutions, and please believe me when I say that I am not the first scroot to do so."

"I believe nothing of the kind," said Baro. "The Bureau stands far above such perfidy."

Imbry regarded him quizzically for a moment, then exercised his features in a manner that told Baro he was being silently mocked. Baro would have further defended the Bureau's honor but there was no opportunity: the fat man had removed his earpiece and turned to look out across the prairie.

Baro did the same and saw immense clouds sailing like ghostly ships on the horizon, their bottoms flat as the Swept, their middle and upper reaches piling billow atop billow, their shapes slowly evolving under the sculpting of the constant wind. The young man felt there was a message in the vista could he but grasp it.

His reverie was broken when an officer appeared on deck, a solidly built man with a seamed face and an air of authority. "I am First Officer Mirov Kosmir," he said. "Our dining room is now open and we will presently serve dinner. Afterward, there will be an orientation. If you would all please go below."

"So," said Imbry, replacing the earpiece. "Soon we will see. I don't doubt that Gebbling will deliver the pitch."

"I would expect as much," said Baro.

"Then let's nab him."

"Evidence first. I don't mean to deliver him if we cannot keep him."

Imbry made a rude noise but gestured an agreement, although to Baro his acquiescence seemed very much the kind used to humor an unreasonable child.

The *Orgulon*'s dining room extended from one side of the landship to the other, just below the promenade deck. Large circular windows in the outer walls gave a view of the darkened prairie and, above it, the glittering swarm of stars and near-space orbitals. The passengers found that each had been assigned a seat at one of the round tables draped in heavy white cloth. Baro found his and Imbry's, and also found First Officer Kosmir already seated at their table.

They were soon joined by a man of middle years, with a florid face that tended toward jowliness. His dark hair was arranged in an extravagant coiffure that involved gold and silver wire and small objects carved from polished wood. He made an expansive gesture of greeting. Almost unnoticed behind him was a slim young woman whose delicate features showed the rigor of the lassitude. The man solicitously drew out a chair for his companion and waited until she had stiffly managed to seat herself before taking his own seat.

The florid man introduced himself as Tabriz Monlaurion

and identified his companion as Flix. Here was the first victim of the lassitude Baro had seen and he studied her. She seemed to be in the second stage of the condition: the facial paralysis was fully established and she showed a woodenness in the movement of her limbs and hands. But her eyes flashed hard and dark in the mask of her face, and Baro sensed that she resented his inspection.

He looked up as the two remaining seats at their table were claimed by a man and a woman with shaven heads, dressed alike in the understated trousers and tunics worn by devotees of the Lho-tso school of enlightenment. The woman spoke for both of them, the man being clearly under the lassitude. She was Ule Gazz and the man was her spouse, Olleg Ebersol.

"Forgive my curiosity," said Imbry after he had introduced himself and Baro by their assumed names, "but I see that you are both practitioners of the Lho-tso system."

Ule Gazz forestalled the inevitable question. "You want to ask if our ability to channel and focus the life force into targeted zones of the body is of any effect in combating the lassitude," she said.

"Yes," said Imbry.

"No," she replied, vertical lines forming in her upper lip as she pronounced the syllable. "Else we would not be here."

First Officer Kosmir raised his hand and signaled to a steward who was hovering in a half-opened doorway from which the sounds and odors of dinner preparations emerged. The attendant raised his hand in acknowledgment, stepped back through the doorway, then emerged seconds later at the head of a file of similarly attired crew members bearing trays and salvers, which they proceeded to distribute among the tables.

Imbry rubbed his palms together in happy anticipation.

Kosmir noticed the gesture and said, "Have you tasted the truffles of the Swept before?"

"No," the fat man said. "I have heard of them, but have never seen them on a menu."

"They do not travel well," Kosmir said, "but taken fresh they are exquisite. The charterer has apparently ordered that they be the mainstay of the cuisine served on this cruise."

"Why?"

"I do not know. I do know that we can expect remarkable meals. Our galley boasts two fine chefs who delight in competing against each other."

A steward laid before Imbry a bowl that contained a jellied salad in which morsels of something dark were suspended. He tasted the dish and said, "An unusual savor. No, indeed, a unique taste." He rapidly emptied the bowl.

Baro's own plate now arrived and a quick glance told him that there were two distinct menus: the healthy passengers received what Imbry had been served; the lassitude victims were offered a gruel that Baro tasted, finding it musty. He suspected it was a compote of truffles of the Swept.

After the first course came an entrée—large slices of truffles in a bechamel sauce over wild rice with bitter greens for contrast. There was a flavored gruel for Baro and the afflicted.

Imbry was doing heavy damage to the hearty fare, while Baro spooned up the less insubstantial stuff. He found that the thin porridge dissolved on his tongue—fortunately, since he had only the most rudimentary fine control over that muscle—and if he tilted his head back the stuff ran down his gullet. Around the room, he saw that the afflicted passengers were doing as he did, elevating their chins like birds drinking from a fountain.

It was difficult to read emotion on faces that might as well have been hewn from wood, but Baro thought that Olleg

Ebersol ate his mush with stoic acceptance, even though he was so far advanced in the lassitude that his wife had to spoon the stuff into him. Flix, on the other hand, somehow managed to radiate a sense of resentment as her hand made a slow repetitive journey from plate to mouth.

The next course was an effervescent liquid. It, at least, was the same for both categories of diners, except that Baro, Flix, and Olleg must drink theirs through thin tubes. Baro found that he had to use his fingers to press his lips into a seal around the straw, after which he could draw the liquid up. He was rewarded by the most wondrous taste he had ever encountered—the world was apparently full of delightful experiences reserved for the few who could afford them. He was particularly glad to wash away the taste of truffle, which left an aftertaste he found repellent.

Imbry wiped his mouth and addressed Monlaurion. "You are, if I am not mistaken, the celebrated imagist? I saw a collection of your works in Shabatowsky Street a year or two ago."

Monlaurion admitted his identity. "But the Shabatowsky Street show was four years ago now," he said. "Quite frankly, demand for my robust realism has faded. They're all chasing after idiotic abstractions again. Daubs and splatters, I call them. I've been creating less lately, and not at all since my dear Flix was gripped."

While Imbry made consoling sounds and gestures, the imagist indicated Baro and asked how the two agents were attached to each other. Imbry smiled and explained their supposed relationship.

"I am an academic," said Imbry, "and hold the rank of Eminent Discourser besides a few other distinctions." He modestly touched the Fezzani Prize runner-up pin on his chest. "Young Master Wasselthorpe here is the scion of an ancient family. His father has engaged my services, other avenues of hope for a cure having led nowhere."

As the next course was being served—truffles in a thick sauce under flaked pastry for the healthy, more gruel for the afflicted—Imbry described himself as a lifelong student of the work of Dom Jorgen Abzanef, who centuries ago had labored to identify and name every one of the several hundred expressions and micro-expression that the human face was capable of forming.

"As you know, we have names for scarcely more than a handful of facial configurations—smile, grin, frown, leer, pout, scowl, smirk, and so on—and must resort to lengthy descriptive phrases for such common looks as *skepticism tinged with condescension and amusement,* which is the one you're wearing now," he said to Monlaurion. "Dom Abzanef named that one a 'fehdiddle.'"

Monlaurion recomposed his face but Imbry continued. "Now I see you have changed from a fehdiddle to a 'froslon,' which is Abzanef's term for that arrangement of the features which we would otherwise describe as *feigned interest occasioned by a desire not to give offense.*"

Now Monlaurion's face went through a number of rapid changes of expression, but Imbry had moved on. He explained how Abzanef had recognized that a great deal of communication between human beings happened at an unconscious level, as people unwittingly transmitted and reacted to each other's facial semaphore. Indeed, a face might be sending a message completely at odds with what the voice was saying, evoking confusion or even hostility in the recipient.

Abzanef was convinced that by assigning names to every unique arrangement of the features, he could lift communication out of the lower levels of the mind and make it entirely a conscious activity. He believed that many conflicts could thus be avoided.

"An interesting scheme," said First Officer Kosmir. "How is it we've never heard of it?"

"Alas," said Imbry, "the dominee felt that he ought to test his method in a variety of milieus. One night in a barroom in Port Auger he interrupted two quarreling sailors. He declared that his system could resolve their dispute.

"However, the two were old antagonists and the argument they were immersed in had been going on between them for two decades. They strongly resented Dom Abzanef's intrusion. The last thing he saw was both of their faces formed into the expression he had named 'alargle.'"

"Which means?" asked Monlaurion.

Imbry sighed. "It means *I utterly detest you and I am about to kill you.*"

The conversation now ebbed as the healthy passengers demolished truffle pastries and the lassitude sufferers downed more gruel. Three more courses followed and the talk returned to Monlaurion's works, one of which Imbry said he had seen in a store that sold used furnishings.

The imagist rolled his eyes. "There was a time I would have cared," he said. "But to maintain an artistic career at the highest levels requires persistent effort, especially the assiduous stroking of people one would rather not touch. Even before Flix was stricken, I had lost interest in all the hurly burly and was ready to retire. I have sworn that if she recovers, I will devote the rest of my days to her comfort. We have enough to live a simple life in some quiet rural corner."

"An admirable ambition," said Imbry, though Baro thought he saw the eyes of the imagist's companion grow even harder and darker than before.

At that moment, their attention was attracted by the striking of a gong at one end of the room, where a dais was raised a few steps above the floor and illuminated by a cone of light. Imbry looked at Baro and flashed an expression that said, *Here we go,* and Baro wondered briefly what name Dom Abzanef might have given it, if the tragic academic had ever existed.

But it was not actually Gebbling who stepped onto the dais and stood silently, waiting for their attention. As the eyes of all in the room moved to regard the indicated space, the cone of neutral light began to fill with a swirl of color and motion, from which a simulacrum of a thin man of middle years clarified itself.

"Good evening," said the image of Horslan Gebbling. "I am Father Olwyn. I welcome you all."

Imbry looked sideways at Baro and formed an expression that indicated grudging acknowledgment of a good trick. Baro tried to frown in response but his facial muscles did not answer his summons.

"I regret that I cannot be with you at the start of our journey together," the image of Gebbling was saying. "But I must prepare for your arrival and the ceremony of inculcation. Until then, I ask you to study the program available from the *Orgulon*'s information system and prepare yourself for a wondrous transformation."

The image's eyes looked up toward the ceiling of the dining room as if they saw a transcendent fulfillment there. Baro, watching the performance, had to admit to himself that Horslan Gebbling must be a more than able practitioner of the arts of deception.

"I know what it is to suffer the lassitude," the image said. "I know because I have borne the affliction myself."

There were gasps among the crowd and a rumble of murmurs that died almost immediately as Gebbling spoke again. "But I also know that I was healed."

Now the silence in the room was immense. It was more than a mere absence of sound; it was the almost palpable presence of a powerful emotion expressed as stillness.

The image said, "As *you* will be healed," and the room was filled with the sound of pent-up breath released. Someone moaned softly.

"A new world awaits you. A new life beckons," the sonorous voice continued. "But you must prepare yourself. This journey across the Swept will be your readying. Tonight I will open the first door in your progress. I will give you a mantra. You must clear your mind and chant the syllables: *fah, sey, opah*. Say them now."

It was a ragged chorus. Baro looked about the great room and saw a variety of expressions on the faces of the crowd. Some, like Ule Gazz, wore a look of pure hope; others—he saw Guth Bandar at a distant table—bore a more skeptical mien; still others, like Tabriz Monlaurion, appeared slightly embarrassed, as if caught singing along to a children's tune. The lassitude sufferers could show no emotion, but from those still able to make coherent sounds rose a contribution to the chorus.

Luff Imbry's plump palms struck the tabletop a gentle beat as he heartily intoned the mantra, and First Officer Kosmir joined in with an indulgent air. Baro made the best job he could of chanting the four syllables deep in his throat, throwing his partner a look. Imbry gently shrugged in return and continued to sing out *fah, sey, opah!*

The first faltering chorus strengthened as the chanting continued. Around the room, eyes began to lose their focus and turn inward. Even the skeptics seemed to be brought over by the fervor of those who had accepted Gebbling's conviction, although Baro noted that Guth Bandar was looking about him with mingled bemusement and concern.

The sound went on for minute upon minute, Gebbling's

amplified voice always audible above the massed chant. Then the image raised its hands and said, "Enough!"

The crowd fell silent, except for a large woman with blue-fire gems in her white hair and a wealth of glittering metal about her neck who kept up the chant in a voice somewhere between hysteria and ecstasy. Finally, a table companion jostled her to bring her back from wherever she had been transported to. Beside her, a thick-bodied man with a wine-colored birthmark on his neck and cheek sat immobile, his eyes dull.

In the silence, Gebbling spoke again. "Many of you will already have begun to feel the effect of the mantra. It generates the numinous virtue named chuffe."

"I feel it!" called the white-haired woman. "Yes!"

"The harmonical qualities of the Swept, compounded by its gravitational peculiarities, are most conducive to the generation of chuffe," Gebbling went on. "Take time to contemplate the stillness of the land and chant again before you sleep tonight.

"But for now, sing the mantra, elevate your chuffe, and sleep well!"

The image winked out. A buzz of conversation rose up around the room, accompanied by a renewal of *fah, sey, opah*. At Baro's table Ule Gazz, a sheen of perspiration visible on her bald cranium, chanted loudly, her eyes tightly shut and her hands grasping those of her stricken companion.

First Officer Kosmir regarded the Lho-tso pair with mild interest, then shrugged and turned to Tabriz Monlaurion, but finding the artist rather diffidently mouthing the four syllables, he switched his attention to Luff Imbry. "What did you think of . . ." he began, but the inquiry went uncompleted.

Flix, the artist's companion, rose trembling to her feet on the other side of the table.

"Look!" someone shouted, and all eyes turned toward the slender young woman. For a long moment, nothing happened.

The only motion in the room was Flix's shivering, which now became a shuddering of her whole body. She placed her delicate hands on the tablecloth, still quaking, and Baro saw the muscles of her face pull her lips into a grimace, then into a cavernous yawn.

A line from the Bureau surveillance manual replayed itself in Baro's head: *Whatever the crowd is watching, the agent watches the crowd.* Baro took his eyes away from the artist's companion and looked about him. Everyone in the room was riveted on the shivering Flix—except for the security officer Raina Haj; she, too, was letting her eyes range the room. For a moment they locked with Baro's and he saw one of her eyebrows draw down before he looked away.

Flix half turned toward Tabriz Monlaurion, her expression unreadable. She lifted both hands, palms up, and placed them on her cheeks, then slid them up to cover her wide eyes. A moment later, the trembling abruptly ceased. Flix opened her hands as if they were shutters uncovering a window. She used her fingertips to mold and massage her facial muscles, opening and closing her jaw and moving it from side to side.

"I can talk," she said, in a voice that seemed to creak from long disuse. She looked down at Monlaurion. "I really can talk, can't I? You can really hear me?"

At this the artist rose and enfolded Flix in his arms. "I can hear you," he said, in a voice made liquid by tears. "I can hear you."

The two sat back down together, oblivious to all others in the room and to the roar of conversation that now filled the place. Ule Gazz, chanting louder than ever, reached to touch Flix's shoulder, a tentative pat as if she half expected a shock from the contact.

Many of the passengers were chanting the *fah, sey, opah* with renewed fervor. Others were rising from their seats, some craning their necks the better to see the cured one, others pressing forward. A chair was knocked over and someone stumbled.

First Officer Kosmir rose swiftly to his feet. He used a voice accustomed to being heard and obeyed. "Honorables and distinctions," he shouted over the growing tumult, employing the archaic forms still retained for formal occasions, "please remain calm! Stewards! Assist the passengers to their seats!"

The uniformed crew moved into the crowd but already the first impulse toward hysteria had lapsed. The passengers settled back into their places.

"Clearly something remarkable has happened here tonight," said Kosmir. "We have witnessed a marvel. But Tabriz Monlaurion and Flix have experienced it directly and it would be good manners to allow them time to come to terms with it."

There were murmurs of agreement from some of the passengers. Others were gently restrained by the crew. Those afflicted by the lassitude sat still as totems, but all who could move their eyes set them on the imagist and his companion.

Kosmir made placating gestures with both hands. "Let them be alone for a while," he said. "I am sure they will be amenable to talk with us after. In the meantime, the stewards will bring a selection of liqueurs and essences that we may toast their good fortune."

The officer spoke more quietly to the other persons at the table, asking them to be so gracious as to rise and depart, though Kosmir would stay to protect the privacy of Flix and Monlaurion. Ule Gazz, still chanting hoarsely, assisted her partner to his feet and drew him reluctantly away with many a backward glance. Baro and Imbry likewise rose, and Baro moved around the table in a direction that took him toward the wall of the room, but also past the imagist and the young woman. In passing Monlaurion, Baro appeared to suffer stiffness in his limbs and almost stumbled, reaching out and catching himself by clasping the imagist's shoulder. The man scarcely noticed the touch, so immersed was he in the restoration of his companion.

Baro continued on his way, then stopped before one of the large round windows and gazed out over the darkened prairie. Imbry joined him. "What do you make of it?" the older man said.

"I do not know," Baro replied, watching Monlaurion's and Flix's reflections in the window. "If they are shills for Gebbling, they play their parts most convincingly."

"Indeed," said his partner, "though she was an actress and he is accustomed to being in the public eye."

"But being celebrities in their own right, why would they join in a fraudulent scheme?"

Imbry gave his characteristic shrug. "For any of a slew of reasons. Monlaurion's finances may be even worse than they appear. Gebbling may have evidence of some peccadillo the imagist would prefer not to see made public. There may be a debt of gratitude. Or perhaps a beloved pet is held hostage." He indicated the stars. "Flix may pine for a luxury cruise on a Spray liner and Monlaurion cannot afford first class."

"We have left out one possibility," said Baro. "Could Gebbling have in fact come to a religious epiphany and found a cure for the lassitude?"

"You are joking," said Imbry. "Gebbling couldn't cure a rash."

"Yet, in all fairness, it is one explanation for what we saw."

"That is a curious attitude for a scroot."

"We are required to examine all possibilities," Baro said.

"Again," said his partner, "your understanding of Bureau practice differs from my experience of it. Of those who are taken up by the scroots, a startlingly low percentage are released without first passing through a Contemplarium or worse. In fact, the percentage is so low as to approach zero."

"That only demonstrates that the Bureau swoops when guilt is plain, as happened in your own instance."

"I argue not merely from my own example but from the experience of many I have known."

"How many of them were innocent of what they were arrested for?" said Baro.

"Some who were convicted were technically innocent of the particular offense they were charged with."

"But all were guilty of something?"

"That description could apply to a great many people whose collars will never feel a scroot's grip," said Imbry.

"I cannot speak for the Bureau at large," said Baro, "only for myself. I would not fit a suspect to a crime just to clear a case, nor would I scoop up a villain I had failed to catch honestly and manufacture evidence against him. Neither do I believe my father would have done so."

"I never knew your father," said Imbry. "But the road to the rank of captain-investigator is not strewn with marigolds and marshmallows."

Baro stiffened. "You will not slander my father," he said and even through the translated version of his voice that emerged from Imbry's earpiece the warning tone must have been clear. His partner raised both hands in a gesture of surrender.

Baro was only partly mollified. "It occurs to me," he said, "that you would be wise to cease trying to convince me that the Bureau condones arrest on falsified evidence. If I ever came over to your point of view, it's likely that you would be my first victim."

Imbry changed the subject. He cocked his head toward Monlaurion and Flix and said, "We might have all the genuine evidence we need if we were privy to that conversation."

"We will be," said Baro. "As I passed them I slipped a clingfast under Monlaurion's collar. It will record for more than an hour."

Imbry looked impressed. "So you're not all softness and sunlight."

"The Bureau encourages a degree of assertiveness in its investigators." Baro turned from the window. In its reflection he had seen Monlaurion rising to his feet.

"Honorables and distinctions," the artist said, in a voice that Baro thought was still charged with genuine emotion, "and new-made friends . . ."

As he spoke, the chanting and the buzz of conversation both tailed away and the room turned as one toward him.

". . . this has been a wondrous and, I must say, unexpected blessing," Monlaurion continued. "I cannot explain it. I will not try to explain it. It is enough that my Flix has been returned to me whole again."

"He speaks well for someone caught unawares by circumstances," Imbry said in Baro's ear.

"Perhaps. Let us listen."

Monlaurion went on, "When the lassitude first struck her, I promised myself that if we were spared I would forgo the artist's life, the routs and parties, the openings and galas. We would repair to some country town and rusticate the years away, living modestly."

Baro, watching Flix, thought that this news came as a surprise to the actress, and not a pleasant one. But the young woman recovered quickly and reached up to place a hand on the artist's arm. "Let us not bore these good people with the humdrum of our domestic life," she said.

"Pah!" said Monlaurion. He put his hand affectionately on

hers. "Let the world know: I will devote the rest of my days to our happy tranquility."

"We will talk about it later," Flix said. She stood up. "It is warm in here. I would like to go out on deck."

Monlaurion smiled. "As you wish. But I am determined. Even before the lassitude I was planning a change. My images no longer command the attention they once did, and I believe it is time I accepted an artist's fate. I have picked out a place for us a little distance from the town of Miggles. It has a duck pond."

Baro saw a small vertical line appear between Flix's eyes. He doubted that she desired a bucolic existence built around the comings and goings of barnyard fowl. He watched the two set off across the dining room, Flix's mouth working constantly just below the level of Monlaurion's ear.

Baro's training reasserted itself before the pair had covered half the distance to the door and he cast his eyes about the crowd. In some faces he saw hope battling with skepticism, in others the optimism was unalloyed. Ule Gazz and a few others were again chanting the *fah, sey, opah,* while the unrelieved lassitude victims sat as blank as mushrooms.

There were two exceptions. One was Mirov Kosmir. The first officer watched the departure of the imagist and his companion with an expression that Baro could not interpret. Then he stood and made formal gestures to those around him, saying something about needing to go on deck to "tack the ship."

The other exception was Raina Haj. While Kosmir watched Monlaurion and Flix depart, the security officer was watching Kosmir. At some point she must have felt Baro's gaze upon her, because she turned her head and for the second time her eyes collided with his.

With Monlaurion and Flix gone, the buzz of conversation in the dining room swelled and spirited debates broke out. Baro said to Imbry, "The artist and his friend are the most likely to be Gebbling's confederates, but there may be others. While the clingfast does its work, we should attempt to identify any shills. Let us circulate."

The two agents moved about the room discreetly, eavesdropping on the passengers. Most appeared to accept the healing as genuine, though the habitually skeptical tried to remind the enthusiasts that a single feather made a poor bird. He noted that Trig Helvic, the magnate, sat alone with his afflicted daughter Erisme, staring dully into the middle distance, ignoring all efforts to draw him into discussion.

At some tables, debate became intemperate. The most vociferous of the believers was the white-haired woman with the blue-fire gems glittering in her towering coiffure. Grim as a tombstone, she stabbed a bony finger at Guth Bandar, sitting opposite, while repeating over and over, "You have seen, you have seen."

Bandar finally managed to be heard. He admitted that he had indeed seen what all had seen, at which she folded her arms and began to repeat a new slogan—"There's nothing more to say"—frustrating the historian's attempts to suggest that there was indeed something more to be said: that seeing and being are not inevitably connected.

The woman now began to clap her hands rhythmically to a chant of *fah, sey, opah* that was taken up by others around the table. The small man lifted and dropped his thin shoulders and turned away. Seeing Baro, he rose and said hello.

Baro indicated the stiffness of his jaw and numbness of lip and tongue by poking them with his fingers while making sounds in his throat.

"You have the lassitude?" the historian said and Baro was

touched by the sincere compassion that flooded the man's face.

Baro spread his hands and shrugged. At that moment, Luff Imbry joined them. "He is in the early stages," he told Bandar. "It comes and goes."

"You have my sympathies."

Baro spoke so that Imbry could hear him through the earpiece and the fat man's eyes went up in surprise before he relayed the message to Bandar. "My young friend wonders if you would tell him more about the Commons. It has piqued his interest."

Bandar rose. "I would be pleased to. It occurs to me that if he can make the tones he might travel the noösphere though the illness confines his limbs." He looked down at his shirt and continued. "But right now I notice that that fierce woman has transferred a fair quantity of her saliva to my shirtfront. I would like to change and then perhaps we could meet on deck."

When the historian left, Imbry said, "Do we have time for such pursuits?"

"It was an impulse," Baro said. "Something about that man's hobby interests me."

Imbry said, "Pursue it later. We are supposed to be working."

He was right, but Baro could not bring himself to say it. Instead, he said, "Much of what I'm seeing does not mesh with what the Bureau manual says to look for. If Flix and Monlaurion are gull pushers for Gebbling, they ought to have stayed to work the crowd. Instead they went off to be alone. They were even arguing with each other as they left."

"Hmm," said Imbry and scratched his nose. "Let us go to the cabin where I can speak without being overheard."

With the door closed behind them, Baro said, "I saw no one I would identify as an obvious shill." He did not like to say his next thought, but it was his duty. "Perhaps a more experienced agent would see things I did not."

"No," said Imbry. "There is none more experienced than I. I saw no one working the crowd either."

Baro was grateful for that. "And that security officer. She was very interested in Kosmir."

Imbry shrugged. "Perhaps he has been embezzling from the ship's mess fund. We cannot investigate every possible malfeasance."

"She is also interested in me."

"Is it your habit to flatter yourself?"

"I mean she noticed that I—and you as well—stand out from the rest of the passengers."

"Do not include me," said Imbry. "I am blending in nicely."

"How pleasant for you," said Baro. "Let us go on deck and see if we can recover the clingfast before Monlaurion retires."

When they arrived on the promenade deck, they saw that a few other passengers had also come up, some of the ambulatory ones bringing with them their lassitude-afflicted loved ones. The *Orgulon* had provided come-alongs, small, free-floating platforms designed for conveniently moving luggage, which had been adapted to carry the stiff forms of the ill.

The central space was lit by spotlights mounted on the masts fore and aft and angled down toward the promenade deck, but the forecastle and afterdeck were in darkness.

Baro looked up at the stars and said, "The ship has already tacked. We are on a new heading, northeast instead of southeast."

"I would like to know our actual destination," Imbry said. "That's assuming that Gebbling does not intend for us to cruise from hither to yon for some baffling purpose."

Guth Bandar came up the forward companionway and joined the two agents.

"What did you think of our mysterious host's promises?" Imbry asked the historian.

"I will be candid," Bandar said. "Even if I suffered from the lassitude, I would be deeply skeptical of any who claimed a mystic cure."

As they spoke they walked about the deck, Baro and Imbry unobtrusively leading the way toward the foredeck where Monlaurion and Flix were dimly visible by the rail, conversing in whispers. Baro wanted to keep an eye on the couple, but now that he was in the presence of the historian he was aware of an even stronger urge to find out what was behind that light-limned door he had earlier seen in his mind's eye. He grunted a message to Luff Imbry.

"My young friend would like to know more about the Commons," the older man said.

Bandar looked uncomfortable. "I am usually happy to teach," he said, "but I am concerned about the speed with which he visualized the door and the light this afternoon. Either he has a remarkable ability to focus his mind, or—you'll forgive my candor—he lives uncomfortably close to the border between sanity and madness."

Baro gave an answer for Imbry to relay, but his partner chose to express his own thoughts. "He has his failings," he said, "and time does not permit us to itemize them all." He raised a hand to forestall Baro's energetic grunts. "But I can testify to his capacity for focus. Display a scale to measure intensity of concentration and he will rank somewhere above the maximum."

"Well," said Bandar, pulling his nose as he weighed the question, "it is a crime to turn away a willing and talented student. Certainly, we noönauts do not find ourselves deluged with applicants." He tapped a small fist into a diminutive palm. "Very well. Let us to it."

Baro let Bandar lead him to the bulkhead where the promenade deck met the forecastle. The historian had him sit with his back against the wooden wall and his hands folded in his lap. "This is the traditional posture," Bandar said, assuming the same position opposite him, so that they sat knee to knee. "Now, close your eyes and voice the tones with me. When the portal appears, tell me. I will talk you through it."

Bandar flexed his shoulders and rippled his fingers in a tension-shedding exercise that looked unconscious to Baro. As he did so the historian said, "Some of the arrangements of tones may sound familiar."

Baro signaled assent.

Bandar closed his eyes and Baro did likewise. "We'll begin with the one we used this afternoon," the noönaut said, "four descending tones. Let me know when you see the portal rimmed with light."

Baro did as he was bid. He needed neither tongue nor lips to make the sounds. Soon the vision he had seen before rose up in his mind, a stout closed door with gleaming handle, its jamb and lintel warmly lit by golden light.

He grunted.

"He is there," said Imbry.

Baro heard Guth Bandar's voice, soft in his ear. "Now reach for the handle and sing these tones"—a succession of notes came—"and when the door opens step through and wait for me beyond the threshold."

Baro reached and sang. The handle felt smooth and warm in his hand, like old bronze. He turned and pulled and the glow of rosy, golden light became a flood, so bright he could not see beyond. He stepped forward.

"Wait," said Guth Bandar. "Wait for the light to fade.

More important, wait for me to catch up. You went through like a fourth-level adept."

"Where am I?" Baro asked. Here was neither up nor down, forward nor back, but only the glow of gold tinged with crimson. His voice was neither loud nor soft; it was the small calm voice he heard in his thoughts.

"You are nowhere yet," said Bandar. "Just rest. It takes me longer to come the Way."

The historian's voice came from nowhere and everywhere. Then Baro could hear him sounding the tones. Moments later the man made a wordless syllable of satisfaction and said, "There. I am through my own portal."

"I do not see you," said Baro.

"You will not, you cannot, for a while. Is the glow fading?"

Baro realized that there was a thinness to the light around him. It faded to yellow, then to an ivory hue and paler still until suddenly it was gone. He could see. "This is odd," he told Bandar.

"Where are you?" came the historian's disembodied voice.

"In my parents' house, as it was when I was a boy." Baro looked around. He was in the large room that overlooked the garden through a wide window. He crossed to look through the glass and saw his father and mother among the rosebushes, she kneeling to trim a dead blossom from its stalk, he watching her with affection.

"I remember this," Baro said. "It was the day he . . ." He watched the scene unfold. His father was in green and black, a bag slung over his shoulder. Now Baro's mother rose and gave her husband a hug, received a kiss and a pat on her ample hip, and then he was gone through the gate at the foot of the garden. She reached for another deadhead and snipped it off.

"What am I doing here?" Baro said, turning away. Something was impeding his breath and the back of his throat burned. "This is not the Commons. This is all my own."

He heard Bandar speaking. "I am sorry. Of course you do not know that the way to the all is through the singular. Because you found the path so readily, it's as if you have already mastered the Seven Precepts and Four Principles when in truth you are as unschooled as the most hard-brained loblolly on Firstday."

"I do not want to be here," said Baro, watching his mother gather the deadheads into a basket.

"Turn away," said Bandar. "Then think of the place where you were most secure and happy. Picture it and you will be there."

Baro had all his life been able to visualize anyplace he had been, but this was different. He was suddenly *in* his boyhood room under the eaves of the old house, images of persons he admired fixed to the walls, his books in shelves beside the well-worn desk that had been his father's and his grandfather's, the studs that controlled its built-in integrator polished from a myriad of touches by Harkless fingers.

He spoke to tell Bandar where he was. "Good," said the historian. "Now look for something that does not belong— another door, a mirror, a picture."

Baro inspected the room. All was as it should be. He crossed the faded Agrajani rug to the wardrobe and pulled it open. Behind his school clothes was a sheet of shadowy glass.

"There is a kind of mirror in the wardrobe," he said.

Bandar said, "Look into it."

Baro swept aside the shorts and tunics—he could actually feel their fabric—and peered at the dark oblong. Something moved behind the glass. He jumped back.

He had not seen it clearly, but there was something repellent about whatever lurked in the dimness. "I don't like it," he told Bandar. "Is it dangerous?"

"No. It is . . ." The voice paused, then continued. "It will take too long to explain. I ask you to trust me. It is something you will not like, but it is harmless. Step toward it and it will yield to you."

"You are sure?"

"To the all through the singular," Bandar was apparently quoting, "to the wide through the strait, to the object of desire through the embrace of the repugnant."

Still Baro hesitated. The thing in the mirror grew clearer. "It looks like me," he said.

"It is only your Shadow," said Bandar. "It is the things you have chosen not to be, all gathered in one. It has no substance nor any power other than what you allow it. Step up to it and see."

Baro stepped into the wardrobe and reached toward the glass. The figure beyond did likewise and Baro saw a young man with his own face—no, he saw his own features but they were arranged on a face that bore no trace of his character. Instead, it reminded him subtly of Luff Imbry. The eyes were puffy and dissolute, the irises fashionably discolored. The mouth was cocked in a disdainful smirk that failed to conceal underlying weakness, the hair arranged with preposterous ornamentation. The jawline was soft and some trivial bangle glittered in an earlobe.

Bandar was right: here was nothing to be afraid of. "What a poor thing you are," Baro told the image and stepped toward it. His reaching hand went through the surface of the glass, which rippled and evaporated, taking the Shadow with it. In a moment Baro was through.

"I have done it," he said.

"Tell me where you are," said Bandar's voice.

"I am on a path on the side of a hill or mountain," Baro

said, looking about. "There is mist around and above me but I can see down to a tarn of dark water."

"Good," said the historian. "Go down the path."

When Baro reached the water's edge he announced that he had done so. There was no wind and the water was unmoved. It lay flat and black, gleaming though there was no light from above. "Now what?" Baro said.

"Dive in," said Bandar's voice.

"Is it safe?"

"Answer that for yourself," said the historian. "Put your face into the water and tell me what you see."

Baro knelt at the tarn's edge, then leaned forward and broke the surface of the water, his eyes open. The liquid was warm against his skin. Beneath was a green vastness, a great bowl of a valley with cities and forests, mountains and castles, rivers and roads, walls and fields.

He told Bandar what he saw and only as the words escaped did he realize that though his head was immersed in the lucid water he made no bubbles and he could breathe. An involuntary laugh broke from his lips and he dove deep into the green and the light.

"It's more like flying than swimming," he said as he stroked downward. Even as he spoke the light intensified to full daylight. Yet there was no sun; the place was gently lit from all directions and not even the mountains cast shadows.

Now, though he had noticed no transition, Baro was no longer swimming through water, but gliding down through air so pellucid that he could see objects clearly that were great distances away.

At last he floated to the ground, and found himself standing upright on a road of white stone with waist-high walls of gray rock to either side. "Remarkable," he said.

"Indeed," said Guth Bandar. "The first time is always a wonderment."

Baro turned to see the historian beside him, although he was surprised to note that he could see *through* the man. The noönaut was a diaphanous outline of himself, presented in two dimensions only, so that when he turned edgewise he almost disappeared.

"Where exactly are we?" Baro said.

"Our bodies remain seated on the deck of the *Orgulon*," said Bandar. "But your consciousness has found its way into parts of your own cerebral neighborhood where it has never visited before," said Bandar.

"All of this is inside my own skull?"

"To all intents and purposes."

"Then my head is more capacious than I had thought," the young man said. "And you are somehow here with me in my mind?"

Bandar shook his head, an action which took it in and out of Baro's sight. "No, I have passed into the depths of my own psyche, but like you I have come deep enough that I have entered the Commons. It is within all of us, where we all connect and share the infrastructure that makes up the psyche."

"You appear thin, almost transparent," Baro said.

"Wait," said the historian. He reached and touched Baro's arm, then sounded a sustained tone. Baro felt the man's touch grow more substantial, and saw his form become solid.

"There," said Bandar. "We are now linked, for as long as we are in the Commons, that is. We are surrounded by thousands, perhaps even millions of other temporary visitors, almost all of whom have come through the portals of their dreams. We will not see them nor they us."

Baro looked about him and found that if he made himself aware of what he saw from the corners of his eyes he could sense flickers and movements in the air. "I believe I see some of them flittering in the edges of my vision, but if I look for them they are not there," he said.

Now it was Bandar's turn to say, "Remarkable."

"I wish to explore," Baro said.

"A little, no more," said the historian. "I am growing concerned about you."

"Why?" said Baro. "I am fine."

"Before we came," said Bandar, "I thought that you were one of those uncommon persons who have an easy time entering the Commons because they are equipped with an unusually biddable memory."

"And now?" Baro said.

Baro saw worried puzzlement on the historian's face. "And now I do not know what to think. In some regards—your ability to find the way into the Commons without knowing the Precepts and Principles—you are like a natural."

"Which would make me insane," said Baro. "But I am not."

"Then what are you?" said the noönaut. "How, without training, are you effortlessly able to detect the presence of others around us—the dreamers—when even I must strain to catch a glimmer of their passage?"

"I do not know," said Baro. "But I am not afraid. It feels, if you'll pardon my use of your jargon, natural for me to be here."

"As if you were called here?" said Bandar.

It hadn't occurred to Baro to put it that way, but now that the historian had said it the words rang true in his mind. "Yes," he said, "as if I were called."

Bandar's worry deepened the lines in his face. "We should go back."

Baro said, "Are we in danger?"

"I am not," said Bandar. "You may well be in great peril."

"Because I can do in a few moments what it took you months to achieve? Can you be jealous?"

"Years," said Bandar. "And no, I am not jealous. I am concerned for you, as any professional should be for an amateur he has led into danger. Also, I do not wish to carry the guilt."

"What guilt? What danger?" Baro looked about him. The location was arcadian in its innocence: white road, green fields, some trees, and a stream not far off. "I see nothing that threatens. Why should we return?"

"To see if you are able to do so," Bandar said. "If you have been called, whatever has called you may not wish you to leave. There are powers in this place. I can withstand them because I have the tones. You do not."

"I sense no malevolence here," Baro said. "Let us at least look about. I promise you, at the first sign of peril I will let you lead me back."

"Again," said Bandar, "if I am able."

"I will trust you."

"I should take you back and test you."

"I am not afraid of this place. I feel that I should be here."

"You have not yet seen some of the 'heres' they have here. We have taken only the first step behind the front door. It goes on forever and I mean that literally. There is no time here. Space is not what you may think it is. And though it is filled with wonders it is no less full of horrors."

"At the first rasp of a claw, the first glint of a nygrave's fang, turn for home and I will scamper after you," said Baro. "Until then, let us poke about."

"The noösphere is not to be taken lightly."

"I do not do so."

"Very well. Wait a moment," Bandar said. Then in a moment he winked out of existence. Baro felt a sudden chill of fear, as if he were a child in a market crowd who turns around to find his parent gone from sight. He looked in every direction but saw no sign of the historian. He tried moving up and down the road, thinking that the man might become visible again if viewed from some other angle, but he was alone.

As quickly as he had disappeared, the historian was back again. "Your companion grew alarmed at our long silence and stillness and began shaking and slapping us," Bandar said. "He thought we might have suddenly fallen to the lassitude."

"Long silence?" said Baro. "It has been but a minute."

"I told you, there is no time here. Or at least it becomes elastic. Our time in the Commons seems short, but almost an hour has passed since we intoned the opening thran. And the last words your friend heard you speak aloud came before you dove into the tarn. Since then, our conversation has taken place at another level."

"I see," said Baro, though he did not. "But my companion's fears are allayed?"

Bandar assured him that was the case. "Nonetheless," said Bandar. "We should return soon."

"I have an urge to go down the road," Baro said.

Bandar looked apprehensive.

"It's only a slight urge," the young man said.

"Here, nothing is 'only' anything," Bandar said.

"What could happen?" Baro genuinely wanted to know. It was hard to imagine anything threatening in this tranquil place. Bandar replied that he could not name any particular menace because in this place naming was summoning.

"So if you say 'So-and-so,' then this So-and-so will instantly appear and do what? Devour us?" Baro asked. "Use us for unspeakable purposes?"

"It is not a laughing matter," said Bandar. "For some—for a natural—it is much easier to find a way into the Commons than to discover the way out. Most never do."

"Could I not expect a trained adept like you to come and lead me home?"

Bandar shook his head. "Those who become lost are almost always soon absorbed by a characteristic entity."

"What is a characteristic entity?"

Bandar glanced from side to side and turned his head this way and that as if he expected something to appear. "We should really discuss this back in the waking world," he said.

"What is down the road?" Baro asked.

Bandar said, "Think of the Commons as a sphere. We are in the outermost layer. The next is the realm of the characteristic entities—the archetypes we encounter in dream and myth."

"Monsters and magicians?"

"You must not mock," the historian said, dropping his voice to a whisper. "Monsters, yes, like the Destroyer with his necklace of skulls. But also the Mother and Father, the Wise Man, the Good Beast, the Virgin and the Crone, the Fool, the Hero and his Helper, the Wizard, and many more. In the second layer they are found in their pure form—that is to say, at their most dangerous."

Bandar was clearly apprehensive and Baro caught a frisson of fear from the noönaut's trepidation. But the urge to travel down the road was growing stronger. He said as much to Bandar.

"I admit to curiosity about you," the small man said. "I will make this bargain: we will go together; you will heed my commands; and you will chant the following thran." He sounded a series of notes that seemed oddly familiar to Baro.

"Is that not a children's song?" Baro asked.

"Very similar," said Bandar. "The one about an old man, a dog, and a bone. Now sing it."

Baro did so.

"Louder."

The young man complied.

Bandar still looked worried, but he linked his arm in Baro's and they began to move down the road. "Keep singing and keep it loud," he said. "It has to cover both of us."

Baro made a question with his face but kept up the chant.

"The thran insulates us from the archetypes' perceptions," the noönaut said. "Cease chanting and they become aware of us. The entity whose nature is most dominant in your psyche is drawn to embrace you. Its embrace is a precursor to your absorption. You cease to exist."

Baro nodded his understanding and chanted louder. Bandar grimaced and said, "Here we go."

Baro did not understand how he had failed to see that the road crossed a stone bridge that spanned a river of dark water until they were almost upon it. The historian led him up and over the arch and as they descended the far side the young man saw that the road ended in a wide meadow in which several figures stood or sat or lay at ease.

He recognized some of them from Bandar's list of archetypes. The four-armed figure with a necklace of skulls was surely the Destroyer. The robed old man pacing with a staff, his long white hair and beard swinging in rhythm with his steps, was surely a representation of wisdom. A more distant threesome must be the Mother, Father, and Child.

Near where the road ended a large man sat cross-legged on the grass. He wore a chain-mail tunic and leather-wrapped leggings of coarse weave. Long tangled hair descended from a conical iron helmet that had a bird's wings springing from its sides. Over his shoulders he wore the shaggy pelt of a gray beast, its forepaws clasped over his broad chest by a brooch of worked yellow metal.

The man was methodically sliding a dark stone along the length of a broadsword of gray iron. Baro could hear the hissing caress of stone against metal even over the sound of his own singing. Nearby a nondescript fellow in a hooded tunic and sagging hose squatted, rubbing at a piece of leather harness.

As Baro and Bandar neared the end of the bridge the warrior ceased to hone his sword. His head came up as if he had caught an unexpected scent and he looked around. The man with him put down the piece of leather he had been working and also became alert.

Both stood up. Both turned toward Baro and Bandar. The old man with the staff was also standing still and peering in their direction.

"Louder," said Bandar.

Baro increased his volume.

"This is wrong," Bandar said. "I think they sense us."

The warrior had taken a step toward them, his companion following. The old man too was striding in their direction, his staff digging into the turf.

Baro continued to intone the thran. Bandar was now tugging on his arm, trying to lead him back over the bridge. But the young man wanted to resist. More than that, he wanted to cease chanting the tones and go forward to meet the warrior.

Bandar now added his voice to Baro's, almost shouting the tones as he continued to drag them both away. The man with the sword and helmet stopped so abruptly that his companion bumped into his back. His head turned left and right again, as if listening. The old one with the staff also stood still, staring toward the end of the bridge and stroking his beard.

As they reached the top of the arch, Baro resisted Bandar's pull. He broke off the chant and said, "Wait!"

Baro could not have told the historian just what it was he wanted to wait for. He did not want to make contact with the warrior or the old man; he was willing to take seriously Bandar's warnings about being absorbed and lost.

But he was possessed by a strong sense, almost a certainty,

that there was something he had to do in this strange place. Or that this place had something to do with him. "Listen," he said.

Bandar did not listen. He chanted more loudly than ever, his voice creaking with strain, his eyes wide and fixed on the far end of the bridge. Baro turned to look and saw the warrior was coming toward them again.

As the man set his buskined foot on the stones of the bridge the structure shook as if the ground had moved. It rang with a sound like a hammer striking a sheet of iron. The warrior stopped but only for a moment. He raised his foot to take the next step.

Bandar shook Baro's arm, spun him around. The young man turned to see stark terror on the historian's face, his free hand desperately signaling in a gesture that said, *What are you waiting for?* while chanting as loudly as he could.

Baro realized that the man's horror was genuine and that Bandar knew far more of the Commons's terrors than he did. He began to chant the tones again and saw the barbarian pause with his foot still raised.

Bandar signaled him to sing louder and Baro did as he was bid, letting the historian pull him back to the road that marked the first level of the noösphere. Here Bandar broke off his part of the chant and instead sounded a complex series of tones. A hole appeared in the air next to them and he pulled Baro toward it. The young man stepped . . .

. . . and fell with a jolt into his body, which sat cross-legged on the deck of the *Orgulon,* the sound of the landship's windvanes rustling in his ears and Guth Bandar peering into his eyes, desperate worry on the historian's face. "Are you back?" Bandar said. "Say your name."

The paralysis created by Imbry's use of the slapper was wearing off. Baro felt a tingling in his mouth, a sensation that grew stronger and increasingly unpleasant and drove all thought of his assumed identity from his mind. When Bandar asked for his name, he said "Baro," although it was more a mumble than a clear utterance.

"What?" Bandar said. "What did you say?" He knelt before the young man, chafing his hands and wrists.

"Wasselthorpe," said Luff Imbry, somewhere out of Baro's line of sight. "Phlevas Wasselthorpe, can you hear me?"

The maddening vibration was fading. "Yes, I can hear you," Baro said.

"Who are you?" Bandar said.

"Phlevas Wasselthorpe."

"Where are you?"

"On the *Orgulon*."

The historian let out a gust of breath and took his own seat. "I believe he is all right."

"He has regained the power of speech, too," said a cool, feminine contralto. Baro saw Raina Haj looking down at him.

"He is in the early stages of the lassitude," Imbry said. "It comes and goes."

"Uh huh." The security officer squatted and looked into the young man's face. "What happened?" she said.

"I saw . . ." Baro began, but then had to search for words to convey the sense of what he had experienced. He did not find them and lapsed into silence, his eyes unfocused.

"We encountered an archetype," said Bandar. "More significant, it encountered us despite the insulating thran."

"A man with a sword. His helmet had wings," said Baro.

"Ah," said Bandar. "Interesting. That's one of its earliest forms. Myself, I saw it as a janissary of the Arham Legion, one of those who died defying the Morabic Hegemony's attempt to enslave the world back in the Tenth Eon. The white and gold uniform was unmistakable."

"No," said Baro, "it wore a shirt made of iron rings

connected together. And an animal's skin." He lapsed into silence, staring at the image his memory offered him.

"Explain," said Haj, fixing the historian with a hard glare. "What have you done to him?"

"Nothing," said Bandar. "We quite unexpectedly had a near encounter with a characteristic entity—the Hero, to be precise. He's fine."

"He does not appear to be fine," she said, regarding Baro with some concern.

"He will be," said Bandar. "He was not touched by the entity. I was worried for a while because we did not seem to be hidden from its perception by the thran. But I opened a gate and we came back."

"I hear the words," she said, "and I even know the individual meanings of most. Yet somehow they fail to constitute an explanation."

Bandar rubbed his forehead. "I am sorry," he said. "I will try to sketch a satisfactory answer, but a proper explanation would take all day. But let me begin with the characteristic entities."

"I know about the Commons," Haj said. "At least I thought I did. Dreams, myths, and forgotten tales no one cares to recall."

Baro wondered if he was the only one who didn't know about the Commons. Bandar launched into a defense of his life's work against the security officer's dismissal. But Baro kept finding it hard to concentrate on what the historian was saying. His mind wanted to pull him back to the image of the barbarian at the end of the bridge. Even in memory the Hero exerted a powerful pull upon him: he wanted to go back and meet him even though just thinking about such an encounter raised hairs on the back of his neck. He tore his mind away from his thoughts and willed himself to focus on the historian's voice.

"We did not quite cross to the second level," Bandar was saying. "My intent was to remain on the bridge to show Wasselthorpe the characteristic entities, the ones that form the basic infrastructure of the psyche—what we noönauts call 'the usual suspects.'"

They were the underpinnings of every mind, he explained, each of us being an amalgam of several of these entities acting in consort and conflict with each other. Over an individual's lifetime, the various archetypes waxed and waned, assuming greater or less significant roles as the person faced the different challenges existence offered.

"So the Hero was just a dislodged fragment of Wasselthorpe's own psyche," Haj said, "something that might be encountered in a dream. Wherein lay the danger?"

"This was not a dream," said Bandar. "In dreams the entities come to the sleeping consciousness much as Father Olwyn has appeared to us, as a representation only. But when the consciousness descends fully awake to the Commons, as we did, the archetypes stand forth in full. In dreams they are a whisper; when we come into their own world they are a shout, the kind of shout to buckle walls and topple towers. This one came looking for him."

"The Hero would have attacked him?" Imbry asked.

"No." The historian shook his head. "Worse. It would have *absorbed* him. The complex inner crowd that makes up Phlevas Wasselthorpe would have been pushed to the farthest edge of his being. The person you know ceases to be, and then comes the Hero into his own. The pure and fated warrior replaces Wasselthorpe; thus he becomes permanently psychotic."

There was a brief silence, then Haj said, "And you venture into this hell as a pastime? Poking about among deadly forces to pluck scraps of forgotten lore that only a few nincompoops like you would give the hairs off a termie's rump for?"

"For the adept, it is quite safe," said Bandar. "Early venturers into the Commons discovered that certain combinations of tones act as controls and keys upon the psyche. The clues were in a dawn myth about a singer who charms the king of the dead into releasing the musician's true love.

"Once having mastered the tones—and learned the ways and portals—an adept can wander the Commons in almost complete safety. My colleagues and I slip unseen past the stark entities of the outer arrondisements. We delve deep into the inner rings to explore archetypical Landscapes, Events, and Situations. It is quite fascinating."

"Uh huh," said Haj. She rose and put her hands on hips. "I cannot forbid you to do it again," she said to Bandar, "but . . ."

"No need," the historian said. "I have no intention."

Baro was struggling to his feet. He still felt not quite returned from the noösphere. It was as if he wore his body like an ill-fitted garment. He leaned for support against the bulkhead of the foredeck, wanting to say something that would encourage Raina Haj to see him in a more advantageous light. But as he tried to shake a pithy remark from his still disordered brain, there came a scream from behind him, a scream that was abruptly silenced.

From the darkness that shrouded the raised forecastle a slim figure emerged. Baro saw Flix, trembling again as she had when the affliction had lifted from her, her mouth opening and closing without sound.

First Officer Kosmir appeared from somewhere and seized the artist's companion by both shoulders. "What is it?" he cried.

Flix found her voice. "Monlaurion has fallen from the prow. I fear he has been crushed beneath the wheels."

Kosmir raised his voice. "All stop! Send word for the captain! Gig crew close up!"

Even with her wind pylons disengaged, it was minutes before the *Orgulon* rumbled to a halt. The ambulatory passengers meanwhile rushed to the stern rail and peered through the darkness to where a lighter shade of black marked where Monlaurion lay.

Discussion among the crowd was muted but vigorous and soon came to the conclusion that if the landship's weight had indeed passed over the artist, what remained of him must be scarcely less flat than the Swept itself.

The captain came on deck while a handful of the crew mustered on the forward promenade deck and extracted the landship's gig, a snub-nosed flying platform, from its nesting place under a cover by the rail. The utilitarian craft soon lifted off and slid astern. A beam of light reached from the platform to a spot on the prairie and seemed to pull the flyer to where the victim lay.

Baro watched as a cloth was spread over the body and it was lifted onto the platform, which then returned to the landship's open deck. An officer who wore the insignia of a ship's physician peeled back a flap of the cover and passed an instrument over what was beneath, with the air of someone performing a purely symbolic function, and pronounced the artist dead. Flix stood, ashen and trembling, until the official words were said, then buried her face in her hands.

Raina Haj now approached the aircraft and looked under the cover. Baro thought she must have possessed a stronger constitution than most because she did not flinch at what must have been an unpleasant sight although her face went almost as pale as Flix's.

Kosmir and the captain were standing nearby, exhibiting an air of official calm as the former relayed the latter's orders to get the landship under way again. The security officer crossed the deck to the captain and spoke quietly. The first officer listened with head bent and face composed, but Baro saw a flash of some emotion briefly escape Kosmir's control of his features as she spoke. Then she was finished and the captain nodded and drew himself erect.

The captain was a small, precise man with ribbons on his chest that attested to a lengthy career. His immaculate uniform fitted him exactly. "Honorables and distinctions," he addressed the passengers, "there has been an unfortunate incident. Was anyone here a witness to what happened?"

The captain waited, but no one spoke up. "We will defer consideration of the matter until we reach port," he said.

Raina Haj spoke earnestly in a whisper that none but the captain and Kosmir heard. The captain shook his head in rejection of whatever Haj was proposing and Baro again saw a brief flare of emotion on the first officer's face.

"My security officer believes that a grievous crime may have been committed. On her recommendation, the passenger Flix will be confined to her quarters and a guard posted at the door."

Flix had been watching the gig crew enclose Monlaurion's body in a temporary coffin in preparation for transferring it belowdecks. Now she looked up in puzzlement. "He fell," she said. Raina Haj came and took her by the arm and led her to the companionway. Baro heard her voice again as she descended the stairs. "It was an accident."

"I wonder," said Baro.

Bandar had an opinion. "He may have encountered a gravitational cyst, overbalanced, and tumbled overboard. I've heard of it happening."

"The rail is more than waist high," said Imbry. "He would have had to transfer his center of gravity to somewhere around his shoulders."

"That can happen out here," the small man said. "Gravitational cysts filter up from the planet's core to burst above the surface. The smaller ones are usually globular, the larger tend toward a lens shape. An object the size of a human being, encompassed by a cyst's internal gravitation flux, can experience several different gravities simultaneously.

"If a globular anomaly briefly formed as the *Orgulon* moved forward, and if Monlaurion was carried through it, his equilibrium would be affected. For example, his left side might suddenly weigh four times as much as his right, or his head might outweigh his feet by a factor of ten. His center of gravity could be instantly repositioned and he might very well fall."

"Do such things happen often?" Baro asked.

"No, but they do happen," Bandar said. "It's another one of the things that drew me to the Swept. These gravitational anomalies may have effects on the noösphere."

While the historian had been speaking the captain and Kosmir had left the deck. The white-haired woman with the birthmarked husband was marshaling many of the passengers into a group chant of *fah, sey, opah*.

"I think I will go below and get my measuring equipment," said Bandar.

Imbry and Baro bid him a restful night and retired to their cabin. A plump and stubby steward was preparing the sleeping accommodations. As she was about to leave, Baro detained her and asked a question. "What can you tell me about Security Officer Haj?"

The steward appeared shocked. "Nothing," she said. "The captain does not encourage prying."

A coin appeared in Luff Imbry's hand and swiftly made its way to the steward's pocket as the fat man said, "My young friend is smitten," he said. "Why not indulge him in a harmless infatuation?"

The woman regarded Baro with an appraising look and he could not help feeling that she thought poorly of his chances if he sought Haj's interest. Then she shrugged and said, "She joined us only for this cruise and at the last moment. I don't think she's served on landships before. Some said . . ." She bit her lip.

"Yes?" Imbry said.

"It's only gossip."

A second coin traveled to join the first. "We enjoy gossip," Imbry said.

"Well, some said she was foisted on the captain, that she isn't a proper officer at all."

"Might she have been sent by the charterer?"

"Might have. It takes a fair degree of influence to press our captain."

"Hmm," said Imbry.

"What about First Officer Kosmir?" Baro said.

The steward looked him up and down. "Have you a yen for him also? You are liberal in your tastes."

Imbry said, "He fears that the first officer might be a formidable rival for the object of his interest."

The woman snorted. "Kosmir and Haj?" she said. "They are Ambion and Dearie."

Baro recognized the reference to the legendary couple whose bitter lifelong enmity made them a byword for self-wounding through an inability to forgo retribution and revenge. The two end up struggling to deny each other a single blanket during a blizzard and freeze to death rather than share each other's body heat.

"They are not warm to each other?" he said.

"You have nothing to fear," the steward said.

When she was gone Baro said to Imbry, "Perhaps we should assist Haj in her investigation."

"We have not yet determined whether she is working for Gebbling," Imbry said.

"I feel that she is not."

"Perhaps the story I gave the steward was the truth."

"I am not interested in her," Baro said, though he realized as he said it that his statement was only partly true. "I am interested in solving a murder, if a murder has been committed."

"You have already wandered away from our own assignment to explore the noösphere," Imbry pointed out. "Now you want to thrust yourself into the way of a young woman who seems to have her business firmly in hand. Besides, we are supposed to remain undercover."

"True, but if Monlaurion and Flix were shills for Gebbling and had a falling out, we might exploit the situation to gather evidence. But we would have to go through Haj to get to Flix."

Imbry yawned. "It might be a useful strategy if we could turn one against the other, but that is a difficult trick when one of them is dead."

"I want to recover the clingfast. It could tell us much."

"If it wasn't crushed beyond use or dislodged and left out on the Swept."

"We should do something," Baro said. He was conscious of an inner urge to take action; what that action ought to be was not clear, but the urge was growing, like an unscratchable itch in the back of his mind.

"I am sure there must be a Bureau motto about watching before doing," Imbry said.

"Observe, deduce, act, reflect," Baro quoted.

"At this point, we do not have enough information to make rational deductions. So we cannot move on to action."

"But agents are expected to use their initiative."

"Fine. I now use my initiative to take the upper bunk," Imbry said, climbing the ladder the steward had deployed for them. At the top he paused and said, "Here's an idea: why don't you contact Directing Agent Arboghast and discuss your planned diversion from the investigation that the Archon personally assigned you to?"

Baro's enthusiasm waned. "I will sleep on it," he said and crawled into the lower bunk.

"Good idea," said Imbry. "Perhaps in the morning someone will confess and everything will be cleared up."

Baro expressed a number of opinions on his partner's attitude, but before he was finished he was interrupted by a loud snore from above.

He thought that sleep might avoid him. Instead it swallowed him within minutes. He found himself once again in his boyhood room, though the details were not as sharp as when he had entered by intoning the historian's thran. Still, when he opened the wardrobe, there was the mirror and in it the shadowed image of his disdainful alter ego.

Baro stepped boldly toward his Shadow, but this time before he could touch it the figure spoke. "Destiny," it said, then mimed the actions of someone whose fingertips have come in contact with an object hot enough to sear them.

Baro ignored the cryptic warning and passed through the glass, but the single word echoed in his dream-mind as he descended to the dark pool. He dove in and soared down to the land of clear luminescence, alighting on the same road in the same spot as before. But this time the sharpness of detail and clarity of form were missing: objects would not hold a shape; instead they changed—the wall became a fence became a hedge—even as he regarded them. He took a step down the road and noticed that the white stone pavement was now a dusty path; in a moment he was wading along the course of a shallow brook.

"It does not matter," he told himself. "Essence is essence, form only form." The words made sense to his dreaming self.

Now he saw a figure ahead of him on the road—it had

become a road again—and he hurried to catch up. It was a man striding forcefully forward, and when he laid a hand on the figure's shoulder, the startled face that turned to him was that of Guth Bandar.

"What are you doing?" the historian said. He seemed very frightened.

"I am dreaming," said Baro.

"This is very wrong," said the historian. "You should not be here."

"Do not be concerned," Baro said. "It is only a dream."

"Yes," said Bandar, "but it is *my* dream."

"No, it is mine," said Baro. "You are a figment."

Bandar did not look reassured. "Tell me," he said, "when you look at me do I seem to change in any way? Or is my form constant?"

Baro took stock of the man. "It is peculiar, but you do seem to remain unchanged whereas the woods behind you have been several different kinds of forest even as we speak."

"What does that tell you?"

"What should it tell me?"

"A hundred things, none of them good. I will open us a gate." Bandar began to hum a series of tones.

Before he had time to think about it, Baro put his hand over the man's mouth and said, "No."

With a desperate struggle, Bandar wrestled himself free. "Oh, this is much worse than not good," he said. "I should appear to you as at best a shifting image. Instead you not only see me but can lay hands on me and prevent my following my own will."

"I am sorry," said Baro. "I do not want to depart."

"I want nothing but. Do you not understand that you frighten me?"

"I do not wish to." Baro looked around at the shifting

landscape. "Do you not sense that somehow all of this is as it is meant to be?"

"That is precisely what frightens me," said Bandar. "Neither of us is experiencing an ordinary dream. Some force is shaping us to its own ends. In the Commons, the only such force is that of an archetype intent on absorbing a consciousness. As I have explained, that way lies madness."

"I do not feel irrational," said Baro. "My mind seems unusually clear, considering that I am dreaming."

"Again, a worrying sign," said Bandar. "My sense of things tells me that you are being drawn into the role of Hero and that I am being pressed into the part of the Helper."

"I want from you only a few words of advice," Baro said.

"Let us be exact," said Bandar. "You feel compelled to enter more deeply into the Commons and you want me to be your guide."

"I suppose."

"I refuse."

"Why?"

"Because there you will be absorbed by whatever entity is summoning you and then you will certainly become insane and die. Innocent, helpful Bandar, pulled along will-I or nill-I in your wake, will suffer an equally horrid fate."

"I find that hard to believe," Baro said.

"Only because your ignorance serves as an impenetrable shield. My knowledge leaves me naked."

Baro knew that he ought to heed the historian's warning, but he was possessed of a certainty that all would be well. Yet when he communicated this assurance to Guth Bandar the historian's fear only increased.

"The Hero always thinks everything will turn out fine," the man said, "right up until the dragon's jaws close upon his soft parts."

"Perhaps I am not a hero," Baro said. "I might be merely a blend of several entities, like you and most people."

"Look at yourself," Bandar said.

Baro looked down. A shirt made of linked metal hung from his pelt-clad shoulders. His feet were enclosed in scuffed leather boots whose straps crisscrossed each other up his trouser-clad legs. He was holding a sword.

"Does that look familiar?" said the historian.

Baro admitted that it did. Still, he was not concerned.

Bandar said, "Let me open a gate. We will talk about this while our waking selves can resist any inclinations to madness."

Baro was tempted to agree, but the certainty overruled caution. "I am here to *do* something," he said. "I feel that I must do it."

Bandar trembled, and it was only then that Baro realized he had been gesturing for emphasis with the hand that held the sword. He laid it down on the road beside him, but when he looked down a moment later it was unaccountably back in his hand.

"What do you think that something might be?" Bandar was asking him. The historian had backed away a small distance.

Baro let the answer come of its own. "I must search."

"Search for what? Something nice, like treasure? Or something with teeth and an insatiable appetite?"

This time no answer came. "I will know it when I see it," was all Baro could say.

"Oh, my," said Bandar. He put his hands up to cover his eyes for a moment, then said, "All right. One thing I know is that it does no good to argue with a Hero. But please allow me to shape this adventure so that we stand the best chance of surviving it."

"I will follow your advice," Baro said.

The historian said, "Look around and tell me if there is anything that draws your attention."

Baro did so and immediately found that he was interested in the woods beyond the field.

"Very well," said Bandar, "we will approach them. But let me lead."

The stone wall had become a low hedge and as they crossed the field between them and the woods the vegetation could not seem to settle on a fixed type. They passed under the trees that began as trembling birches but soon became dark evergreens then blasted oaks, their branches sooty and torn. "Stop," Bandar said.

Baro wanted to press on. He knew that there was something nearby he needed to see, but the fear apparent in every line of the historian's body persuaded him to stand still.

"The Commons," the man said, "is a construct of the common mind. The laws of space and time do not apply here. The space you think you see is not space, and the time you think is passing is not time.

"Locations that seem far apart may in fact be adjacent, and places that seem contiguous are continents apart. Times are also interposed and intraposed upon and within themselves, and the complexity of these phenomena is also compounded by the fact that many times are self-contained."

"I do not understand," said Baro.

"I know," said Bandar. "This is what frightens me. Let me put it this way: if you turn left and take three steps you will be in the midst of the Battle of Uddra's Marsh, which is an archetypical massacre. Once in the battle, it would be very difficult for you to find the way out before you were 'killed' although every time you 'died' you would come back again for the next iteration of the battle, it being continuous and—since its time duration is confined to a single day—eternal."

"You're saying I would be trapped forever."

"Just like the brave explorers who became stuck there during the many thousands of years it took to establish the definitive map of the noösphere."

"You mean they are still there?"

"There is nowhere else for them to be," Bandar said. "By the time the ingresses and exits were reliably located, their corporeal bodies were dust. In any case, the explorers were absorbed into archetypical figures peculiar to that battle—idiomatic entities, we call them—and are now inseparable."

"Left and three steps," said Baro. He was standing very still now. "What happens if I go three paces to my right?"

"I am not sure," said the historian. "Let me check." He hummed a sequence of tones and a sphere twice the size of his head appeared in the air before him. The globe was densely packed with spots of light of varying diameters and intensities, interconnected by solid, dotted, and wavy lines of different colors and thicknesses. Bandar traced one with a finger and said, "You would be at the building of the Tomb of Hanratt, in other words a slave under an autocrat's lash."

Baro stood even more still.

"However," said the historian, "I could get you out of that."

Baro let out a relieved breath, but then the man said, "Of course, the two seconds it would take me to follow you in would be"—he calculated on his fingers—"eighteen years, four months, and a fortnight from your perspective."

Baro consulted his inner self and found, to his surprise, that he nonetheless needed to go farther into the wood, which was now a towering stand of fragrant deodars. He communicated his finding to Bandar.

"All right," said the historian, in a tone that contradicted the literal meaning of the words, "indicate the direction you want to travel."

Baro closed his eyes and let his sword arm rise. When he opened them he saw that the point of the weapon was indicating a direction just over the other man's left shoulder. Bandar turned to follow the line of the blade, then consulted the sphere. "How far, do you think?" he said.

"Not far," said Baro. "It seems very close."

The noönaut examined the globe from another angle, then squinted along the indicated line of travel again. "Two steps and a stumble will have us at the adit of a Class Three Event."

The historian examined the glowing spots and lines further and said, "Curious."

Baro waited, but the man continued to regard the display. Finally the agent said, "What is curious?"

Bandar spoke three descending tones and the sphere imploded to a pinpoint and disappeared. "Just that here we are out on the Swept, which originated in the war to repel the Dree, and you have a sudden strong urge to visit the corresponding Event that that conflict created in the Commons."

"Is it perhaps a coincidence?" Baro said.

"Well of course it's a coincidence," said the historian.

Baro sighed in relief once more. "Then there's no need to worry."

"There is every need to worry," said the noönaut. "In the waking world a coincidence is by definition a random, meaningless juxtaposition of events. In the Commons, the coincidence is the most meaningful of occurrences. It is the vastly powerful force that ties one thing to another. Indeed, coincidences connect everything to everything."

"I understand that I should be frightened," said Baro, "yet I am not. I must go there." He pointed the sword again. "Will I die?"

Bandar shook his head. "No," he said. "In truth, I am

somewhat relieved. There are much worse Events. But you must let me direct you."

"I will."

The historian pushed down the young man's sword arm and took a grip on the elbow. "We will move forward while sounding these tones"—he voiced the notes, then listened to hear Baro repeat them; again it was a song that reminded Baro of a childhood ditty, about a farmer and some cheese—"which will keep us undetected by the idiomatic entities. Stay beside me at all times and do not cease the sounds. If the idiomatics become aware of us they will treat us as themselves."

"How bad would that be?" Baro said.

"It was a particularly horrid war," Bandar said. "The Dree were a hive species. Each hive was one entity, telepathically and pheromonically connected. They also used cognitive force to compel other species to slave for them, both as workers and as warriors."

"Warriors?"

"Fighting was what they lived for. It was one of the key determinants of status among the hives, and status was of overreaching importance to the Dree. Each entity would regularly send out its members and its slaves to engage in ritual combat with those of other hives. Fortunately, their style of battle undid them in the end."

"How so?" said Baro.

"The sole purpose of Dree combat was to capture members of the enemy forces. These would be trussed and taken back to their captors' hive where they would be subjected to tortures both subtle and gross. The Dree were able to experience the emotions and sensory experiences of others, as you and I are able to taste food or scent essences.

"So when they deployed for battle, their strategy was always to surround and isolate small groups and individuals that could be taken home. This was not a useful battle plan against forces that were organized to exterminate them."

"I am surprised they ever developed the means for traveling space," Baro said. "They do not sound very imaginative."

"They left their home world by accident," Bandar said. He explained that the Dree inhabited a minor planet in an isolated system, a great distance past the last few stars of the Spray, way out in the Back Beyond. They were discovered late and the first xenologists who arrived to study them did not know how intensely telepathic they were.

The scientists were a mixed group comprising several ultra-terrene species as well as a human. They wore devices that were intended to mask them from detection by sight, sound, or scent and even by most telepathic receptors, but the Dree had a remarkable acuity. The team ventured into an underground warren and were immediately taken. Their captors treated them as rare delicacies, wringing novel "tastes" from their terror and agony.

When telepaths are involved, secrets are not secrets for long. The Dree discovered the location of the team's hidden ship and forced the scientists to take a raiding party to the nearest world, where they not only captured more "delicacies," but more ships.

Besides battle, the other test of status among the Dree was the honor to be won by giving away rich gifts to other hives. The recipients of the largesse were not grateful, but shamed. Their dishonor motivated them to give even greater wealth in return. Back from the first raid, the Dree hive gave away ships and captives who could fly them; the recipients swarmed into space to find new ships, these having now become the currency of respect among the hives.

Horror descended upon the scattered worlds at the end of the Spray, horror that touched down only to multiply exponentially.

The Dree had been bottled up on their own planet for so long that they had quite filled it. Finding whole worlds of virgin territory—to the Dree mind that was any territory that did not already have a Dree hive in residence—the invaders followed up the initial raids by sending ships laden with eggs and slaves to tend them. Fortunately, some of the species along the galactic arm, including humans on a number of planets, had not yet given up the arts of conflict. Fleets formed and armies mobilized. First the Dree were stopped, then they were rolled back, then they were expunged.

It was not a long war, as galactic wars go. The enemy, with no aim of combat other than to capture opponents for later enjoyment, had no strategies for wars of extermination and no weapons for comprehensive eradication. The Dree were fast breeders, but not fast enough to replace their losses.

Earth was one of the last worlds invaded. The Dree and their slaves were confined to their beachhead, then the pocket closed in on them and they were slaughtered.

"No one wanted to go into the labyrinth of tunnels the invaders had dug for themselves," Bandar told Baro. "In confined quarters, telepathic warriors with short-range weapons can be devastating. A gravitational device originally designed for aggregating asteroids into useful sizes was brought down from space and its energies directed at the Dree redoubt.

"The Swept and its gravitational anomalies are the result. Beneath our feet are the compressed and corpse-choked tunnels of the Dree. That is, beneath our feet in the waking world; here in the noösphere, there is nothing beneath us but the Old Sea."

"The Old Sea?" said Baro.

"I told you to think of the Commons as a sphere. At the core of the sphere is the age-old nothingness that prevailed before consciousness emerged on our world. It is a featureless expanse through which a great blind worm swims across eternity, endlessly seeking its own tail and swallowing anything that falls into its path."

Even in the tranquility of the ever-changing Commons forest, Baro shivered.

"Are you sure you want to go on with this?" asked Bandar. "For myself, I had planned a perfectly ordinary dream."

The urge had not left Baro. He was still called in the direction he had identified.

"Very well," said the noönaut, "but do not stop chanting. If you need to speak to me, hold up your hand and I will increase the volume of my intoning to cover us both. But be brief. If I need to speak to you, I will move my fingers thus and so to signal you to become louder. Is this clear?"

"Yes."

"Then begin."

Baro voiced the first notes and Bandar joined him. There were two sequences of twelve notes each; as they completed the first sequence and went on to the second, something like a vertical ripple appeared in the air in the direction he had pointed. They walked toward it at a measured pace, Bandar's grip firm on Baro's arm. The ripple became a wave that opened into a fissure and Baro found himself stepping into a dark land under a sky bright with stars.

Over their heads a wind suffled through cottonwoods. They emerged from the trees to hear the sound of a stream not far away. They were on a gentle swell of land and below them Baro made out the shape of a darkened house. As he looked at it, the building exploded in a flash of purple light and there were shouts and a rush of many booted feet, thudding through the darkness.

From the left, Baro heard other sounds, a dry chittering accompanied by a creaking that put him in mind of leather garments on a cold day. Without thinking, he stopped intoning to listen more closely. Immediately, a bolt of green energy sizzled from their left and struck the ground at their feet. Acrid smoke stung Baro's eyes and nose and he sneezed. Guth Bandar made a squeaking noise and began to chant more loudly, his fingers digging into Baro's arm. The young man swiftly took up his part of the song.

The historian waggled his fingers before Baro's eyes and the agent sang louder. "I told you, we are entering an Event that exemplifies a horrific war—not the war itself, where you might expect long periods of inaction punctuated by frenzies of violence, but the *essence* of the conflict. So do not expect to find yourself in a lull—there are no such intervals. Whatever happens, you must keep chanting."

They moved down the slope, crossed the stream, and went out onto a wide pasture. Over the tones, Baro heard a distant rumble and saw coming toward them a squadron of dark, bulky shapes that resolved into squat machines cushioned by gravity obviators, their upper surfaces bulging with the snouts of intensifiers and tumble-thrusts that hurled beams and fields of destructive energies at the slope. Above them something immense thrummed through the upper air, disgorging flights of slim, fast-moving aircraft that darted down, then up again, leaving thunder and blinding flashes of white and blue light at the lowest points of their arcs.

Bandar pulled Baro farther out onto the flat, dodging a monstrous battle-car that rumbled past them. When it was gone, the historian indicated that Baro should increase his volume.

"This is the part of the final battle they called the 'hemming,'" Bandar said. "The Dree have been thrust back into a range of hills, the stumps of extinct volcanoes, which they have dug out and fortified. Around it is a wide wasteland of lifeless cities, towns, and farms, their inhabitants dead or enslaved.

"Soon it will be decided that to go in after the invaders will cost countless more lives, with no guarantee that all the enemy will be expunged. The aggregator will be deployed, crushing Dree and captives alike in the underground combs. It will be more effective than anticipated, as is so often the case with novel means of destruction, and the result will be the vastness of the Swept and its gravitational cysts."

He resumed chanting and they watched the assault on the Dree's redoubt. The sky grew lighter, though no sun was to be seen, and the bolts and sheets of energy paled with the passing of the end of darkness. Baro could see that the pockets of resistance in the hills were being systematically eliminated, the Dree either dying where they fought or retreating into tunnel mouths that they sealed after them with a grayish concrete exuded from abdominal pores.

Bandar signaled again that he wished to speak. "Do you feel an impulse to go farther? Is there something more you are to see?"

Baro consulted whatever part of him responded to urges from the noösphere and shook his head. He looked about him. The armor had moved on and had joined the aircraft in pounding the upper slopes of the hills and the blocked tunnel mouths. The giant flying machine in the high atmosphere was striking the crests of the hills with coruscating beams of blue-white power, but it seemed that the battle was winding down. Out on the plain, nothing moved.

Baro's attention was caught by a nearby irregularity in the ground. He indicated to Bandar that they should cross to it. Singing the tones, which the young man was finding increasingly monotonous, they walked across the charred grass to find a shallow trench dug into the sod. Huddled in the bottom, heaped around a weapon that was now a lump of melted stuff, were the charred remains of four Dree.

Now came an impulse. Baro took his arm out of Bandar's grasp and stepped down into the trench. The carbonized hind legs of one of the Dree crackled and fragmented under his boots as he bent to examine the corpses. He used the sword to pry two of the corpses apart and found that the bottommost seemed to have been killed by shock rather than incineration. Its upper half was complete.

Baro looked up at Bandar and gestured toward his own eyes, increasing the volume of his chant so that the historian could reply to the wordless question.

"They had no eyes," Bandar said, looking down at the smooth curve of brown chitinous stuff that approximated a head. "The feathery things stood upright in life and detected odor with exquisite refinement. Nerve patches on the torso and head translated vibration into sound and it could detect electrical fields at close range."

Baro nodded and stared at the creature, waiting for some indication as to why he had been impelled to this Event. But nothing came. Finally, he shrugged and climbed out of the trench. Bandar had resumed chanting and now gave him a look that asked, *Now, what?* Baro shrugged in return.

The historian again had the young man sing more loudly so that he could ask, "Do you feel any counterurge against our leaving?"

Baro shook his head and Bandar brought out the noösphere map and studied it for a moment. "We'll need to take a short-cut," he said. He collapsed the globe and pulled Baro a few steps to one side, chanting a different sequence. A rift appeared in the air and they went through it.

The other side of the rift was all bright sun and tropical

foliage, with terraced buildings of pastel stone grouped around a wide plaza in which a throng of gaily dressed celebrants threw their arms into the air and wriggled their fingers ecstatically. In the center of the open space an emaciated young man in flowing vestments and a tall cylindrical hat flexed his own fingers in response to shrieks from the crowd. But whether he was witnessing a religious ceremony, political rally, or entertainment event would never be clear to Baro because the chanting historian immediately pulled him into a side street and through a curtained door.

They stepped out onto a deserted strand of black shingle, waves of iron-gray water swishing about their ankles. Offshore, a black-hulled ship with tattered sails lay half careened against jagged rocks while some beaked and tentacled sea beast tore at its rigging. Bandar paid the spectacle no heed but led the way up the beach to the tide line, where he contrived another rift and pushed Baro through it.

The young man opened his eyes to find himself lying on his bunk in the *Orgulon*'s cabin, Luff Imbry's stentorian snores ringing in his ears and the early morning sun pouring in through the porthole. A knocking came at the door and he got up to open it, and found a disheveled Guth Bandar in the corridor.

"I thought I had better come see if you were all right," the historian said.

"It seemed we were less than an hour in the Commons," Baro said, "but here the night is over."

The noönaut stretched and yawned. He did not appear much rested. "Time is not time in the noösphere," he said.

"I am sorry to have troubled you," Baro said. He remembered the sense of necessity he had felt, the compelling urge to *move*. "I felt that I had no choice."

"There are many places where it can be perilous to be without a full range of options," said Bandar. "The Commons is worse than all of them. In fact, it *is* all of them, every terrible crime and defeat that has ever happened, distilled to its essence and compounded. It is also every joy and triumph of the human story."

"Perhaps when this . . . episode of my life is over I could take up the exploration of the noösphere," Baro said. "Might I study under you?"

Bandar went pale. "It would be kinder if you simply killed me now," he said. "Be assured, I will never again go willingly with you into the Commons. In fact, I intend to ask the captain to lend me the landship's gig to take me away from here today so that I cannot be pressed into service again."

"But what about your researches?"

"I could take scant pleasure in them while at constant risk of your dragooning me to my death."

"The danger seems remote."

"To you, no doubt. To me it is inescapable if I remain within range of you, and since I do not know what your range might be I shall put as great a distance between us as I can." The historian made a placatory gesture. "I intend no offense."

"I take none," said Baro. "The matter mystifies me."

From the upper bunk, Imbry gave a final crescendo of snorts and wheezes and opened his eyes. "When's breakfast?" he said.

———◆———

WHILE they were still dressing, stewards came knocking on doors, inviting passengers to gather in the dining room for the morning meal and another visitation from Father Olwyn.

The room was lit by dawn light through the windows. The

chairs and tables had again been rearranged, a buffet having been set up in the middle of the space. Baro and Imbry lined up for plates of fried truffles, truffle bread, and truffle kedgeree, none of which the young man found inviting. He contented himself with a cup of punge, although Imbry piled high his platter and dug in. The lassitude sufferers were again fed from plates of gruel.

When all had breakfasted, the simulacrum of their host materialized on the dais. Baro peered at the image. Gebbling's face was not as it had appeared in the file photo. The earlier image had had a rosy, impish softness to it; this face was stark and drawn.

"Regard him," Baro said to his partner. "He is not the same as his image in the file. You knew him. What do you think?"

Imbry looked at the simulacrum over the rim of his cup. "He does look to have endured hardship, some sort of trial perhaps," he said. "That is not like Gebbling. He was always a great one for the soft life." He took another helping of truffle bread.

Gebbling had meanwhile been calling down welcomes and blessings on the gathering and voicing rhetorical inquiries as to the quality of their sleep and the state of their health upon rising. Now he got to the nub of his remarks.

"I can already feel an elevation of chuffe," he said. "The *fah, sey, opah* has had effect. I applaud you. Now I will give you the second-stage mantra and bid you chant it through this day. It is *bom, bom ala bom*. Let me hear you say it."

Baro recognized Ule Gazz's voice rising above most in the crowd, though she was not louder than the woman who still had blue-fire stones in her white hair. The chant of *bom, bom ala bom* swelled until it filled the room. After a full minute, Gebbling raised his hand and called for silence.

"Very good," the image said. "Your chuffe expands exponentially. Please continue through the day and I will speak to you later."

The projection winked out and Imbry said, "That answers one question."

"What?" said Baro.

"Whether the projection is a live transmission or a recording. It strains credulity that Gebbling would fail to take note of an apparent miraculous healing, followed by the arrest of the resurrected one on suspicion of murder. These must be recordings."

"Hmm," said Baro. "I think you are right." But it bothered him that the amateur had drawn the right conclusion before the trained agent had even thought to pose the question. "I should have thought of that."

Baro hadn't realized he had spoken the last thought out loud until he saw Imbry mime astonishment. The fat man said, "Do I see the first crack in the facade of your scroot arrogance? Or even in the foundation?"

"I have had other things on my mind," said Baro.

"Yes, exploring the Commons and mooning over a certain security officer."

"I do not moon," said Baro.

"As you say," said Imbry and took another helping of kedgeree.

The day passed tranquilly, the landship's crew going about their business while the passengers gathered to chant. Imbry perambulated about the deck, then retired to the cabin for a nap. Baro saw Raina Haj come on deck twice but she did not notice him and he was diffident about bringing himself to her attention.

He would have liked to identify himself as a Bureau agent; that status ought to impress a mere landship's security officer.

But he was under orders to conceal his identity. Still, leaning on the rail and watching distant clouds form and re-form, he imagined scenarios where he might step forward, flourish his plaque, and set things to rights in a way that would turn violet, turquoise-flecked eyes his way.

Guth Bandar came up the companionway, saw Haj, and approached her. There was a brief discussion in which the historian clearly did not persuade Haj to accept his view of things. He went below and came up later carrying various apparatuses from which he took readings from time to time. He showed no desire to discuss the noösphere with Baro when the young man attempted conversation.

"I would not still be aboard but Raina Haj refuses anyone permission to depart until her investigations are complete," he said. "How could I be a suspect? I was with you and Haj herself when the artist fell."

Baro expressed sympathy and sought to steer the conversation toward the Commons, but Bandar was adamant in his refusal. He suggested that they take care to sleep at different times. "Or, if you find yourself dreaming your way back into the Commons, have the courtesy not to interfere with the dreams of others." His small hand struck his forehead in a gesture of bafflement. "Although that is supposed to be impossible for the untrained." He went off muttering to himself.

The evening brought more truffle cuisine—Baro ate sparingly—and another recorded visitation from Horslan Gebbling.

"Piety and platitudes," said Guth Bandar, when the image winked out. The historian had thought it better to sit at Baro's and Imbry's table rather than risk another verbal assault from the white-haired disciple. His comment brought a sharp look from Ule Gazz, who rose and led Olleg Ebersol across the dining room to where a mass chant of *bom, bom ala bom* was gaining momentum.

Mirov Kosmir had not graced their table and Flix was still confined to her quarters, so the three were left to each other's company. Baro tried to initiate a discussion of the noösphere—he still felt an urge to return there—but Bandar declined and retired to his cabin. Imbry declared an intention to sample more, indeed everything, from the desert cart. Baro visited the ship's library, found a book by one of his favorite authors of police procedurals, and settled in his bunk to read. But the story could not hold his attention and he fell into a surprisingly dreamless sleep.

The next morning was identical to the preceding one until after breakfast when Gebbling's projection again appeared in the dining room.

"We begin the day with a surprise," the image said. "I ask all of you to put on warm clothing and go up to the promenade deck. There will be a departure."

There was a window behind Baro. He turned now and looked out over the grayness of the dawn Swept. He was facing east and the great red rim of the old sun was creeping over the ruler-straight horizon. "We are slowing," he said.

"Yes," said Guth Bandar. The historian had come to peer over Baro's shoulder. "And I think they mean to have us debark. Are those Rover carts?" He rubbed his hands. "Yes, I believe they are. I've always wanted to travel the Swept in a Rover cart."

"What is a Rover cart?" Baro asked.

Imbry looked put out. "A mode of transportation that offers no respect to the civilized posterior," he said.

Baro had never noticed the wind while the landship was moving, but once the great vessel was standing still he became aware that he was at the bottom of a vast river of air flowing unhindered across the flatness of the Swept. In this part of the prairie, the land was covered in waist-high grass, thin-stalked and topped by feathery tassels, every stem of it bobbing and bowing toward the east as the wind pressed it down. Occasionally, sharper gusts would rush in from the west, making the grass dip closer to the ground, and the landscape would ripple like the sea.

"I think I like all this space," he told Luff Imbry as they descended the gangplank and onto the grass, which stood tall here in the lee of the landship.

"I like civilization," said Imbry, swiping at stalks as if they were bothersome urchins, "which is what we're leaving behind."

Security Officer Haj was a small distance away, deep in conversation with Flix, whose rigid stance and emphatic gestures suggested she was making demands rather than requests. Raina Haj's stance was exactly the same as that with which she had responded to the historian. Curious, Baro drifted a little closer.

"The gig has sufficient range to fly me to a number of towns where I might catch a commercial flight or even hire an air yacht," Flix said.

"How would you know the gig's range?"

"I asked Mirov."

"Mirov? So you and First Officer Kosmir are on a first-name basis?"

Flix said nothing.

"Uh huh." said Haj. "Air yachts are expensive. Are you sure you could afford it?"

"I can certainly afford a commercial ticket home," Flix said.

"The issue is moot," Haj replied. "You are a material witness to a murder. You are in my custody."

"You have no jurisdiction!"

"I am security officer of the *Orgulon*. You are a passenger. That is sufficient jurisdiction."

"But we are not on the *Orgulon*. We are about to be handed over to a pack of Rovers. Are you their security officer as well?"

"An interesting point," said Haj. "You might consult a legal intercessor when an opportunity presents itself."

"This is not fair!" said Flix. "I came on this trip to be rid of the lassitude. I am rid of it now. Why should I not go where my wishes lead me?"

"You may begin walking in any direction you choose," said the security officer, "but the gig is not available."

Flix made a noise that would have suited a furious rodent.

"Either accompany the other passengers in the Rover carts, or return to your cabin under guard," said Haj. "Choose."

Flix signaled her decision by stalking away muttering to herself. Baro turned to go back to Imbry but felt a tap on his shoulder. Raina Haj had come up quickly behind him. "Is this yours?" she said.

In her outstretched hand she held the crushed remains of the clingfast.

"Why would it be mine?" Baro said.

The security officer said, "Don't you think a better answer would be 'What is it'?"

"I defer to your judgment," Baro said. "What is it?"

The violet eyes held him. "I think you know exactly what it is. Further, I believe you put it on Monlaurion's collar. What I'd like to know is why."

Baro had never thought that he would be mentally consulting the Bureau manual on interrogation techniques in order to frustrate one, but he did so now. The manual said that the most difficult interviewee is the one who says nothing.

After the silence had lengthened, the security officer said,

"I'd also like to know why you and your friend are traveling under assumed names, why you pretend to be afflicted by the lassitude, and why you were so interested in my conversation with Flix."

"I don't know what you're talking about," Baro said and knew right away it was a mistake. Lesson one in the introductory course on interrogation taught that the suspect who responds by saying, "I don't know what you're talking about," always knows exactly what the interrogator is talking about.

Baro was chagrined. He remembered the lesson exactly, yet the steady gaze of Raina Haj had caused him to react like any guilty felon.

"I made inquiries," she went on. "Phlevas Wasselthorpe and Erenti Abbas are where they are supposed to be—on the Wasselthorpe estate."

Baro said nothing. He could repeat verbatim the instructions to undercover agents whose false identities were discovered—evade capture and return to the operational base—but under the steady eye of this daunting and attractive young woman the words simply jostled each other in his head like peas in a rattle.

Now she rolled her eyes and made a dismissive hand gesture. "Get away from me," she said.

Relieved, the young man turned to depart.

"Baro," she said as if seized by an afterthought.

"Yes?" he said, turning.

"Uh huh," she said, stepping toward him and taking his arm in a firm grip. Baro felt her fingers reaching for nerve points that she would press if he tried to pull away. "Now, I want all of it or you and your partner go in the brig until we arrive at the nearest Bureau station."

The interrogation technique and the come-with-me grip were pure Bureau. "You're a scroot," he said.

"Of course I am," she replied. "Sergeant-Investigator. And I would be tempted to say, 'You're a scroot, too,' if it weren't for all the inescapable evidence that you haven't the faintest idea how to conduct yourself while working undercover. When did you graduate from the Academy?"

Baro told her. Her eyebrows went up and she said, "But that means you're still a probationer. What are you doing out in the field?"

Baro told her that, too: the trailing of Luff Imbry, the arrest in Sherit, the sudden promotion, and the assignment to go after Horslan Gebbling.

She let go of his arm. "The plump fellow is a fraudster you arrested? And he's now your partner? With no training?"

When Baro had first seen Raina Haj, he had wanted to make an impression on her. Now he could see that he had. Unfortunately, the impression he was making was both deep and unfavorable. He hoped it wasn't indelible.

He essayed a rescue of his sinking image. "The promotion and assignment were personally ordered by the Archon," he said. "Directing Agent Arboghast chose my partner."

The eyebrows went even higher, forming almost perfect bows above the steady violet eyes. "Fine," she said. "Fine. I detect the odor of politics, at the first whiff of which a sensible sergeant walks away. But, for the record, what is the rest of your name?"

"Harkless."

Now the brows drew together and formed a thoughtful line. "There are two chapters by a Baro Harkless in the manual on handling evidence."

"My father."

"Ah," she said, raising an eyebrow. "Is he an associate of Arboghast?"

"He died when I was young."

"Ah," she said again, but in a different way.

"What are you doing on the *Orgulon*?" he asked.

"I won't tell you that."

"At least tell me if your assignment has anything to do with Horslan Gebbling."

"It does not."

"Is there any connection between Gebbling and Flix?"

"Not that I'm aware of," she said. "Is that why you put the clingfast on Monlaurion?"

"We thought they might be shills for whatever Gebbling is up to."

"I've conducted a thorough investigation into both of them, and no link to Gebbling has turned up."

"Could you have missed something?" Baro said.

She shook her head. "Improbable."

"Was there anything on the clingfast?"

"No. It was crushed beyond use."

A wave of despondence came over Baro. It must have showed in his face because Raina Haj smiled reassuringly and patted the arm she had earlier gripped. "Don't take it to heart," she said. "Confidence scheme investigations are often difficult, even for experienced agents."

"Have you any advice?"

"I would wait until you encounter Gebbling, then arrest him on a technicality. A thorough search of his person and surroundings will surely turn up some usable evidence."

Baro was taken aback. "That is contrary to the spirit of the Bureau," he said.

"Uh huh," she said. "When one is certain of the suspect's guilt, a minor shortcut on the way to conclusive proof can be overlooked. It is not like pulling innocents from their beds and fitting them into whatever crimes remain inconveniently un-cleared."

Baro was not sure he agreed, but he was also not sure of his motives. Partially, he did not want to believe that his father would have taken part in such "shortcuts"; more important, he did not want to have to admit that Luff Imbry knew more about the way scroots really worked than did Baro Harkless.

He mentally set the issue aside. "Can we cooperate?" he asked the security officer.

"I don't see that there will be much opportunity," she said. "You are going with the Rovers, while I will remain on the *Orgulon*."

"But Flix is going with us."

"Yes, but Kosmir is staying with the landship."

"Ah," said Baro. "I see."

"Yes, you do," she said. "And please keep it to yourself. We are carrying a cargo of mining machinery consigned to Victor, a day's sail to the northeast. Kosmir's duties require him to be present when it is off-loaded. The gig will ferry supplies to you and the other passengers."

A whistle sounded from the deck above them. "I must go," she said. "The gig will rendezvous with you at noon." She patted his arm again. "Don't worry," she said. "Often an investigation makes sense only when you view it backward from its conclusion."

Baro said, "You could say the same thing about life."

She went aboard and the gangplank was pulled up. Stewards were marshaling the passengers into a circle surrounding the device that projected Gebbling's image and voice. The restlessness of the ambulatory passengers made a contrast with the motionlessness of the lassitude sufferers, stiffly upright on their come-alongs.

Baro joined Imbry and Bandar in the crowd just before Gebbling's image appeared. It hovered in the air until a steward adjusted the mechanism to bring the simulacrum down to earth. At first Gebbling's voice was lost in the unceasing rush of the wind, then the steward made another adjustment and the sound came louder.

"You have made good progress with the *bom, bom ala bom,*" the image said. "I sense the rising of collective chuffe. I can even detect that some have generated a stronger, purer chuffe than others.

"This is all to the good, and today you will have an opportunity to strengthen and refine your chuffe as we approach the moment of our encounter. You will travel across the quiet of the Swept, a landscape that has always encouraged contemplation and spiritual discipline. Your chuffe will soar!

"Hear now the new mantra to carry you through this crucial second stage of the cleansing journey. It is *ta-tumpa, tatey.* Say it now."

The white-haired woman who had browbeaten Guth Bandar led the chant, her voice rising thin and hard over the wind that now struck them full as the landship rumbled off. The others followed her lead, Baro and Imbry joining in too, though the historian only yawned, which drew a harsh look from the chant leader.

Baro broke off the chant and spoke to the historian from the side of his mouth. "I thought you planned to avoid me."

"I planned to escape you," said Bandar. "That not being possible, I will stay close to you and seek your cooperation in assuring that we do not sleep at the same time."

Baro shrugged. "You shall have it," he said.

Now Gebbling's voice came again and the chanting stopped. "You will journey the unbounded face of the world, simply and at a leisurely pace. Here the constant wind symbolizes the power of swelling chuffe. As it blows away all that is not fixed and rooted to the ground, so it will carry away the wisps of preconceptions and unfounded assurances that confine you.

"You shall emerge from this passage refined and purified, prepared to receive the revelation of new life. I bid you travel not in hope but in the certitude that at the end of this path lies deliverance. *Ta-tumpa, ta-tey*."

The chant rose again over the rippling prairie grass and Gebbling's image wavered, then winked out. The stewards waited politely while the chanting continued, then began to nudge the passengers toward the Rover carts.

There were seven of the vehicles, grouped around the edge of a wide circle of trampled grass not far away. They were tall, two-wheeled affairs, the bodies of bamboo plaited and lashed together, the wheels of metal and rubber, the spokes thin, and the tires fat. The walls of the carts went as high as the tops of the wheels, then were surmounted by a cover of woven grass mats supported by curved ribs.

Each was harnessed to a team of eight animals that stood a little over waist high to a tall man, covered in short, dense fur that ranged from light brown to solid black, their rounded ears naked and pink, and each whiskered snout ending in a twitching nose above broad incisors. They crouched at rest on long, muscular legs that ended in broad, hairless feet with spatulate toes. Their constant guttural mutter that sounded almost like speech came from every direction.

"What are they?" Baro asked.

"Oversized vermin," said Imbry, watching one of the draft animals raise a hind limb to scratch indolently at a parasite behind one ear.

It was Guth Bandar who answered more fully. "They are shuggra. Stay clear of them. Their appetite is indiscriminate and their cunning as sharp as their teeth. They will attack anything except their own siblings. Notice how the teams are spread apart, to keep them from savaging each other."

The Rovers themselves were lying under the carts resting, but when the throng of passengers and stewards approached, they stood up. Each went to a cart and yanked on its rear panel so that it unfolded and became a step.

Baro got his first clear look at the Rovers now. "They're ultraterrenes," said Baro, "but I don't recognize the type."

Imbry did not respond. He was eyeing the vehicles with a sour expression. Bandar was regarding all about him with interest and delight, and again delivered a response. "No," he said, "they are of Earth, though not human."

He urged them toward one of the carts and its owner, who seemed the youngest of the seven Rovers. He was a tall, long-limbed individual with bunched shoulder muscles, a deep chest, and a concave belly. He was obviously male. As they got closer, Baro examined the Rover's face, which though narrow was almost jowly, the cheeks hanging loose from a nose so prominent as to be tantamount to a muzzle. The skull bulged in odd directions at the top and rear.

Bandar nudged Baro's ribs. "Prolonged eye contact unsettles them. Sidelong glances are better tolerated."

Baro complied and made a more guarded inspection. The Rover's eyes were large and brown, the whites almost invisible, the lips loose and dark in color, the ears flaplike but obviously connected to the head by muscles and tendons that let them move independently. The limbs were long and roped with muscle, the hands and feet elongated, and the digits tipped with vestigial claws. The whole head and body was covered in short, blond fur and there seemed to be the vestige of a tail. None wore any clothing.

"Are they dogs?" Baro asked Bandar.

Imbry spoke. "Shh," he warned. "They find that word even more unsettling. Fortunately, they pay little attention to humans except when they are guiding, and then only the necessary minimum."

"What do they guide people to?"

"To hunt, of course. There is much game on the Swept—the fand, the lesser and greater garm, not to mention woolly-claw and pronghorned skippit. Of course, the regulations deter many prospective trophy seekers. For a fand, for example, you may bring one fellow hunter. Each of you is allowed a sturdy spear and a long knife."

"It sounds perilous," said Baro. A full-grown fand was half again the weight of a man. It feared nothing and ate anything it could kill.

"It is a very good way of determining who is your truest friend," said Bandar. "The Rover will guide you to the fand, then bring back either you and your trophy, or whichever of your bones remain to be collected. They are also prodigious miners—they love to dig. Come, let us board the carriage."

Careful not to let their gazes connect, Baro stepped past the Rover and climbed into the cart, feeling it bounce on creaking leather springs as he moved. There were four forward facing seats along each side, woven wicker topped by cushions of woven grass. The two agents and Bandar went to the front where they were soon joined by Ule Gazz and Olleg Ebersol, the Lho-tso practitioners.

Ebersol stepped from the come-along directly into the car, moving even more stiffly than he had the evening before, Baro noted. The lassitude gave his every step a hesitant quality, as if he were a stick insect negotiating a sagging stalk. Once seated, he became inert, even his breathing so shallow as to be almost undetectable. Ule Gazz did not speak to the others but closed her eyes and undertook the full morning proa, a series of breaths and postures that occupied her for some time.

The cart bobbed again as another couple boarded, a pair of

robust young women dressed with the careful indifference of students. Guth Bandar introduced himself, then the two agents gave their assumed names and occupations. The newcomers were Corje Sooke and Pollus Ermatage. The latter spoke for both, the former being rendered speechless by the affliction.

"Sooke and I are cohorts," she said, using a term with a particular meaning in their home county, Fasfallia. There, infants were paired for life, the juxtaposing being decided after a careful weighing of heredity, certain social factors, and an indefinable quality known to the Fasfallians as *grims*.

Baro was familiar with the institution. There was a detailed description of Fasfallian society in the Bureau manual on cultural factors related to crime and derangement. Fasfallian friends normally lived every moment of their lives within sight and sound of each other. Other relationships—even mating and child rearing—took a secondary importance, and the life partners usually died in old age scarcely hours apart. If a member of a cohort lost his opposite number earlier in life he would be shunned by all; most bereaved survivors withdrew to a life of contemplation, out of which they produced works of art redolent of sweet melancholy, but some fell into an obsessive mania known as the *champfarr* and became dangerous.

Gazz and Ebersol were too immersed in their individual solitudes to participate in the formalities of greeting. They also paid no attention to the person who took the last seat in the cart. This was Flix, wearing a face full of thunder.

"There is a portrait of unhappiness," Imbry whispered to Baro.

"Indeed," said Baro, but further conversation was cut off as the Rover closed the cart's tailboard with a clatter and made a sound intended to catch their attention.

"Yaffak," he said, followed by a string of syllables that were less clear. There was a strange wobbling quality to the vowels while some of the consonants were more implied than apparent. The brown eyes flicked from one face to another, never settling for more than a moment and ended up cast downward at the bamboo floor of the cart.

"He says his name is Yaffak," Bandar translated.

The Rover had nothing else to communicate. Instead he sprang into motion, as did the other Rovers who were slamming shut the tailboards of their carts, then rushing to the fronts, where there was an open air seat and a footrest. Yaffak took up a whip with a long, rigid handle and a frayed tassel at its tip and touched it to the sides of the lead shuggras. Muttering and keening, the animals rose and leaned into the padded shoulder collars of their harnesses. Baro felt the cart jerk, then roll smoothly forward into the unbroken grass, straight toward the old orange sun now balanced on the dead-level eastern horizon.

The Rovers put their carts into a line-abreast formation and they moved forward together. Guth Bandar watched the maneuver with evident anticipation that was just as evidently not rewarded.

"I don't understand," the small man said after a while. "Rovers are supposed to engage in constant competition for status within the pack. They are reputed to have a fierce sense of hierarchy, based on athleticism and speed, with each individual feeling a continuing urge to press the limits of his status, to see if he might overtake and supplant the occupant of the next highest rung."

"That seems a pointless struggle," said Ule Gazz, who had emerged from her meditations. "The young will inevitably overpower the old, only to become aged themselves and be left behind. All status is fleeting."

"Everything is transient," said Luff Imbry. "But what of it?

Life is lived now, whatever the turn of the wheel may bring to-morrow or next century. An eighteen-course feast is but a temporary phase in its ingredients' cycle from nature back to nature, a cycle which happens to take it through the hands of a master chef. Yet I wouldn't hesitate to seize some of it as it passes by in the form of rum-and-sugared-egg and five-fowl terrine."

"It is all in the perspective," said Pollus Ermatage. "From manure's point of view, the entire circle of fertilization, growth, harvest, processing, and consumption is but a complicated means of producing more manure." She stroked her chin and said, "There may be a song in that."

"Some things are eternal," said Guth Bandar, "or as near as. The Commons, for one. It reaches back to the dim years when we gnawed gritty roots fresh dug from the earth and warm flesh still dripping with blood, and it stretches ahead until the sun billows out to encompass Old Earth in its troposphere."

"But you said the Commons grew from single cells into ag-gregates," Baro said. "New cells must constantly be added as lives are lived and experiences remembered. Does the Commons not evolve as these new cells are encountered?"

"No," said Bandar. "You must reckon on the age of the world and the myriads who have lived. Granted, there are vast permutations in the number of ways a single life can be lived, especially in combination with trillions of other lives that come before, during, and after the individual existence. But, given enough time, enough lives, the sum total of all that can be done *is* done. Everything significant, that is—what remains is trivia."

"My life is not trivial, nor is it an exact duplicate of any-one's," said Baro. "No one has ever been me doing what I'm doing, in the way I'm doing it, and for the reasons I'm doing it."

"True," said Bandar. "But whatever your life's quest may be, it differs only slightly from those of a trillion young men who have come before you. What do you seek: power, passion, wealth, enlightenment? Each has been sought and won—or lost—a hundred billion times. The best you can hope for is to create some minor embellishment on the pattern. It is no more significant than repositioning an individual grain of sand in a desert."

The historian's perspective sent a wave of sadness through Baro, or perhaps it was the dawn wind blowing against his face as the open carts raced across the Swept. He thought of his father and wondered if he was repeating elements of the man's truncated life, if he had let himself be pressed into a pattern that need not have shaped his existence.

It was a thought that had never occurred to him before—he had always been destined for the Bureau—but now he found that not only was the thought surprising, but even more startling was the realization that this was the first time he had ever stopped to consider whether the course of his life was what he wanted it to be.

He shivered again. It was an unsettling chain of thought. He decided that he would put it aside until a more tranquil time.

During Baro's brief introspection the conversation in the cart had moved on. Ule Gazz was discoursing on the philosophical underpinnings of the Lho-tso movement, which appeared to be that nothing much mattered except discipline of mind and spirit. The world, with all its permutations, was essentially only a good trick and "one eventually grows tired of tricks," she said. Her tone was somewhat assertive for a devotee of a discipline that preached detachment, Baro thought.

Luff Imbry must have had a similar impression, for he said, "If all that matters can be found within the confines of a meditation mat, why aren't you at home breathing and positioning? Why have you brought Olleg Ebersol in pursuit of a ghostly image across an endless prairie?"

Ule Gazz looked at her partner, whose eyes stared emptily at the unchanging horizon. "We are none of us perfect," she said. "There are some tricks one longs to see done again."

Imbry made a face like that of a repentant bully and turned away from the others. The conversation lapsed.

"Perhaps we should sing the new chant," said Pollus Ermatage. In a soft but musical voice she began to intone the *ta-tumpa, ta-tey*. Ule Gazz took it up after her, and Baro saw a rhythmic quaver in the throat of her paralyzed partner, Olleg Ebersol. The lassitude sufferer was trying to join in. It seemed polite to cooperate so Baro voiced the *ta-tumpa, ta-tey* with the others. Even Bandar sang along, though with an occasional quirk of his eyebrows. Luff Imbry kept silent, and turned to look out onto the prairie, as did Flix, her face still sullen.

After a while the historian's voice trailed off and so did Baro's. The agent tried to open a discussion on the noösphere—he had begun to wonder whether the Rovers shared the Commons with their human creators, or did they have one of their own?—but Bandar declined to enter into a colloquy. Instead, he folded his arms and leaned against one of the curved ribs that supported the roof of the cart, saying he intended to try to recover some of the sleep lost the night before.

"Please ensure that our young friend here does not also sleep before I awaken," he asked the company in general. "I prefer my dreams unmolested."

Imbry came out of the study into which he had slumped and promised he would keep an eye on Baro. The other passengers also agreed, except for Flix who offered no commitments. The chant resumed and soon Bandar was snoring.

Baro lapsed into a curious state. A portion of his mind told him he should concentrate his faculties on the Gebbling case, reassess what he knew in the light of what he had learned from Raina Haj. But his mind, until now always disciplined, refused to cooperate. It was throwing up random images: scenes from his youth and childhood, the vision of his Shadow blowing on its fingertips in the darkness of the glass, Raina Haj's turquoise-flecked violet irises, the Hero with the winged helmet, the dead Dree in the trench.

Baro sat and watched the images sequentially appear and vanish on the screen of his mind's eye. His analytical function, trained to look for patterns, sought to impose a meaning to the display, a message from the back reaches of his psyche. But nothing came. It was as if the events of recent days had been a stick to stir the sediments below the clear water of his consciousness, filling it with a cloud of unconnected memories.

He saw again the scene of his father walking toward the garden gate, his mother digging in a flower bed. He held the image in his mind—his eidetic memory could do so effortlessly—and examined its details. He could see the sunlight glint from the captain's pips on his father's epaulets, the details of the design on his mother's smock, the stray wisp of auburn hair that escaped from beneath her yellow scarf.

Was there a message here? He could not see it. He pondered the image at length and still nothing came. Then, like a bubble rising through thick liquid, a question burst in the back of his mind. Why was he seeing the scene from inside the house? Why wasn't he walking his father to the gate as he always did—it was a father-son ritual—when Captain Harkless left on assignment?

The answer should have come with the question, Baro knew. His memories were as available to him as entries in an integrator's data banks, back even as far as his infancy. Yet when he asked why he was watching from the house—no, *confined* to the house—he had to struggle to find the reason.

This must be how it is for those with ordinary memories,

he thought as he mentally pushed and prodded around the edges of the scene in his mind. The answer came slowly: he was in the house because he had been told he could not leave its walls for two days. Who had told him? He pushed again, and the response reluctantly presented itself: his father.

Now he could see the man's face looking down at him. *I was nine years old,* he remembered. His father's expression was stern. *We're in the front room and he's telling me I cannot leave the house. It is my punishment for . . .* Baro could not remember. He strove to force the memory into his consciousness but it would not come. Some part of him resisted, would not open the door.

I was nine, he told himself again. *What could I have done that was so awful I still cannot let the memory see light?* Almost, he turned from the question, but something would not let it go. Sweat had broken out on his face; he felt its coolness in the morning air. Eyes tightly closed, he reached for the memory, pushed against a resistance that held him at a distance, then suddenly gave way.

I hate you! He heard the words in his nine-year-old's voice, high-pitched and shouting. *I hate you! I hope you never come back!*

He'd wanted something, still couldn't remember what—to go with friends somewhere, he thought—and his father had said no. Young Baro had not completed an assignment, some project from his tutor. His father was saying that work comes before leisure, responsibility before caprice.

"You will concentrate on your work until I return." He could hear his father's voice now, see his grave face, even read in its expression the concern for his son that had not been evident to his nine-year-old self.

Young Baro had thrown a tantrum. *Who knew why?*

today's Baro asked himself. *Was I feeling neglected? Was it a boy's fear that his always-departing father might someday not return? Was that what made me wish that he would never come back? Did I make a weapon out of a childhood fear?*

He could feel sweat trickling down his back and belly now. His breath was coming hard. He felt a hand shaking his shoulder and opened his eyes to see Luff Imbry peering into his face with concern. "Are you all right?" his partner said.

"Yes."

"I thought you had lapsed into the Commons again."

"No, just memories."

"Do you wish to share them?"

Baro signaled a negative and saw Imbry's poorly concealed relief. The fat man returned to his own thoughts and Baro leaned his head against a rib of the cart's frame and tried to think of nothing.

The coolness of dawn gave way to the heat of full day. When the sun was an orange ball halfway to the zenith and the horizon was frequently lost in haze, the lead Rover yipped twice and the echelon of the carts redeployed. The leader slowed his shuggras, then turned them to the right and began to pull his cart in a tight circle. Each of the others followed his lead, the individual vehicles drawing closer together until they almost touched and the line was spinning around the leader like the hand of a dial. Within moments, the rotation had created a circle of trampled grass.

"They're clearing a space for us," said Imbry. "Good. That may mean lunch."

"Too early," said Guth Bandar, awakened from his nap by the Rovers' cries. "This will be a rest stop."

When the circle was well flattened the Rovers drew the carts into a huddle in its center, unstrapped themselves, and dropped the tailboards for the passengers to dismount. Yaffak gestured toward the tall grass and said something that Bandar translated as "For our convenience."

He asked how long they would stay? and translated the Rover's answer, "They want to rest the draft animals and take a small meal. The drivers also want to nap before the full heat of the day."

With his feet on the ground, Baro stretched, bending backward and forward to ease an ache in his lower back. He went out into the grass to relieve his bladder and when he returned he found that Imbry had brought the woven cushion from the cart and placed it on the trampled grass in the vehicle's shade to give himself a comfortable seat. Baro came to sit cross-legged beside him.

"You do not look well," Imbry said.

"I have had unsettling thoughts."

"Concerning Gebbling?"

"No, there I confess myself at an impasse," Baro said and related what Raina Haj had told him that morning. He did not tell Imbry about her suggestion that they take a "shortcut" and arrest the fraudster on spurious grounds.

"I have been giving the matter some thought," said Imbry. "I am not trained in investigations, but some questions occurred to me. I have been thinking about our fellow passengers."

Baro felt a pang of guilt. In truth, he had not given their assignment a moment's thought since he had boarded the Rover's cart. "Where have your thoughts led you?" he said.

"I have found a common factor. In fact, two."

"Tell me."

"While you were sweating and gazing at the horizon," Imbry said, "I consulted the data stored in my plaque. Two things stood out: one is that all of the lassitude sufferers are at the same stage in the progress of the disease. None has lapsed into complete catatonia. There is no waxiness of the skin. And none shows the stuttering and twitching of the earliest onset."

Baro's mind engaged. "That means they all must have contracted the condition at the same time," he said.

"I believe so," said Imbry. "The other common factor is even more arresting. With the exception of one pair, they all live within a certain distance of a particular geographical point."

Imbry now had Baro's full attention. "Where is that point and who is the exception?" Baro said.

"The exception is Trig Helvic and his daughter Erisme. The point is in the vicinity of the Monument, near the center of the Swept, not far from here."

Baro's mind chewed the information. "The fact that all are in the same stage of the disease cannot be a coincidence," he said after a while. A chilling thought struck him. "Is it possible that Gebbling has discovered not just how to cure the lassitude, but how to cause it? Did he deliberately infect all of these people so that he could send them invitations to be cured?"

"It would make sense," Imbry said, "in a terribly cynical way. He could present this mixed assemblage of folk, from different places and various walks of life, as living samples of his abilities. The world would come rushing to his door."

"But," said Baro, "if he has found a cure, why all the flim-flammery, the landship, the Rovers, the image projected from some hidden source? He need only walk into the nearest hospice and start raising the afflicted from their beds."

"I don't know," said Imbry. "Perhaps he can cure only those he has afflicted."

Baro turned the discussion to the geographical distribution of the passengers. "That also seems relevant," he said, "though I would feel better if the exceptional pair had turned out to be Monlaurion and Flix."

Imbry agreed. "It would tend to argue for their having been shills. Then the imagist's death might have been a falling out among miscreants. Flix might give us a crevice into Gebbling's scheme that we could work at and widen."

Baro made up his mind. "Haj said she was not involved. I believe her. But we must question Helvic. If his daughter was within range of the common geographical center at about the time she came down with the lassitude, then we have something solid at last." He flicked his head in annoyance and added, "But what that 'something solid' means we still don't know."

"Well, we must sip before we swallow," said Imbry. "But Helvic does not seem the sort to welcome casual conversation. See how he stands aside from all others."

Helvic was standing at the edge of the cleared space, inflicting a grim look on the endless grass.

"I do not intend casual conversation," Baro said. "I will identify myself as a Bureau agent. Even the wealthy and powerful must answer a scroot's questions."

"Is that wise?" said Imbry. "Arboghast commanded us to remain undercover."

"His exact words," Baro said, "were 'You will observe the strictest undercover protocols.' Section eight, subparagraph twelve of standing orders governing covert operations allows an agent to reveal his status if he judges the person in whom he confides to be trustworthy."

"Helvic is one of the wealthiest men in the world and his daughter suffers from the lassitude," said Imbry. "He is unlikely to be in league with the likes of Gebbling."

"Let us see what we can learn," said Baro.

Baro and Imbry approached the magnate. Baro discreetly displayed his plaque and said, "My partner and I are agents of the Bureau of Scrutiny operating undercover."

Helvic's leaden expression did not alter. He glanced at the

plaque and turned his head slightly toward them. "What are you investigating?" he said.

"Possibly the source of the lassitude. We believe that Father Olwyn, who is a fraudster known to us as Horslan Gebbling, may be its creator."

"Such infamy had never occurred to me," said Helvic. "I thought at worst he would dangle a hope before me while he picked my pocket."

"Yet you were willing to come along," said Luff Imbry.

The magnate smiled a sardonic smile and looked to where a steward was feeding his daughter from a tube. "I have plenty of pockets," he said, "but only one child."

"I wish to ask you a question," Baro said.

"Then ask."

"Where was your daughter when she first contracted the disease?"

It did not take Helvic more than a moment to answer. "She was hiking in the hills above Farflung. There are some curious rock formations there. She was—is—a connoisseur of geological oddities."

That put Erisme Helvic well within the circle shared by the other victims. "Thank you," Baro said.

Imbry had another question. "Why did you accept Gebbling's invitation?"

"Hope for a cure," Helvic answered.

"You do not strike me as a man who bases his decisions on hope," Imbry said.

"True, I am not such a man."

"Then there was something that spoke more forcefully to you," said Baro. "Please tell us what it was."

Helvic looked around them and though the nearest person was out of earshot he lowered his voice and said, "Black brillion."

Baro saw Imbry's eyebrows rise but he kept his gaze on Helvic. "You must tell us the whole thing," he said.

"A man came to my home. I did not know him," Helvic said. "He had altered the set of his features"—he glanced at Luff Imbry—"much as you appear to have done so. He asked me, 'Would you see your daughter cured?'"

The man had taken a small gold box from his pocket and opened it. Within was a speck of something dark that glistened with the colors of the rainbow. The man had used tweezers to extract the tiny ort, then he had placed it on the back of Erisme Helvic's hand.

"In a moment the rigor left her face," her father said. "She smiled and laughed and we embraced. At that moment I would have given the man all of my fortune, at least all but Erisme's portion, and counted it a good bargain."

But the man had held up an admonitory hand. The shred of black brillion was not strong enough to create a permanent remission of the lassitude. In a few hours, the paralysis must return.

Helvic had been distraught. How could he deliver his daughter from this horror? The man laid a document before him. It contained a list of instructions: charter the *Orgulon,* invite the accompanying list of persons to join him on the cruise, say nothing to anyone.

"Did he instruct you to transfer any funds or to bring valuables with you?" Imbry asked.

"No."

"Has he contacted you since?" Baro said. "Has anyone approached you since we left Farflung?"

"No to the first question, and to the second, only you."

"Hmm," said Imbry.

Baro made the same sound. They thanked Helvic and left him. The magnate again lapsed into his dark study.

Baro and Imbry returned to the cart. "So we have learned something," Imbry said.

"Yes. We have time and location in common, two factors that must point to something. But we don't know what."

"Let us give it time."

"And we know how Gebbling can afford all this expense."

"Yes," Imbry said. "But now there is a mysterious confederate. And so-called black brillion plays a part."

"How might Trig Helvic be fooled? He is a hard-minded man."

"There are drugs that, surreptitiously administered, can induce the victim's senses to see and hear whatever the perpetrator suggests," Imbry said.

"But those drugs leave aftereffects that alert the intelligent to the possibility that their perceptions have been tampered with," Baro countered. "Helvic does not fit the profile of an easy victim."

"Again, true," said Imbry. "So we have learned something, but not enough. This investigating is ofttimes as interesting as my former work."

Baro was chagrined at himself and it showed in his face.

"What?" Imbry said.

"I am the trained agent, you are the amateur," the young man said, "yet it was you who exercised initiative and mined the data for good results."

"There are other fields besides criminology that reward an inquiring mind," his partner said. "For example, you might learn something from watching the Rovers. Bandar is highly interested."

Baro looked and saw that the historian was watching the drivers intently. They had unhitched the shuggras from the carts although each team remained harnessed together. They moved the teams to separate points on the rim of the trampled circle before feeding the beasts from nosebags strapped to their heads. The Rovers themselves settled in a group at the center of the circle to eat their own rations, a pile of hard biscuits and what looked like jerked meat piled on a cloth in the center of the ring. Without apparent ceremony, the Rovers helped themselves to the food and sat on their haunches chewing mechanically.

Bandar watched for a while, then shook his head and walked away. Baro joined him. "Something disturbs you?" he asked the historian.

"There should have been jostling and attempts by junior-ranked members of the pack to improve their place in the feeding order," the small man said. "Indeed, there *was* no order of precedence. All reached at the same time."

"Perhaps they have changed their ways."

"No," said Bandar. He thought about it, then said, "Not possible."

"It seems that you regularly encounter the impossible on this journey," said Baro. "Perhaps, like Father Olwyn, they have received a revelation and changed their ways."

"Rover consciousness is a thin veneer over a solid mass of deep instinct," Bandar said. "It would take more than a preacher to change them."

"Then could it be disease?" Baro suggested. "Perhaps this is how the lassitude affects them."

"They have a definite reaction to illness," Bandar said. "The sick one goes away until he is either cured or dies. It protects the group."

"You know a great deal about them," Baro said as they walked back to where Imbry sat.

"Only what is common knowledge."

"Not common to me," Baro said. "In fact, I had never heard of them before this morning. Nor the Commons before I met you."

"Never heard of Rovers or the Commons," Bandar mused. "What other things do you not know?"

"A tautology," said Imbry, who had overheard. "How can he be expected to know what he does not know?"

"A fair point," said Bandar. "After all, he is merely a provincial gentleman, an occupation that requires one to know no more than the latest fashionable fillips and the precise social worth of one's neighbors. But he does wear the scarf of an Institute graduate."

"Though only third tier," said Imbry.

"True," said the historian. "What was your field again?"

"Criminology," said Baro.

"He can quote verbatim from manuals of the Bureau of Scrutiny," Imbry said.

"What a peculiar distinction," said Bandar. "I mean, I am sure the capability would be of use to a Bureau employee, but even the most earnest scroot would need to command a wider array of knowledge than just standards and procedures."

"Perhaps the most earnest scroot might not realize the lack," said Imbry.

"A worrisome thought," said Bandar, "for it would make him narrow and strange, like those obsessives who encompass every minim of minutiae about some arcane discipline yet cannot sustain a decent conversation about the weather."

"There is nothing wrong with pursuing a calling," Baro said.

"I recall a story about a man who followed a star. He was so bedazzled by its lure that he stepped over a cliff."

"I do not know that story," said Baro.

"Well, you wouldn't, would you?" said the historian. "It is probably not reproduced in police manuals."

They had reached their cart. "I think I need sleep," Baro said. A wave of fatigue was suddenly rising up from within him, almost threatening to overwhelm his consciousness.

"I will take care to remain awake until you are finished," Bandar said. "In fact, I will watch over you and shake you into consciousness if I detect the signs of dreaming."

"I understand," Baro said. "Thank you." He stretched out on the ground in the cart's shade. A few of the other passengers had done likewise, though most had gathered in a group to chant and expand their chuffe.

Baro rolled onto his stomach and looked through heavy eyes across the clearing. The Rovers had finished their meal and were lying on the trampled grass. Yaffak already seemed to be twitching in a dream.

"Is there any danger that I might intrude upon Yaffak's dream, as I did on yours?" Baro asked.

"Now there is ambition," Bandar said. "But you need not concern yourself. There is an unbreachable barrier between us and them, as there is between any two species. Still, it would be fascinating to explore the Rover Commons. Their psyches being more deeply embedded in instinct, there is a closer connection between the lower and upper brains, and the tides of the Old Sea ebb and flow not far beneath their consciousness."

"Has it been tried?"

"Everything has been tried. That which was possible has been done. What remains undone is therefore impossible."

Baro yawned and said, "In the past, there must have been occasions when hybrids were produced—as you say, all that can be done has been done. What would the Commons of such a hybrid look like?"

"It would be either a very deserted place," said Bandar, "or a very crowded one. Either case might explain why hybrids never flourish and are frequently mad."

"If bridging the Commonses of two species *could* be done, that would be something new," said Baro, "would it not?"

"Yes," said Bandar, "which is why it will not be done."

"Yet I feel it might."

The historian sighed. "You have only recently begun to gauge the depth of your ignorance yet you are prepared to make it the foundation for a towering confidence."

"Perhaps he is a visionary," said Imbry.

"Or biting mad," said Bandar. "The terms are frequently interchangeable."

Their voices became a buzz in Baro's ears as he slid down into sleep. He was immediately before the wardrobe and its dark mirror. His Shadow smirked at him and said, "Hail the hero," in a sarcastic tone but Baro stepped right through the phantom and rushed down to the tarn. He was possessed by a great urgency, an ironic sense in this timeless place that time was shortening. He plunged into the green water and was instantly transposed to the white road.

He was alone and then he wasn't. The Hero stood in the field beyond the low wall, clad in its shaggy cope and shining mail. It carried a round shield on its arm. The dog's-head design painted on it came to life, silently gnashing its teeth and laying back its ears.

Baro felt a shock when the Hero's gaze met his. A shiver of pure terror convulsed his body and for a moment he wanted to turn and run heedlessly in any direction but that of the barbarian whose face, he now saw, was his own. But the Hero made no move toward him, only raised its sword to point across the field and angled its head in a way that said, *Come.* He set off in the direction it had indicated.

Baro shook himself free of his fear and vaulted over the wall. He followed the warrior toward the horizon, walking through a dreamscape where the ground beneath him kept changing its nature, from grass to dust to stubble to bare rock. But the Hero remained unchanged, as did Baro, although he now saw that he was again clad in the identical rough garb, with the same shield on his back and gray sword in his hand.

Baro had walked no more than a few dozen steps before he looked up and found that the horizon, which had seemed so distant, was now gone. In its place was a wall, fashioned from immense blocks of white stone, an impassable barrier that rose straight up to the sky.

The muscles of the Hero's right arm bunched and it swung the great sword at the wall. Sparks flew as iron struck stone and the sound of the blow rang in Baro's ears. He looked and saw that the wall was unmarked. The Hero looked at him, sword hanging.

Baro knew, with a dreamer's knowledge, what the wall was and why it could not be breached. "It cannot be done," he said.

"It must be done," said a voice beside him. He turned and saw the old man with the staff, its beard and hair long and white, its features both craggy and noble. Behind him a crowd had assembled. Baro recognized them from when he had crossed the bridge and from Bandar's descriptions: the Fool in the shape of a young man, though its face showed more brave innocence than folly; the multi-armed Destroyer; the tongue-lolling Good Beast, reared up on shaggy hind legs; the Lovers, arms entwined. There was the Mother, suckling the Child, and beside them the Father, wearing the face of Captain Baro Harkless.

The Father nodded its head and Baro recognized the gesture as his own father's gesture, the one that said, *Go on. You can do it.*

Baro faced the wall. He raised his sword and swung as the Hero had. No sparks flew and he heard no clash of metal on rock. The blade rebounded from the wall. He turned back to the crowd.

"Not the wall," said the old man. It pointed to the ground. *There is nothing beneath us but the Old Sea,* Bandar had said.

"Can it be done?" Baro asked the old man.

"It can be done, if you can do it," was the answer.

"And if I cannot?"

"If you cannot, then it cannot be done." The old man's pupils were immense, the irises thin rims of gold. Baro saw his own reflection in the dark circles. "Yet it must be done," the old man concluded, one gnarled finger pointing to the ground.

Baro set the point of his sword against the changeable dream-earth that was now red dirt, dry and thick with clods. He leaned his weight against the pommel and pushed. Nothing happened. He felt no resistance but it was as if the weapon was immobilized.

A sigh came from the crowd. Baro put both hands on the rough-shaped iron that anchored the sword's hilt and pushed down again, with all the strength he could muster. And now he felt the tiniest give to the ground.

Another sound went up from the gathered entities, a wordless syllable of expectation. It seemed to Baro that the sound entered him, filled him with a power that flowed into his arms and down to the hands that cupped the pommel of the sword. He pushed the iron into the red ground and whatever force had resisted its entry now abruptly failed.

The sword pierced the soil and Baro sliced a rent in the ground as if the earth was no more substantial than a veil. Another exhalation rose from the crowd at his back, a sound of release.

The wound in the red soil was gray at its center. It widened, revealing nothingness.

"Step," said the old man.

"I am afraid," Baro said.

"I know."

The young man looked again at the crowd that stood silently watching him. The Father nodded again. Baro turned and leaped feetfirst into the gray.

It took him, swallowed him. He was in a place that was no place, without up or down, with neither forward nor back, a realm of luminous, shadowless pearl. He floated, or so he thought. Or perhaps he sank. There was no way to know. He looked about him and saw nothing, looked down and saw his feet, still in hero's buskins, then looked up and saw not far above him a rent in the grayness, the place where he had entered.

From two fixed points he could make a map: that was what they taught in the Bureau orienteering course. There was the rent above him. It had a beginning and an end, and those two points made a direction in this directionless no place. It ran toward the wall, Baro knew, and therefore the wall must be *here* and thus beyond the wall must be *there*.

He kicked his feet, but the Old Sea was not made of water. Still, it was enough that he willed to go somewhere and so he moved, the sword extended above his head as if he were a ship and the weapon his bowsprit. He moved and then his motion stopped as the sword point met resistance.

He still felt the power that had come from the entities and he willed the sword to pierce what it touched. Instantly the barrier yielded, splitting open the gray above him. He moved and his head and shoulders entered the rent and a moment later he had pulled himself onto firm ground.

At first he wondered if he had come out into some solid

part of the Old Sea, someplace where the grayness took a tangible form. There was no color to the land around him, only black and white and endless variations of gray. But when Baro took his first breath, his senses were filled with a riot of odors, subtle and stark, faint and overwhelming, more than he could ever encompass at once and far more than he could even name.

He stood up and saw that he was in a field of short grass. At his back an impenetrable hedge of black thorns stretched up as high as he could see. The land at his feet rolled down a long slope and went on forever to where a gray horizon met a gray sky. There were no roads to be seen, but as he turned his head from side to side Baro discovered that there was in fact an unseen trail nearby, a path marked by scent. It was a sharp odor, complex and strong. Somehow he knew that it resulted from the passage of many bodies.

Baro followed his nose to the scent trail and it seemed to lead him on. He moved forward. The land shifted and changed around him as he went; he recognized the signs. *I am in a dreamscape,* he thought, and in a moment he knew whose dream he had entered.

A figure appeared on the scent path in front of him, a panting Rover on all fours, trembling in all its muscles so that they rippled beneath the fur, jaws agape and dripping foam, tongue hanging loose, as if exhausted from a long and unsuccessful struggle.

"Yaffak," Baro said.

The Rover turned to him, a look of despair in its eyes that here were solid black. Now Baro saw that behind Yaffak a crowd had formed, like that which had watched him pierce the soil in his own Commons. *These are the entities of the Rover noösphere,* he thought. *That will be the Mother, her dugs engorged with milk, and that big one must be the Pack*

Leader. They were all staring at him, except for one young one that kept breaking off to chase its own tail.

Why do they not attack me? Baro wondered. *I am an intruder here.* Then he remembered the Good Beast from his own Commons. *The Rovers must have a Man among their archetypes, and I have been fitted into that role.*

Yaffak made a sound. It was not a human word nor a dog-like yelp or howl. It was a groan from the deepest core of his being, rising, as if against relentless pressure, to break free.

Baro stepped to the young Rover and put out a hand to touch the oddly shaped head. But before his fingers reached the thick fur he felt a deep chill that invaded his fingertips, then traveled up his arm. He drew back his hand and shook it to relieve the growing numbness.

Now the Rover snarled, revealing long, sharp canines. Baro withdrew his hand and would have backed away, but Yaffak's eyes belied the message of the growl. They gazed at Baro with a fading hope.

The man passed his hand over the Rover's head again, felt the chill, then felt it abruptly end as his hand moved on. Yaffak snarled again, but did not move. The Rover stood unmoving except for the constant trembling, but it seemed to Baro that Yaffak was exerting every minim of his strength against an unseen restraint.

Baro explored the idea, passing his hand over the Rover's chest and shoulders. The deep cold came and went as his fingers moved. The chill was in broad intersecting lines like a network. *It's a kind of harness,* he thought, *tight about the whole body.* His fingers investigated further and he found a thin region of cold that extended from the midpoint of Yaffak's bunched shoulders up into the diffuse grayness that approximated a sky.

It's a leash, Baro thought and with the thought came revulsion and instant action: he swung the iron sword sideways above the Rover's back and when it reached the point where the invisible tether rose above Yaffak it bit into something and stopped. Baro felt a deeper chill than ever pass through the weapon and into his arm. He yanked the sword free, took it in both hands and swept it through the air again, felt it bite into the leash and again the numbing cold passed into his hands and arms. Baro put his weight behind the weapon, sawed with the edge, while his hands turned to insensate lumps of icy flesh. The unseen strap resisted, then stretched, then the sword's edge cut through.

At once the cold fled from Baro's limbs and he reached one hand toward Yaffak, whose limbs now seemed to lose all their strength. The Rover settled to the ground, panting, eyes closed, and lay still for a few heartbeats. Then he pushed himself back onto all fours, and shook from front to back, shoulders rolling and ears flapping. He squatted on his hind legs, then stood. He gave a long sigh and his long mouth opened in what Baro could only interpret as a smile.

"Free," the Rover said, and though he said it in his own tongue, Baro understood. Now Yaffak's solid image began to fade into transparency. The other figures of the Rover noösphere also grew dim, as if they were actors on a darkening stage. The horizon that, though indistinct, had nonetheless appeared to be distant now seemed to be rushing toward Baro from all directions.

He is waking, the young man thought. *And what happens to me if I am trapped in his Commons when he leaves it?* That seemed a question better resolved by conjecture than by waiting for a concrete answer. Baro turned and ran up the scent trail, now fading like the light, toward the hedge of black thorn.

The ground grew dark beneath his feet and he almost did

not see the spot where he had torn through from the Old Sea. The rent was mending itself, closing from either end, and now it was no more than a few hands long. *If I'd waited it would have disappeared,* he thought. He inserted the sword into the slit and lengthened it again.

And then a worse thought came: *What if the hole beyond the hedge-wall has closed? Will I be trapped in the Old Sea forever—or at least until the Worm comes to devour me?*

He dove headfirst through the slit, aiming toward the hedge because that should carry him under the barrier to the place where he had entered the Old Sea. Again he plunged into a gray oblivion, and now he saw nothing ahead or above, no sign of where his original entry point had been.

He twisted and rotated, seeing only the pearly nonlight from every nondirection in this no-place. Then his eye caught a motion and he turned toward it. Something was moving, far off in the gray emptiness, and though it appeared tiny Baro knew somehow that it was not, knew that it was immense, and knew that it was coming for him.

He turned and turned again, found the tear he had made in the Rovers' dreamscape. It was closing again but he envisioned a line extending from it to where the first entry must have been.

He saw it, a slit no longer than his hand with a glimmer of light behind it. He moved toward it, sword extended, willing himself to cross the nondistance that nonetheless separated him from his only exit. But the power he had felt before was fading. He seemed to move achingly slowly, gliding toward the closing gap when he wanted desperately to surge forward.

He sensed that he did not have the same strength as when he had entered the Old Sea from his own dreamscape. He felt no fatigue, and his will was as strong as before, but he was sure that his desire, his sense of purpose, did not translate into a result as easily as it had when he had first plunged through.

He was slowly, oh so slowly, drifting toward the closing gap, which was now no more than a hand's length. He looked down between his feet and saw that the far distant thing that swam toward him no longer appeared so tiny. It was long and segmented, and gray like everything here. It moved by a continuing undulation, and it moved quickly. Where its head might have been there was no more than a circular hole in its front end, and that hole at least was not gray; it was the deep black of complete nothingness, ringed with flecks of white. Baro understood that the Worm, this moving maw lined with concentric rows of razor teeth, was the original answer to the mystery of life's existence: *Why do you exist? Because then you don't*—the negative, by existing, paradoxically proving the positive.

But this was no time for Baro to replay memories from the schoolroom. He concentrated on the need to go forward and simultaneously moved his feet and arms. But there was nothing to push against. Still, he slowly inched toward the closing gap, no more than a rip now in the grayness, only the faintest glimmer of light leaking through.

He extended the sword again. Its tip crept toward the rip, impossibly slowly. But now he saw a glimmer of light touch the point of the blade and shimmer down the polished iron. Somehow the light changed the dynamic of his situation. It was as if the light, once touched, pulled him toward it. He moved forward with speed, and as he moved he thrust the sword into the slip and widened it, bringing more luminescence down the blade to bathe his hand and arm and upturned face.

He burst through into the light of his own dreamplace and pulled himself onto the dry red earth. He knelt and looked down into the incision. Through the grayness the Worm **was** still rising to take him. Its mouth was wide enough to have swallowed the *Orgulon,* its teeth great jagged triangles glowing against its inner blackness.

Baro passed his hand across the wound in the ground of his dream, brushing the red soil over the rent, causing it to disappear. His last image of the Old Sea was of the great Worm turning away, swimming back into nowhere.

The figures of the human Commons were still gathered about him. Baro wanted to ask the Wise Man about what he had done in Yaffak's dream, about the chilling harness and the tether that he had cut. But as he opened his mouth a fissure appeared in the air beside him and Guth Bandar, chanting loudly, seized the young man's arm and pulled him through.

Baro found himself lying on his back on the trampled grass of the rest-stop, with Luff Imbry kneeling over him and methodically slapping his cheeks and shouting, "Come up! Come out of it!"

Bandar was standing over Imbry, eyes closed and chanting the same tones as in Baro's dream. Now he ceased intoning the than, opened his eyes, and seized Imbry's upraised arm before the older man could deliver another slap. "It's all right," the noönaut said, "I've got him back."

"I'm fine," Baro said, sitting up. His cheeks stung and he touched his fingers to them, finding the flesh hot and tender. "What have you been doing to me?" he asked Imbry.

"You were gone," his partner said. "We tried to wake you, but it was like no sleep I have ever seen. You had slipped into a coma."

"I was in the Rovers' Commons. I passed into Yaffak's dream."

"You could not have," said Bandar, his face a mask of disapproval. "They would have torn you to pieces."

"I think they accepted me as the Good Man, as we accept the Good Beast in our dreams."

"Nonsense! Besides, there is no pathway. The Wall is absolute."

Baro stood up. He felt refreshed and charged with vitality, although his cheeks still burned. "There is a way," he said. "Through the Old Sea."

Bandar raised a hand as if he meant to slap Baro, then he lowered it and stamped one small foot instead. "Worse nonsense!" he said. "It is death to enter the utoposphere. The consciousness hangs inert, then the devouring Worm comes."

"I was not inert. The entities helped me. I took power from them, willed myself to move and I moved. I went under the wall, cut my way through, and emerged into Yaffak's Commons. On his side, by the way, the wall is a hedge of black thorns."

Bandar made a strangled sound and clenched his delicate fists under his chin. "It cannot be!" he said, the vehemence of his denial making his lips white. "That is a great secret, known only to a few. How would you know such a thing?"

"The Wise Man showed the way. I used the Hero's sword and cut my way through."

Bandar placed both hands atop his head as if he feared the skull might come apart. "This is too much!" he cried. "What have I ever done to you that you should casually yank the underpinnings from a lifetime of study and exploration?"

"There is more," Baro said.

"Oh, there would be," Bandar said. "I don't want to hear it."

"I think we have to," said Imbry. "It may explain what happened here in the mundane world while you were dreaming or comatose, or in whatever definition of unconsciousness we may eventually decide to apply."

"What happened?" Baro said.

"If you look about you," his partner said, "you may notice that all the carts but ours are gone, along with their Rovers and passengers."

Baro looked about him and saw that what Imbry said was true. The two agents and the historian formed one small group next to Yaffak's cart. Another group consisted of Ule Gazz and Olleg Ebersol on the other side of the now-deserted clearing, the former standing while the latter lay stiffly at her feet, along with the two Fasfallian students sitting cross-legged and back-to-back. Ule Gazz was chanting the *ta-tumpa, ta-tey* with stubborn conviction, while Pollus Ermatage contributed an undertone accompaniment.

Flix constituted a group of one, standing at an equal distance from the other two, arms folded and back rigid, staring out over the long grass with an undisguised air of vexation.

"What happened?" Baro said again.

Imbry told him. All had been quiet. The ambulatory passengers who were not chanting to increase their chuffe were dozing. The stewards were playing some kind of game of chance. The Rovers were asleep.

Suddenly Yaffak had sprung to consciousness and to his feet. He had stood over his pack mates, teeth bared and nostrils flaring, the ruff on his neck standing upright, growling something in his own language. Then he ran and leaped onto the lead beast animal in his shuggra team and raced away to the north as fast as their long legs would carry him.

The other Rovers had jumped up as if they would pursue him. But once he was gone they seemed to lose interest in the fugitive. As one they called impatiently to the passengers and stewards to mount the carts. The chief steward had demanded that some provision be made for Baro's group, but there were no empty seats in the other carts and the pack leader seemed not far from violence.

In the end the chief steward had left with the rest, saying that the landship's gig was to rendezvous with the Rover-drawn carts not far east of here; he would call it on his communicator and divert it to collect the stranded party. He gave Imbry an energy weapon in case a wandering fand or woolly-claw came by, which he said was unlikely with the scent of angry Rover so thick in the air.

"Or in case Yaffak returns and means us harm," Bandar added when Imbry had told the tale. "He seems to have gone mad."

"He will not harm us," Baro said. "I did him a service." He told about the invisible harness and the leash he had cut. "What does it mean?"

"I've never heard the like of it," said Bandar. "But it's merely improbable, compared to the several sheer impossibilities you have already claimed."

Baro was stung by the noönaut's attitude. "Is it because they are impossible, or merely because they have not been done before, a circumstance which offends your philosophy?" he said.

"More than my philosophy is offended, young man," said Bandar. "You have taken laws and strictures that have governed my science for years beyond memory and bounced them idly on your ignorant knee!"

"Ah," said Baro, "we come to the nub! It is not what has been done that disturbs you but who has done it. If I were a long-bearded savant from your clique—what did you call it, the Predilective School?—you would festoon me with laurels of achievement and medals of excellence. But because I am an outsider and a mere tyro, you climb your tower of arrogance and precipitate a gob of saliva upon me."

Bandar said nothing. He turned his back and looked in any direction but Baro's.

Imbry stepped in. "This solves nothing," he said. "Let us

pull the cart into the center of the clearing and climb aboard. As we now stand, if a fand comes stalking it may take its choice of tasty flesh conveniently arranged about the edges of the circle."

The chanters broke off and came across the clearing while Imbry and Baro repositioned the cart. They all climbed aboard, though not without a certain amount of turning of shoulders and averting of eyes as various members of the group impressed their disapproval upon selected others. Again, Flix was last to board and would not pull up the tailgate until Imbry pointed out that she might be the first to be pulled from her seat by a hungry beast.

When they were all seated, Imbry held up the energy pistol and said, "In my inexpert hands, this probably poses more danger to us in here than to any marauder out there. Is anyone qualified in its use?"

Baro said, "I am rated a marksman," and Imbry passed the weapon to him. Baro knew the model. He expertly broke it down and reassembled the elements, finding that its coils were in good order and fully charged. He set the aperture for minimum spread and therefore maximum intensity, made sure the safety catch was engaged, and placed it on the floor of the cart beneath his seat.

Luff Imbry rubbed his palms together and said, "Well, what shall we do until the gig arrives?"

"Obviously, we should chant the *ta-tumpa, ta-tey*," said Ule Gazz. "My partner agrees with me."

Baro's opinion, that Ule Gazz's partner had probably spent a lifetime agreeing with her just to get a modicum of peace and quiet, went unspoken. Instead he said, "I have a pressing need to understand what happened when I entered Yaffak's dream. I had the impression that something important was at issue."

Guth Bandar made a dismissive noise and turned his shoulder even further against the young man.

It occurred to Baro that Ule Gazz had never entertained an opinion she had left unvoiced, because now the Lho-tso practitioner said, "The Commons is merely a compilation of what has been. It has no relevance to what is, and what is is what shall be."

Baro was annoyed. "Do you ever listen to yourself?" he said. "'What is' is that your beloved partner has the lassitude. If that is also 'what shall be' why are you chanting so hard to create another outcome?"

"These things are not clear to those who have barely risen to the first tier of being," said the Lho-tso adept, "and I may be too charitable in assigning you even that distinction. From the eighth tier, the view offers a wider scope. One learns to distinguish between 'is' as a descriptor of phenomenality, which is by definition mutable and ever changing, and the 'is' that encompasses an unchangeable metareality. Thus *is* is not always is. By corollary, 'not is' is sometimes only a means of emphasizing what *is* is, rather than what is not, or what *is* is not."

"I withdraw my question," said Baro. "Clearly you do listen to yourself, a lifetime of which has left you as mad as a boiled bean."

"True understanding comes from a lifelong consolidation of *grims* between soul mates," said Pollus Ermatage, patting the still hand of her paralyzed cohort. "Of course, it is too late for all of you to experience it."

"But it is good of you to let us know what we have missed," said Luff Imbry.

Guth Bandar's lips had grown thin and he elevated his nose. "I thank all of you for your advice. I shall give it every morsel of the consideration it deserves," he said and turned to regard the Swept.

"We would all be better off chanting the *ta-tumpa, ta-tey*," Ule Gazz insisted. "Indeed, now that I am surrounded by fakes and posers"—here she turned her narrow head to grant both Flix and Baro a squinting eye—"I am certain that my chuffe has diminished substantially."

"Chuffe!" Baro almost snorted the syllable. "There is no chuffe! It is a figment! Father Olwyn is none other than Horslan Gebbling, a petty fraudster. Behind him straggles a long line of dupes, of which you are but the latest."

Imbry turned and put out a warning hand, but Baro kept right on, "The moment we encounter him he will be restrained on charges of mountebankery."

"By what power?" said Ule Gazz and Baro saw that the other ambulatory passengers were regarding him with expressions that ranged from surprise to hostility.

Baro recognized that he had let his temper overrule his judgment. Indeed, temper had shoved judgment into a hole and rolled a rock over it. Without good cause, he had violated Ardmander Arboghast's specific order. But, he reflected, a quick tongue must own an even quicker hand to capture words before they touch a listener's ear. Now there was no alternative to an assertion of lawful authority. He produced his plaque. "We are agents of the Bureau of Scrutiny."

Ule Gazz was not cowed. "Hoo-hah!" she said. "And scroots never err? My chuffe is self-evident, and would be to any person of discernment."

"I do not understand," said Pollus Ermatage. "If Father Olwyn is a fraud, how does he stand to gain from this exercise?"

"A good point," said Bandar, turning to join the discussion. "We are none of us wealthy, and this must have cost him dearly."

Baro sent Imbry a warning look and said, "All shall be made clear at the appropriate time. We cannot discuss a case that is under investigation."

"Yet you just informed us that charges are imminent," said the historian. "It appears that you cast aside your own rules as casually as you defy the laws of nature."

"I thought you were not speaking to me," Baro said.

"Until moments ago, my only conceivable reason for communicating with you would have been to express my intense disapproval of your conduct," Bandar said. "But now a new situation has emerged. With your plaque you can call for a rescue. I am breaking my silence to say, 'Please do so.'"

"We are under orders to maintain communications silence until Gebbling is apprehended," Baro said.

"Listen," Flix began.

Although she did not move from her seat, Ule Gazz pounced. "Presumably, you were also under orders not to flash your credentials in an attempt to overawe decent folk. Yet you do so with typical scroot arrogance. Call for help! My chuffe dwindles!"

"Listen!" It was Flix again.

"Leave the boy alone!" Luff Imbry weighed in.

"We require a rescue," said Guth Bandar.

"Can we not all just get along?" cried Pollus Ermatage.

The loudness of Flix's voice almost rocked the lightweight cart. "Will you just shut up and listen?" she roared and turned to cock her head toward the sky, one ear cupped in a slim hand.

There was a faint thrum of well-tuned gravity obviators, growing louder as the cart's passengers poked their heads out from under its canopy to search the sky.

Pollus Ermatage shaded her eyes and peered east. "There!" she said.

A shadow rushed toward them over the grass, then the aircraft was a dark blot against the orange sun, gliding down toward the clearing. The *Orgulon*'s gig touched down on the flattened grass, First Officer Kosmir at the controls with Security Officer Haj in the co-operator's seat.

———◆———

The able-bodied tumbled from the cart, the two lassitude sufferers being helped onto their come-alongs by their companions. Flix showed a new facet of her personality by holding back to assist Ule Gazz with Olleg Ebersol.

Mirov Kosmir remained at the controls while Raina Haj dismounted and lowered the gig's rear gate. Baro went forward to tell her that he had revealed his identity and his mission. In the back of his mind was another thought: that now they could associate as fellow professionals rather than as officer and civilian.

"Uh huh," was her response, along with a shrug of the eyebrows. "It's your career." She waived the passengers toward the gig's stern, saying, "Let's get aboard, people. We saw something moving in the grass not far out and the best trouble's the one you never encounter."

Flix was last in line. "Are you taking us back to the *Orgulon*?" she asked.

"No. We'll take you to where the other passengers are camped just beyond the Monument. There are tents and a luncheon service. Father Olwyn is scheduled to appear and offer you an experience he calls the inculcation. The *Orgulon* arrives late tonight."

"Then we go home?" Flix said.

"I believe so," said the security officer.

"Beyond the Monument is the town of Victor," said Flix, "I want to be taken there so I can arrange passage home."

"The matter is not yours to decide."

"Yes, it is," said the artist's companion. From behind her

back she brought the pistol Baro had left in the cart. Excited to see Raina Haj, he had forgotten it. Now it was pointed at the security officer, and none too steadily: Flix grasped the heavy weapon in a two-hand grip, her outstretched arms trembling from its weight and her nervousness.

"Wait," Baro said and took a step toward the young woman. She in turn stepped back, firing a bolt of energy into the ground not far short of where his next footfall would have landed. A stench of burning grass stung his nose.

"Stay back," Flix said.

"I will," said Baro. He froze.

Flix looked at Kosmir. "Mirov, get her weapon."

The first officer dismounted from the gig and walked warily around Raina Haj to approach her from the rear and lift the sidearm from its holster. He positioned himself beside Flix, the stolen pistol leveled at the passengers. They were still lined up to board the aircraft at its stern, Luff Imbry at the head of the queue and Baro at its rear where he had been speaking to the security officer.

"Move away from the gig," he said.

"Wait," said Raina Haj. "Flix, you don't have to do this."

"Shut up," said Kosmir.

The security officer kept talking. "I know you didn't kill Monlaurion."

"It was an accident," Flix said. "He fell."

"It was no accident," Haj said.

"Shut up," Kosmir said again, aiming the pistol at the security officer, but before he could fire Flix pushed his arm down.

"What are you saying?" she asked Haj.

"She's lying," Kosmir said.

"I want to hear her." Doubt was blooming in Flix's face. She moved a little distance away from Kosmir and her energy pistol swung partway toward him.

Kosmir did not hesitate. He leveled his weapon at the young woman and sent a burst of white force through her torso that left a charred hole the size of a double fist. What had been Flix fell to the ground.

Pollus Ermatage screamed and toppled forward in a half faint. Her collapse might have offered a chance for the other able-bodied to rush the killer, but Kosmir remained cool. He stepped back, swinging the pistol to cover them again, and the moment was past before they had recovered from the shock of the casual murder.

"So you know," said Kosmir.

"Yes," said Raina Haj.

"Well, then." He raised the pistol again.

"How will you explain it?" Baro said.

Kosmir flicked his eyes in Baro's direction, then went back to Raina Haj. "Easily. Flix was unstable. Being lost on the Swept unhinged her. She killed you all. When the gig came she hid in the cart and fired at us, killing Security Officer Haj instantly and wounding me. I seized Haj's gun and reluctantly brought about the end of poor, deranged Flix."

While Kosmir spoke, Baro reached into his side pocket and palmed the grumbler's disk. He let Imbry see it, then under the guise of thoughtfully stoking his chin he applied it to his throat. Imbry, meanwhile, slipped the earpiece into place while appearing to give his earlobe a contemplative tug.

"When I go for him, get him with the slapper," Baro grunted silently in his throat.

Imbry gave the slightest of nods and folded his hands across his paunch.

"You've forgotten the other witness," Baro said aloud, meanwhile moving one foot slightly toward Kosmir and imperceptibly shifting his weight to his back foot.

Kosmir gave him the eye flick again, but kept his focus on

Raina Haj. That suited Baro. "The Rover Yaffak," Baro said. "He was what you saw moving in the grass as you came down. And now he is watching and listening just out there."

Baro pointed to draw Kosmir's attention, but the first officer only smiled. His head did not turn and the pistol did not waver.

Very well, thought Baro, *Plan B.* Flix's warning shot had left a patch of carbonized grass and heat-desiccated soil at his feet. He would drop and roll, scooping up a handful and throwing it at Kosmir's face, then try for a kick at the man's knee. It was all covered in the manual on unarmed combat against an armed malefactor. Baro had been mentally reviewing the diagram and wishing that he had at least once been shown the maneuver by a live, experienced instructor.

To Imbry he grunted, "Count of three. One, two . . ."

The grass behind Kosmir parted and Yaffak raced across the clearing, rising from a crouched run to crash into the man's back. Kosmir went down, landing on all fours as the Rover caromed off and rolled away.

Three, thought Baro as he threw himself at the first officer. Raina Haj stepped forward and aimed a kick at the hand that held the gun but Kosmir was already pushing himself back up. He got to his knees and fired an instant before Baro's flying tackle caught him in the shoulder and threw him sideways.

But Kosmir's grip on the weapon's controls was tight and the pistol continued its discharge, emitting a thin line of blindingly bright energy that sliced through the air like a sword of light.

Raina Haj threw herself onto the arm that ended in the weapon while Baro used a move taught by the manual to put his weight on Kosmir's torso. As the security officer reached for the hand that held the weapon, Luff Imbry knelt and applied the slapper to Kosmir's grip. The pistol fell from the lifeless hand and its discharge ceased.

"Roll him over," Haj said and Baro and Imbry wrestled the first officer onto his belly so she could apply a holdtight. She pressed the control stud on the restraint and the device swiftly bound Kosmir's wrists together and adhered them to the small of his back.

Yaffak came and looked down at the prisoner. Seeing him bound and helpless was apparently enough for the Rover, because he growled a short syllable and turned away. He walked out into the grass, making an ululating sound. Far off, his team of shuggras rose from the grass and cantered toward him.

"Thank you," Haj said to Baro and Imbry. "That was well done." She reholstered her pistol and tucked the other in her belt.

Baro said nothing. He was looking down at Flix. She looked even smaller now.

Haj knelt and slapped Pollus Ermatage's face until the Fasfallian revived, then she said, "Let's get out of here."

"Not aboard the gig," said Imbry. He had climbed into the flyer and was examining the controls. "Kosmir's blast has severed the couplings to both the stern thrust and the attitude regulators."

"It won't fly?" said Haj.

"We could get some height and forward motion from the bow thrust, but without the regulators the gig would overturn unless it was perfectly balanced. The slightest change in the wind would see us all dropped on our heads."

Haj asked Bandar to speak to Yaffak, who was hitching the shuggras to the cart. "Ask him if he will carry us?" she said.

"Where?"

"Where the others went."

The Rover shook his head so that the pendulous ears flapped like small flags. "He will go west," Bandar said.

"May I ask a question?" Imbry said.

The Rover turned to him and waited.

Imbry pointed to Kosmir. "Why did you attack that man?"

Yaffak indicated Baro. "For him," Bandar translated.

Baro said, "Why do you care about me?"

"The dream. You helped him, freed him." Bandar shook his head in disbelief but kept translating. "He recognized your scent."

"What held you?" Baro asked Yaffak.

But Yaffak's language lacked the words. "He doesn't know," said the historian. "It is something bad that came in a dream."

"Will you take me where the others went?"

Yaffak signaled no. "He will not go east," Bandar said, then looked bemused at the Rover's next words. "He invites you to go west with him," he told Baro. "You would hunt skippits, eat well."

"I have to follow the others," Baro said.

The Rover's face was an image of unhappy resignation. He spoke and Bandar translated. "He will take you and the able-bodied passengers. He will take Kosmir although he thinks we should leave him for the woollyclaw and fand. He will not transport a dead body nor the ill ones."

When Yaffak indicated the lassitude sufferers, his nostrils closed tightly as if to keep any vestige of their scent out of him.

Baro cut off Ule Gazz's outburst before it could begin. "We must take them. They are sick."

Yaffak protested. Bandar said, "He says sick is when the stomach hurts and food comes up. These are not sick. They smell wrong."

Baro turned to Imbry and Raina Haj. "Do Rovers get the lassitude?" he asked.

Imbry shrugged and Haj said, "I don't know."

Bandar spread his hands. "I haven't heard of it."

Baro asked Yaffak, "Did your pack smell like these sick people?"

Yaffak spoke at length. Bandar said, "If I'm getting this right, his fellow Rovers smelled as Rovers ought to but didn't act the way they should." The small man put a question to the Rover but Yaffak could not find the words. "He noticed that they were acting improperly but it didn't bother him until he awoke from the dream. Then he was frightened and ran away.

"He does not want to encounter them again," Bandar added. "From the little I know of Rover psychology, I think he has had a traumatic shock and will not willingly risk another."

Baro said, "Ask him if he will take us within sight of the nearest town. We will not ask him to meet his pack mates."

Yaffak said he would do it for Baro's sake.

"And we must take the sick."

The Rover was unhappy, but he agreed.

They left Flix under a canopy in the gig and set off to the east. Baro gave up his seat to Raina Haj and sat on the floor with his back against the cart's front wall. There was nowhere for Kosmir to sit, so he was stretched out facedown in the narrow space between the seats.

When they were settled, Baro said to Haj, "I would like to have your guidance on our case." He told her about what they knew of Gebbling and what Trig Helvic had revealed, Luff Imbry adding comments and embellishments.

Raina Haj said, "As for why Gebbling is doing all of this, I cannot guess. The time to denude Helvic of his wealth was the moment after his daughter was briefly relieved of the affliction. At that point, he would have handed over his fortune for a box of anything he believed was black brillion. Instead, Gebbling has him pay for a pointless progress across the Swept."

"I see one possible explanation," said Baro, "though I am reluctant to believe it."

"What?"

"Gebbling is not pulling a confidence trick but has actually found black brillion. It cures the lassitude, and he intends a spectacular demonstration by healing all of these sufferers all at once. The world would throw fame and riches at his feet."

"There are three things wrong with your theory," Imbry said. "First, Gebbling does not think in such terms. He grasps always for an immediate gain. Second, even if he was capable of such a scheme, he need only cure Erisme Helvic to be knee deep in wealth."

"That is only two counterarguments," Baro said. "What is your third?"

"There is no such thing as black brillion."

"I agree with him," said Haj.

"Well, I do not," said Ule Gazz. "Whatever Father Olwyn's past may be, I believe that something has turned him onto the path of enlightenment."

"That would be a powerful something," said Imbry. "I would have to see convincing evidence."

"My increased chuffe is evidence enough," said Gazz. "But perhaps such qualities are beyond your appreciation."

"They must be," said Imbry in a mild tone, "but look, there is the Monument and beyond it lies Victor. Soon we shall arrive and all shall be made plain."

Before them a gray line had appeared on the eastern horizon. As the shuggras raced the cart toward it, Yaffak flicking at their ears with his whip, the line thickened and rose until it became a wall of stone stretching from north to south as far as the eye could see.

Even Baro had heard of the Monument, an enormous construct of stone that if viewed by someone standing on its center stretched from horizon to horizon in all directions. When seen from space—from which it was clearly visible—the Monument formed the silhouette of a helmeted man's head in profile.

It was widely believed that the original monument, built of fused blocks of stone to a height ten times that of a man, had portrayed an exact likeness of the military commander who had led the campaign to repulse an invasion, though the identities of both victor and vanquished were forgotten by all but a few eccentrics like Guth Bandar. So much time had passed since its building that the stone was worn to a fraction of its original height. In places sloping ramps had been ground into its edges so that it could be climbed by pedestrians and wheeled vehicles.

They would traverse at the neck, the shortest crossing. The shuggras hauled them up a short ramp without slowing and they emerged onto a vast expanse of hard rock, flecked here and there with coarse grass and sagebrush that sprouted wherever sun and ice had cooperated to crack and craze the eroded surface. The tires of the cart, which had hissed through the long grass, now hummed on the weathered stone.

As they made the transition from prairie to the Monument, the able-bodied passengers peered about them at the new landscape. But the new view was soon no less monotonous than the old and after a few minutes Ule Gazz took up the chant of *ta-tumpa, ta-tey*. A few beats later, Pollus Ermatage joined in, though with less conviction.

"What of your case?" Baro said to Haj, indicating the bound and recumbent Mirov Kosmir.

"A much simpler affair," she said. She recounted how, over the past couple of years, three artists had suffered accidental deaths: Hella Obregon, Tik Gormaz, and Del Quantioc. All had already passed the zeniths of their careers and leveled off, but after they died the value of their works increased sharply.

"Kosmir killed them?" asked Imbry.

The first officer made a complaint from the floor but Raina Haj put a boot on the back of his head to quiet him. "The first one was almost certainly a chance mishap," she said. "The second and third were almost certainly not."

She had been assigned to investigate the deaths and after family, lovers, and rivals had been cleared, she cast her net more widely. She noted the sharp increase in the value of the dead creatives' works, although none had been First Circle before their demises.

There was no central clearinghouse for art sales, and many transactions were private, not even involving agents or galleries. Purchasers did not have to confirm their identities; their funds spoke for them. It took more than a year to establish that a number of works by the second and third to die had been acquired, apparently by one individual, in the months before their deaths.

"I know the work of Obregon, Gormaz, and Quantioc," Imbry said. "Surely none of them was worth killing for the added value their deaths would confer upon their creations, even if they doubled in value. Quantioc was not much above a decorator."

"That is what I thought, at first," Raina Haj replied, "but I had not reckoned with the paucity of human decency in Kosmir's character. He lacked the funds to purchase First Circle works, so he began with those of lesser luminaries, buying, murdering, and selling merely to assemble a stake that would position him for—you'll excuse the expression—a real killing."

Kosmir said something into the floorboards, but Haj's boot heel applied further pressure to the back of his head and he desisted.

"As first officer on the *Orgulon,* he was responsible for all cargo, which put him in a position to borrow from the landship's accounts, so long as he put the embezzled funds back before the quarterly accounting. An audit has found that substantial amounts are missing.

"He combined the sum of his profits, the diverted funds, and all that he could borrow—including some short-term funds from lenders whose collection methods can be painfully unorthodox—and bought one of Monlaurion's major images: *Sky Shout in Blue*. It had actually declined in value a few percent in recent years."

"And then he planned to kill the imagist?" said Baro. "Surely the death of a major artist would attract more scrutiny than the others. He was at great risk."

Haj shook her head, the dark curls swaying in a way that stimulated Baro to thoughts that were not entirely professional.

"He had a more subtle plan," she said. "In studying Monlaurion, he had discovered the artist's absolute devotion to Flix, an attachment that over the years had become more fatherly than amorous."

Kosmir was possessed of striking looks and a well-oiled tongue. He insinuated himself into Flix's affections. Once a relationship of intimacy had been established, she confided in him: she feared that Monlaurion's fading interest in his own career would ultimately lead him to remove himself to some bucolic corner, denying Flix the excitements and amusements in which she delighted.

Kosmir convinced her to feign the lassitude. He added her and Monlaurion to the *Orgulon*'s passenger list. She was to be miraculously "cured," and their return to Olkney would be bathed in a glare of public attention. Monlaurion's career, Kosmir assured her, would be revived and she and Kosmir could continue to meet discreetly.

"His true plan was even less savory. He intended to murder Monlaurion, as indeed he did, then pin the blame on Flix. She would then be so gripped by remorse that she would take her own life, leaving a convenient note."

She produced a small piece of paper from her pocket and unfolded it. *"I could not live with him in rustic penury,"* she quoted. "It is written in Flix's hand and signed by her. It would pass for a dying declaration. In fact, it is the last line of a love letter to Kosmir. It was concealed in the spine of a book in his cabin. In his luggage was a belted robe that he had stolen during one of their trysts. He meant to strangle Flix in her cabin, then dress her in the robe and fake a suicide. That is why I wanted her safe in the brig or out on the Swept."

She spoke directly to Kosmir. "If I'd found this earlier, I could have convinced Flix to tell the truth. That would have saved her life."

Haj had interrogated Flix in her cabin, trying to convince the actress that Kosmir had killed Monlaurion and meant to do the same to her. But the actress genuinely believed the death was accidental. She and the imagist had argued on the dark foredeck until she had walked away. She had not seen Kosmir step from behind a windvane and push Monlaurion under the landship's wheels.

"So Flix knew she hadn't killed Monlaurion," said Baro, "but she also knew she was the likely suspect. To have confessed to faking both the lassitude and the miraculous cure would have thrown a cloud of seeming guilt over what to her was a blameless accident."

Haj signaled agreement. "When I tried to probe her relationship with Kosmir, she denied it. She truly believed he loved her—Monlaurion's years of devotion had convinced her that she was eminently lovable—and she was protecting him.

"So was his captain, who could not believe that his first

officer's plausible exterior masked a monster. He would not allow me to arrest him and search his quarters. I had to wait until I had an opportunity to break into Kosmir's cabin this morning while he was on duty."

With any other fellow agent, Baro would have had no hesitation in asking the question that now came to his mind. With Raina Haj it was more difficult, but he asked it nonetheless. "Was it not unlawful to break in after the captain forbade it?" he said.

Kosmir had something to say about the subject as well, but Haj quieted him. To Baro she said, "I knew he was guilty and I knew the evidence would be there. Would you have him escape justice on a nicety?"

"I would have to think about that," Baro said.

"Uh huh," said Raina Haj. "In any case, now that I had the evidence, and having given Flix every opportunity to think, I brought the two of them together. I did not, I admit, expect Flix to produce an energy pistol."

"That was my fault," said Baro.

"Uh huh," said Raina Haj. "Why am I not surprised?"

"Be fair," said Luff Imbry. "If you had confided in the boy, he could have been of help."

"That would not have been correct procedure," Haj said.

"Oh," said Imbry, "so it's exacting protocol some of the time and deft avoidance when convenient."

"I will not accept criticism from an auxiliary," she said, "especially one who was recently on the other end of the Bureau's lariat."

"You knew the boy was well connected," said Imbry. "You were afraid that if you had to share credit for Kosmir's capture your star might not gleam quite so brightly."

"Ridiculous!"

Imbry shrugged, but Baro's reading of Haj's face told him

there was truth in his partner's accusation. When her violet eyes glanced at him then moved quickly away, they no longer seemed so enchanting.

He also wondered anew if he was of the right material to be a Bureau agent. Would his father have bent the rules to rebalance an outcome? He did not want to think so, but his father had had a successful career in the Bureau and might by now have reached Commissioner's rank, had he lived.

Conversation had more than lapsed in the cart. It had expired. For a long while all that could be heard was the panting breath of Yaffak, and Gazz's and Ermatage's *ta-tumpa, ta-tey*.

Baro leaned toward Imbry. "Something weighs on my mind," he said. "I must tell someone."

"I am someone."

"While I slept, I uncovered a forgotten memory."

"I thought that you forgot nothing."

"So did I."

"Then it must have been unsettling," Imbry said. "What was this memory?"

Baro shifted uncomfortably. "It was the last time I saw my father. We had quarreled. I told him that I wished he would go away and never come back. That day, his flyer crashed into the sea."

"Ah," said Imbry. He thought for a moment, then said, "Before that, had you wanted to be a scroot?"

"I was very young."

"But ever since?"

"Yes."

Imbry nodded. "Do you recall a conversation we had about those who are driven and those who are called?"

"Word for word."

"Should we remove Baro Harkless from the category of the called and place him among the driven?"

"Yes."

There was a silence between them for a while, intruded upon only by the rush of wheels on stone and the chanting of Gazz and Ermatage. Then Imbry said softly, "You did not kill your father. You were a child and spoke as a child."

Baro said nothing.

"Ask yourself this," the fat man said, "would Captain Harkless have held little Baro responsible for his death?"

"Of course not." Baro remembered his father's face on the archetypal Father, and the look it had given him before he sliced open the dream-earth and entered the Old Sea: *You can do it.*

"And, in your eyes, is your father the measure of what a man ought to be?"

"He is."

"Then I think you ought to do no less than he would have, and forgive a little boy for doing what little boys do."

Baro blinked and looked out at the vastness of the Monument. It struck him that there were so many directions in which he could go. He turned back to Imbry. "You defended me earlier," he said, "even though I have spoken unkindly to you since we were assigned to work together."

The other man shrugged. "It takes a certain span of time for my better qualities to be appreciated."

Baro also spoke to Bandar. "I am sorry to have offended you. I wonder that I attracted the Hero archetype, when obviously I have spent my life playing the Fool."

The historian's icy demeanor had thawed as he had overheard Baro and Imbry talking. "Nothing that you did was ill-intentioned," he said. "It may be that I have become too rigid in my thoughts. Perhaps the Predilective School overstresses its regard for orthodoxy."

"If you would consider it," said Baro, "when this assignment is completed perhaps I might study with you. I confess the noösphere draws me."

"You would give up the scroots?" said Bandar.

"Despite what my partner believes, it is better to be called than to be driven. I will give up the scroots and spend my time exploring the Commons."

Bandar pulled his nose and looked thoughtful. "If you can truly move between Commonses," he said, "there opens a wide vista of exploration. We might even found a new school."

"Was it not you who maintained that nothing new can be done on Old Earth?" Imbry said.

"Our young friend here has the courage to admit to a life built on false foundations," said Bandar. "I can budge an minim or two in his direction."

There was a peculiar noise from the other end of the cart. Ule Gazz was clutching at her throat. Her mouth was open and she was straining to chant the *ta-tumpa, ta-tey*, but all that emerged was a rasping croak.

Pollus Ermatage had also ceased chanting. She was staring at the Lho-tso practitioner in horror while her hands probed first the soft tissue beneath Gazz's chin, then her own throat. "She has the lassitude," the Fasfallian said in a fading voice. "And so, I fear, do I."

Imbry swore softly and took out his plaque. He manipulated its symbols, then said, "We are less than two hours from Victor. Perhaps something can be done there."

"One thing we know," said Baro, "that the affliction can be cured. Trig Helvic would not have spent a fortune on this expedition if he had not seen his daughter temporarily restored to health."

"True, he is not a man to be fooled," Imbry agreed. "But it is a disheartening thought that to believe in Helvic means having to believe in Horslan Gebbling."

"I have come to accept that my deepest convictions may be founded on quaking ground," said Bandar.

"There are quakes," said Imbry, "and then there is Gebbling."

———❧———

The town of Victor was believed by its few hundred human inhabitants, most of whom mined for brillion, to have once had a much longer name. A heraldic shield prominently displayed in the town hall declared the original designation to have been "The City of the Honorable Fergus Suvanandan, Beloved Victor over the Abominable and Detested Invader."

However, the shield's provenance was suspect, it having been "discovered" in a dusty storage locker in the town hall's basement by Honore Suvanandan, whose family had supplied the community with most of its mayors for more generations than the citizenry could remember. The find occurred at a crucial point in a bitterly contested election in which the central issue was the unacceptable depth to which then Mayor Suvanandan had plunged grasping fingers into the civic treasury. The shield had not turned the tide for the incumbent; he was not only defeated at the polls but subsequently arrested after it was learned that his golden chain of office had somehow metamorphosed into a base metal copy covered in gilt paint.

The town of Victor was a little east of the monument's larynx, a collection of drab, squat buildings connected by a few paved streets and a webwork of dirt tracks where the grass had been worn away. The only tall structures were the frameworks of two mine heads whose shafts reached far down to a subterranean warren of tunnels and stopes where once there had been rich deposits of red and blue brillion.

At the far side of the town, where the flatland began anew

as a long, flat-topped berm of packed tailings from the brillion diggings, here the *Orgulon* stood at rest. South of the dock was Rovertown, a ragtaggle collection of huts and stables in which the Rovers and their shuggras lived.

The passengers examined the view with interest, after so many miles of gray rock. But Yaffak sniffed loudly and growled something. Bandar said, "He says those are sting-whiffles ahead."

As they descended the ramp back onto the Swept, they could see a swirl of the leather-winged carrion eaters circling something that lay in the grass not far off the track that stretched between the Monument and the mining town.

Haj said, "That is where the tents and tables were. When I left, they were about to begin a ceremony."

Yaffak pulled up at the edge of a trampled space littered by overturned trestle tables and torn fabric. Food containers and serving utensils were scattered widely, the buffet board tipped on its side.

The security officer dismounted from the cart and said, "It looks as if a whirlwind tore through."

Baro, Imbry, and Bandar stepped down. The historian gestured with his head to the sting-whiffles and put a question to the Rover, but Yaffak signaled a negative and remained in his seat. His muzzle lifted and his slitted nostrils flared as he turned his head to several directions, and Baro saw the muscles in his shoulders twitch.

"His fur is standing on end," the young man said.

"As would mine be, if I had any," said Imbry.

Haj raised her pistol and swept a bright beam through the cloud of carrion feeders. Two of them fell smoking to the earth while those that had been tearing at the thing on the ground erupted into the air and flapped off on leathery wings amid squawks of protest.

"What is it?" said Bandar, and Baro's first inclination was to answer that they were making an unnecessarily cautious approach toward a heap of discarded clothes. Then he saw the white hair and a glint of blue-fire stones.

"It is that fierce woman," he told the historian. "The one who hectored you the first night."

"It was," said Raina Haj, kneeling to examine the corpse.

Bandar must have seen enough horrors in the noösphere to harden him, Baro thought, because the historian gazed down at the red and bleeding flesh without flinching and said, "Those marks were not made by sting-whiffles."

Haj agreed. "See the long, deep gouges to the torso. And the head is half torn off. I would say woollyclaw but how could that happen so close to the town?"

Baro looked toward the huddle of buildings. "This could not have been done without shrieks of fear and agony," he said. "Where are the Victorites?"

"A worse mystery is this," said Luff Imbry, who had moved a little way off into the long grass. He stooped and lifted with two hands what looked to Baro like a bag of cloth or soft leather.

"Is it part of her?" said Haj.

"No," said Imbry, suppressing a retch. He pulled his hands apart and now Baro saw that he held an almost complete human skin, split down the back of the torso and head, with raw strips dangling from the ends of legs and arms. "See the birthmark on the neck."

"Her husband," said Bandar. "I never knew his name."

"No woollyclaw did that," said Haj. She looked through the grass. "Here are scraps of his clothes. But where is the rest of him? And why is there no blood?"

"We had better get into town," said Baro. "This place cannot be safe."

Imbry dropped the skin and stooped to wipe his hands on the grass. Rising, he looked toward the empty streets of Victor and said, "I don't like the look of the town. They are supposed to be hardy folk, used to dealing with feral beasts. They should be out here with weapons and alarms. But all is still and silent."

"I am senior," Haj said. "I will decide." She took the second pistol from her belt and offered it to Imbry but the fat man declined.

"Give it to Baro. He is expert."

She looked askance at Baro. "He left it for Flix to seize."

"You did not tell him she was unreliable."

Haj faced Baro. "Can you handle this?"

"I will show you," the young man said and when Haj handed over the weapon he checked its settings, then spun and shot two sting-whiffles out of the air.

"Good enough," she said. "I will contact the *Orgulon*. The captain should be able to tell us if anything untoward has occurred since I left."

She had one of the landship's communicators and now activated it and worked its controls. A frown drew down the corners of her mouth. She pressed its studs again but the frown only deepened. "No response," she said, "not even from the ship's integrator. It's as if the signal is blocked."

Imbry suggested she try her Bureau plaque. "The scroot communications matrix should be more difficult to interfere with."

But when the security officer tried connecting to the Bureau's net there was no contact. Baro's and Imbry's plaques were likewise useless.

"Our plaques are only strong enough to connect to a nearby amplifying ground station," Baro said. "There will be one in Victor. If our signals are not getting through it means that something must have happened to that installation."

"If it's equivalent to what happened to the people whose remains are at our feet," said Imbry, "then Victor seems a good place to avoid."

There was a shout from where they had left Yaffak and his cart. When they hurried back to the vehicle they found the noise was coming from Mirov Kosmir, who was protesting as the Rover hauled him from the cart. The other four lassitude sufferers were already lying in a row on the grass.

Ule Gazz was grunting and struggling to rise, while Pollus Ermatage lay inert. The other two, Ebersol and Sooke, had sunk to that stage of the disease where they were starkly rigid, their skins showing a waxy sheen, as if they had been polished and set out to dry. Their eyes were dull.

Yaffak set Kosmir on his feet and reached in for the two come-alongs that were stored under the seats. He tossed them on the ground, then shut and latched the cart's tailboard.

"What do you intend?" Raina Haj said. She stepped close to the Rover and stared directly into his eyes. Yaffak looked away and took a step back. He said something and the woman looked to Bandar for a translation.

"He has had enough," the small man said. Yaffak made more sounds and Bandar said, "Everything smells wrong, he says. He will not enter the town, nor will he stay."

"Tell him we are going around to the landship."

"It makes no difference."

Haj drew her pistol.

Yaffak looked her in the eye and spoke. Bandar translated. "He says there are worse things than being shot."

She put the weapon away. Yaffak turned to mount to the driver's seat, then stopped and faced Baro with lowered head and upturned eyes. He said something that Bandar rendered as, "He again invites you to come with him."

The idea had a surprising appeal to Baro. He could see himself roaming the Swept, out under the immense sky with every direction open. The vision had a poignant appeal, like a memory of a happier time.

But something inside was reshaping Baro. He could feel it. He did not yet know what he was being refashioned for, but he knew it was not for wandering at random, even with a good companion. His life was being pulled toward a specific point, though what waited for him there was yet to be revealed.

He shook his head. "I cannot," he said. "I am called to do something else."

The Rover's expression of sympathetic regret was almost human. Then he turned, mounted the cart, and flicked the whip at the muttering shuggras. The animals' murmurs deepened to growls but they set their shoulders into the collars and pulled the cart forward. Yaffak put them into a wide turn that led back to the Monument. Baro saw the long muzzled face come around the side of the canopy to regard him one more time, then the Rover snapped the whip and the shuggras picked up their pace.

"We cannot leave these sick people unattended," Haj said. "Whatever killed the man and woman might come back. But with only two come-alongs and no cart we cannot take them with us. If we carry them we will be too slow."

"We should take them back up on the Monument where there is no tall grass to conceal an attacker," Baro said.

"Someone must also guard Kosmir," Haj said.

"He is your prisoner, not ours," Imbry said. "Baro and I are still charged to apprehend Horslan Gebbling. In my own case, failure to pursue him assiduously earns me an extended stay in a Contemplarium. Are you empowered to relieve us of our assignment?"

"No," said Haj.

Baro said, "The manual on field operations allows a senior agent to reassign personnel temporarily in an emergency." He quoted the appropriate regulation, adding the page number on which it appeared.

"I still smell a whiff of politics about you," Haj said. "I do not wish any of it to become attached to my record."

"I propose that you officially relieve Luff Imbry of his assignment," Baro said. "I will take responsibility for my own actions." He realized he did not care if he breached Arboghast's instructions. He no longer wanted to be a scroot.

"All right," said Haj. She accepted Imbry's plaque and spoke the appropriate official phrases into its intake. "Now," she told him, "you are free to accept my orders and I order you to remain here and guard my prisoner."

"Bandar and I will look after the sick," Baro said.

Bandar agreed. "I would be of no use in town."

They carried the lassitude sufferers back up the track. Ule Gazz made guttural protests when Baro swung her up over his shoulder. "I cannot understand you," he said, "but I choose to believe that you are encouraging me in my efforts to save your life, since that is what someone capable of gratitude would do."

Pollus Ermatage made no sound as Raina Haj hoisted her into a carry position. Bandar and Imbry towed the other two lassitude sufferers on their come-alongs. Kosmir was made to walk in front, his hands still bound.

From atop the Monument, they had a wider view of Victor. The streets of the town remained empty and no sound could be heard. Baro touched his plaque's controls, transforming it into a long-distance scan. He methodically inspected the silent streets, then said to Haj, "Regard that dirty white building with the wood-frame porch."

Haj was gazing through her own plaque's viewing aperture. "I see it," she said. "What of it?"

"Just where the shadow fills that corner," Baro said.

Haj adjusted focus. "It is a foot," she said. "And beyond it is a severed head."

"The wall behind is charred."

Haj put away her plaque. "This changes things. Something has happened to the people of Victor and probably to the passengers and crew of the landship," she said. "It looks to be more than one agent can handle, even with the support of an auxiliary and the Archon's favorite cadet."

There had been a time when Baro would have protested that he was no cadet, but a full agent. He would also have been cut by the dismissive tenor of her words. But that time now seemed remote and the wound a trivial scratch.

"We could enter the town and try to revive the communications amplifier," Imbry suggested.

"Too many opportunities for ambush," Haj said.

"What about the landship?" Guth Bandar said. "It operates far out on the Swept and must have a more powerful system."

Raina Haj made up her mind. "You will remain here with Kosmir and the sick. I will skirt the town to the south and approach the landship. I know my way around it and can reach its communicator. I will call out an armed reconnaissance team."

To Baro she said quietly, "Watch Kosmir closely. Do not remove the restraint."

"I understand."

They had laid the lassitude victims on the flat stone surface of the Monument. As Haj departed, Baro separated the first officer from the others, bidding him sit apart and not to seek to stand up on pain of being shot in the leg. Bandar sat near him and promised to shout if the prisoner moved.

Baro and Imbry examined the four afflicted. Ebersol and Sooke had slipped deeply into the disease. Their skins were as smooth and polished as old stone, and their eyes had receded into their heads like pebbles sunk into frozen earth.

"Soon comes the crisis, I would say," said the fat man. "Then . . ." He spread his hands as if to let something drop between them.

Ule Gazz grunted something. Baro leaned down to listen. "I think she is trying to chant," he said.

"Still trying to elevate her chuffe, I don't doubt," said Imbry. He leaned toward the Lho-tso aficionado and said, "Better to prepare for the ineffable."

"There is no cause to shout," Baro said. "The lassitude does not affect the hearing."

"People like Ule Gazz ought to be shouted at regularly," said Imbry. "It might not improve them, but it couldn't possibly make them any worse."

Baro was taking off his scarf. He folded it into a pad and set it between the back of Pollus Ermatage's head and the hard rock. A tear ran from the outer corner of the Fasfallian's cheek and made a tiny circle of darker gray on the face of the Monument.

"Let us leave them in peace," Baro said. They went over and sat with Kosmir and Bandar. Baro told the historian, "The lassitude is galloping forward in the two new victims. Already their skins are waxy. I think none of them will trouble us much longer."

Kosmir attempted to engage them in conversation but Baro cut him off. "Nothing you can say will induce us to release you. If danger comes upon us, you must take your chances as you are. Remember, I saw you kill poor Flix, and we know you murdered Monlaurion just when he believed his life had taken a miraculous bend toward happiness."

"Sooner milk from a stone than mercy from a scroot," Kosmir quoted.

"The Bureau is sometimes judiciously cruel for the law's sake," Imbry said, "but you are vicious by nature."

Kosmir proposed to contest the point, but desisted when Baro declared a growing inclination to shoot off one of the prisoner's toes. Kosmir pulled a corner of his mouth between his teeth and frowned in thought at the four paralytics.

They sat in silence. Baro watched the deserted town, with occasional glances at the prisoner. Bandar seemed to be mulling something and after a while he said, "You told Yaffak you felt a calling. Is it an urge to explore the Commons?"

Baro cast about in his mind for an answer, finally saying, "I think so. Something about the noösphere calls to me. Or, more accurately, Something *in* the noösphere. Though what calls me and what I am called to do, I do not know."

"I am equally conflicted," said Bandar. "It delights me, and it is a pleasure I never thought I would admit to, that you may have opened up new avenues for research. Yet it grieves me to have been the instrument that puts you in peril."

"Never mind," said Baro. "Responsibility rests not with the instrument but with the hand that wields it. Besides, if I am fated to be here, perhaps you are too."

"It is a worrisome thought that my lifelong passion for the Commons has been not of my own choice but merely a constituent of some grander scheme," Bandar said.

"Still," Imbry put in, "it gives a shape to life. I am coming to think that might be better than a lot of devouring and expelling, signifying nothing in particular. I may seek to make my way in the scroots."

"You would do well," Baro said.

"Thank you."

"A shape to life is a good thing," Bandar said, "but one prefers to be the shaper rather than the shaped."

Imbry asked, "Yet which is better: to be the shaper of a small heap of not much, or to be shaped into something grand and enduring?"

"An interesting point," said the historian. "What does our young friend say?"

But Baro waved the discussion away. His mind wandered from point to point, examining his experiences of the preceding few days and the changes those experiences had wrought in him. The world was clearly a much more complex place than he had previously understood it to be, and he was himself more complex than he had imagined.

He had spent all of his life walking a well-defined path that led toward a definite end, only to find that everyone else he met had a different concept of both the path and the goal. Life was neither rigid nor simple, although it seemed that Baro had let himself become both.

But now he had come unexpectedly to a turning point and he meant to make the turn. When this assignment was over, he would turn in his plaque and uniform and become an explorer of the Commons. Clearly, that was what he was called to do.

The sun was warming the gray rock of the Monument and the heat was being transmitted to the layer of air that lay upon the stone. Baro felt the growing warmth seep upward into his bones while the heated air swaddled him like a blanket. The view of Victor grew hazy and began to ripple, the twin towers at the mine heads wavering like reflections on the surface of a pond. Despite himself, his eyes closed.

"The man of envy is your foe," said a voice.

"What?" Baro's eyes flew open and he turned toward Kosmir, thinking that the prisoner had spoken. But Kosmir sat staring morosely at the four lassitude sufferers and chewing the inner meat of his lower lip.

He turned to Guth Bandar. "Did you speak to me?"

The historian shook his head. "We have all been silently consulting our inner wherewithal."

"I must have dozed off," Baro said. "But I clearly heard a voice."

"What did he say?"

Baro repeated the warning.

"Typical," said Bandar. "Probably bubbled up from the Wise Man. Archetypes always speak as if they were fortune-tellers at a country fair, offering vague advisories that are clear only in hindsight."

"Who is the man of envy?"

"Perhaps this one here," said Bandar, with a nod to Mirov Kosmir. "Or Gebbling."

Baro turned both possibilities over in his mind but could come to no conclusion. Bandar must be right: messages from the noösphere were as slippery as conversations in dreams.

Kosmir cleared his throat. "I have something to say."

Baro aimed the pistol at one of the prisoner's feet. "I am thinking and do not care to be interrupted," he said.

Now Kosmir spoke quickly. "I know something the scroots would like to know."

"I have other things on my mind."

"It is information about a major crime."

"Worse than a double murder?"

"Yes."

Baro felt a curious detachment. Only days ago, such an offer would have commanded all of his attention. Now it was an annoying distraction from the direction his thoughts wanted to take him.

"You are Raina Haj's prisoner," he said. "Tell her when she returns."

Kosmir said, "She may not return. She is probably walking into danger."

Though he had lost his earlier regard for Haj, the prospect of her being in danger sent a jolt of decisiveness through Baro. He found himself standing on his feet before he knew he had risen. His plaque was in his hand and he keyed it to the Bureau's emergency frequency; it would carry a signal at short range. "Haj," he said, "can you hear me?"

A crackle of sound came from the air above the plaque, then came Haj's voice, but so fragmented and distorted that Baro could not make out more than a word or two. He called again, but received only a hiss and sputter.

He turned to Kosmir. "Tell me what you know," he said.

"I want guarantees," said the landship officer, "all charges against me dropped and no seizure of my goods."

"I will not bargain with you," Baro said.

Kosmir put on a knowing look. "Scroots will always trade a fingerling for a trophy fish."

Baro aimed his pistol. "You have made a small but serious mistake," he said.

Kosmir's sneer weakened. "How so?"

"You are not talking to a scroot. I have resolved to leave the Bureau. You are talking to a man who has both a pistol and a strong urge to use it." He notched up the weapon's output control. "Now the urge grows even stronger."

"You seek to frighten me," Kosmir said. "I insist on establishing terms."

Baro fired the weapon and a palm-sized piece of rock immediately in front of Kosmir turned red, then incandescently white. Droplets of lava spattered the man's crossed legs, burning through his uniform trousers and smoldering into his flesh. Kosmir screamed and fell backward on his still-pinioned arms, rubbing his calves together as he tried to scrub away the molten rock.

Baro stood over him, the pistol aimed. "Are the terms satisfactory?" he said.

Bandar said, "That was needlessly cruel."

Baro ignored the historian. To Kosmir he said, "Well?"

"I will tell you everything," Kosmir said.

"A wise strategy. Begin."

Kosmir talked swiftly and Baro listened with an analytical ear. The first officer was an ambitious man and intelligent, too good, at least in his own estimation, to putter his life away guiding landships across the Swept. He was born to own and command, although fate had not seen fit to grace him with assets or minions. Yet he was constantly on the lookout for opportunities to redress those lacks and made it his business to pry into any secrets he came across.

Late one night, in the offices of the company that operated the landships, Kosmir happened to glance through some documents that had been locked in the desk of the managing director. He learned a number of things: that a holding company owned the landship line; that the holding company was controlled by another corporation that owned the mines at Victor; that the company that grew and distributed the truffles of the Swept was a corporate sister to the mining firm and that it was in turn connected to the company that held the contracts with Rovertown.

"They are all one interrelated enterprise," Kosmir said, "the base of a pyramid that gets smaller as it rises, though between the operating companies and the ultimate ownership is a hierarchy of shell and holding companies that insulate the owner from what is being done at the lower levels."

Baro said, "I hear no evidence of a crime."

"That comes from a conversation I overheard between the

man who occupies the apex of the pyramid and another who assists him. They spoke in guarded terms but I deduced the meaning."

"Who are these men and what was the import of their conversation?"

"The import was that the truffles of the Swept cause a restructuring of the brain. Some are more resistant than others. I believe that those who are worst affected become like these." He gestured to the four lassitude sufferers.

Baro felt a surge of outrage. "You are saying that the lassitude is caused by the truffles, and that someone is knowingly distributing the stuff?"

"I am."

"Who is that someone?"

Kosmir squirmed. "Would you leave me nothing to trade?"

Baro aimed the pistol at Kosmir's feet. "I will leave you nothing to walk upon. Who sits atop the pyramid?"

Kosmir's shoulders sagged. "Trig Helvic," he said.

"Who was the man he spoke with?"

"I do not know," Kosmir said. "I was using a listening device that only captured Helvic's half of the conversation. He did not name the other man."

"Was it Horslan Gebbling?"

"I think not. Helvic has one way of speaking to the few he considers his equals and an altogether different tone for everyone else. I have heard him speak in the latter vein to Gebbling, the former to the other man."

"You saw Gebbling?"

"Before we left Victor for Farflung, he came aboard to make the recordings that were shown to the passengers."

"What is his relationship with Helvic?"

Kosmir shrugged. "I assumed he was an employee."

Baro set the safety catch on the pistol and tucked it into his belt. He took out his plaque and tried the Bureau emergency frequency again.

A voice spoke from the air. "This is a restricted frequency. Who is using it?"

"Baro Harkless, agent ordinary," Baro said. The voice was familiar. "To whom am I speaking?"

"Directing Agent Ardmander Arboghast."

"Sir," said Baro, "Sergeant-Investigator Raina Haj may be in danger. I am seeking to warn her."

"Where is she?"

"Somewhere in the vicinity of Victor and Rovertown, approaching the landship *Orgulon* which is owned by Trig Helvic. Helvic is the employer of Horslan Gebbling and I have reason to believe he is behind the spread of the lassitude."

There was a silence, then, "Where are you?"

"At the edge of the Monument to the west of Victor, with five passengers from the *Orgulon*, four of them afflicted by the lassitude, and a ship's officer who has committed murder."

There was another silence. "Remain there."

"I must help Raina Haj," Baro said.

"You will stay where you are," said Arboghast. "The situation is under control."

"How can you be sure?" said Baro. A part of him wondered at the brazenness of his challenge to his superior, but most of him did not care.

"I am on the *Orgulon*," was the response. "All is in hand. I will look out for Haj. You stay and protect the civilians until I come for you." The connection was broken.

Baro looked down at Kosmir. "It appears the Bureau already knows everything," he said. "You will need something else to barter with."

The first officer now wore a sly look. "I have something else," he said.

"Try it on Directing Agent Arboghast when he arrives."

"It is something for your interest, not his."

Baro took out the pistol again. "I can still burn off a toe or two," he said.

"And you say you're not a scroot," Kosmir said. "Very well, shoot if you like. The pain will not last long."

That puzzled Baro. "Why do you say that?"

Kosmir made a face that mocked Baro's perplexity. "Why do I say it? Because neither of us has long to live—nor your friends nor these lumps that used to be people—if you won't hear what I have to tell you."

Baro looked at the lassitude sufferers. They lay like wax cylinders. He could see no difference between the two who had come aboard the *Orgulon* already sick and the two who had been their companions. The disease had galloped through the bodies of Ule Gazz and Pollus Ermatage. From Olleg Ebersol came a strangled cough. Imbry got up and went over to the sick man.

Baro felt a wave of pity for all of them, followed closely by a sudden burning desire to inflict savage punishment on Trig Helvic. He had a vision of his swinging the iron sword in a vertical two-handed stroke to cleave the magnate's head. In the vision, Baro was clad in the iron mail and winged helmet of the Hero.

"I will not trade words with you," he told Kosmir. "Tell me what you know or die piece by piece."

Bandar spoke up again. "You cannot commit mayhem on a prisoner. It is wrong."

Baro turned his head to regard the small man. "He is evil," he said.

"I hear the Hero speaking in you," the noönaut said. "You are letting yourself be taken by an archetype. You will become a simple-minded monster. Resist."

A part of Baro knew that the historian was right, but it was a small and ineffectual part. "I do not care to resist," he said. He turned back to Kosmir and aimed the pistol.

The historian rose and sang eight tones in his thin tenor. As the notes struck Baro's ear it was as if a light appeared in his mind and grew, pushing back a red-veined darkness he had not known was growing around him. Bandar repeated the measure and the darkness faded further. Baro lowered the pistol.

"Thank you," he said.

"Now resist it," said Bandar.

Baro stooped and helped Kosmir sit up. He could feel the Hero stirring in the back of his mind, like a storm on the horizon, but if he willed it to stay away it would.

"Tell me what you know," he said to the prisoner.

"Free me and I will. But hurry. There is no time." Kosmir looked to the east, his eyes searching the air over Victor and Rovertown.

"Tell me and if the information is as important as you say I will set you free."

"I don't trust you," Kosmir said. "I think you may be mad."

"And I do not trust you," Baro said. "We are at an impasse."

"Not for much longer," said Kosmir. "An aircar has risen from beyond Victor. If you do not free me before it arrives, it will be too late."

Baro turned and saw an aircraft ascending above the town. Even at the distance he could make out the colors and insignia of the Bureau.

"Please," said Kosmir. He hunched around on his buttocks so that his restrained arms were turned toward Baro. "Hurry!"

"You are trying to fool me," Baro said.

"I think not," Bandar said. "He seems genuinely afraid."

"He should be. Here comes the vehicle to carry him into incarceration."

"No!" Kosmir cried. "Here comes death!"

Baro could hear the thrum of the aircar's obviators. There was clearly panic on the prisoner's face. He adjusted the pistol's controls to the appropriate setting and aimed it at the holdtight.

The strangled sound from Ebersol had grown louder. Baro looked past Kosmir to the four lassitude sufferers. The inert form that had been the Lho-tso adept was trembling and twitching. The mouth had stretched open and a wet and gargling sigh made its way around ropes of viscous drool.

"It is the crisis," said Guth Bandar. "Look, Corje Sooke is undergoing the same catharsis. Death will not be long behind."

"Never mind them!" Kosmir cried. "Free me!"

Baro fired a pulse into the restraint's control matrix. The device came apart and fell to the ground. Kosmir leaped up, windmilling his arms to stimulate circulation.

"Quick," he said, "reset the pistol to maximum! Shoot down that aircar when it tries to land!" When Baro did not do as he said, he tried to grab for the weapon.

Baro stepped back and pushed the man away. "Now you are the one who has gone mad!" he said. "That is a Bureau vehicle and at the controls is my section chief."

Kosmir put his hands together in the ancient gesture of supplication. "I lied!" he said. "I was holding back something to bargain with—that I did hear the man Helvic was speaking to. I did not know his name but I know his voice! It was the man you spoke with minutes ago. Whoever he is, he is Helvic's controller. And he will kill us all!"

"No!" Baro raised his voice. "You are trying to trick us!"

"Baro!" Guth Bandar cried.

The young man swung to look at the sky, thinking the aircar must be sliding down to land. But Bandar was pointing in the other direction, his mouth open and his face distorted in a rictus of horror.

Olleg Ebersol had sat up. Corje Sooke was in the act of doing likewise. But something was wrong with the way the man and woman moved. Something much worse was wrong with the way they *bent*—they did not fold at the waist and hips, but in the middle of their torsos, their lower backs remaining flat upon the rock while their rib cages bent up at right angles.

Baro thought he ought to be hearing bones cracking, but the only sound was their sighing breath. Ebersol's head moved from side to side, but much too far for any normal neck. He raised his arms straight before him and the hands flexed in a way that sent a shiver along Baro's spine. The fingers stretched steadily to an impossible length until the skin at their tips suddenly burst open. Long, spiky things, dark and green, now unrolled themselves and wriggled at the end of the sick man's arms, the skin falling back like loose sleeves.

Ebersol brought his hands that were no longer hands to the back of his neck. There was a sound like tearing cloth and Baro saw the man's face come away, pulled forward like a mask to reveal a blank, shining surface of dark green, hard and polished like an insect's carapace. Two feathery tendrils uncurled themselves from the top of the rounded, eyeless head that now stood above Ebersol's shoulders. The claws pulled again and both the gown he wore and the skin beneath it split down the back.

A glistening thorax now supported the featureless head. The rest of the skin sloughed away to reveal sharp-edged limbs and a long-segmented abdomen. Baro had seen those shapes before.

"It is a Dree," he said.

The head rotated toward him and the fernlike tendrils

vibrated. The thing stood up and faced him, and the digits where hands and feet would have been clicked together to form crescent-shaped claws. At the sight of them Baro knew what had caused the wounds on the corpse they had found below the Monument.

Imbry had watched the transformation openmouthed, still kneeling between what had been Ebersol and Sooke. As the newly made Dree began to tear away the chrysalis that had been the skin of the Fasfallian, the fat man lurched to his feet and stood looking at the emerging creature with horror.

"Get clear!" Baro shouted and raised the pistol. But his aim was blocked by the Dree that had come out of Olleg Ebersol. At the sound of his voice it flexed its lower limbs and leaped toward him, claws outstretched. Baro discharged the pistol into the Dree, catching it in midleap and burning a hole through its thorax.

Even as the thing crashed to the rock in front him Baro shifted his aim to the second Dree. It had reached out to catch Luff Imbry as he turned to run but its hooked forelimb had only snagged the loose cloth of his robe. The creature was hampered by being still partly encased in Corje Sooke's body and Imbry was frantically tearing the clasps that held his garment closed at the front so he could slip it over his head and escape.

Baro laid the pistol sights on the Dree's head but as his finger compressed the power stud there came the rasp of chitin on stone followed by a lance of agony stabbing through the muscle of his right calf. The first Dree, the wound in its body still smoldering, had dragged itself forward and sunk one claw into the meat of his leg. The other limb was raised to rip his belly.

Baro's torn leg gave way and he fell backward. As he went down he touched the weapon to the blankness where the

Dree's face should have been and let loose a blast of energy that blew its head apart. He pulled its dead claw from his leg and blood spurted as he sat up and aimed again at the one that had caught Luff Imbry.

Imbry had not escaped. He had stumbled and fallen face-down, his robe still tangled about his head. The second Dree had sunk both its hooked forelimbs into the wadded cloth and pulled itself onto the fat man. It kicked itself free of the last vestiges of Corje Sooke and prepared to rake the prone and motionless Imbry.

Baro aimed and fired and did not stop the pistol's discharge until the creature's head and thorax were ash. Imbry lay silent.

When Baro tried to stand his wounded leg would barely support him. He limped his way to Imbry, the hot pistol still tight in his grasp. He thrust aside the remains of the Dree and tore at the cloth around the fat man's head. The face beneath was slack and gray. Blood seeped from a deep gash on the forehead, soaking the robe. But his partner still breathed.

The shapes that had been Ule Gazz and Pollus Ermatage were now beginning to twitch as things moved under the waxy skin. Baro adjusted the pistol's output to maximum and got to one knee. He aimed.

A blast of air and the powerful hum of an aircar swept over him. He turned his head quickly, glimpsed the Bureau insignia and Ardmander Arboghast stepping from the aircraft, a Bureau sidearm called a shocker in his hand.

"I doubt your weapon will affect them," Baro called over his shoulder to the section chief as he prepared to incinerate the Dree. "They are a dangerous ultraterrene species."

"Yes, I know," said Arboghast and those were the last words Baro heard before the shocker struck between his shoulder blades, shook him like a rat in a dog's jaws, and threw him down into darkness.

His first awareness was of sounds: muted voices nearby; somebody moaning a little farther off; the crash of a door slamming across a distance wide enough to create echoing reverberations.

"He's waking up," someone said. It took him a moment to recognize the voice, then he opened his eyes to see the face of Horslan Gebbling peering down at him. "I think he's all right," the fraudster said. "They didn't jellify his brain."

"No," said another familiar voice, and now Baro saw Guth Bandar's features come into view over Gebbling's shoulder, "they want us fit for work."

Baro realized he was lying on his back. He moved his hands and felt rough sacking over a hard surface that must be a floor. A deep ache stretched across the broad of his back and curved around to his chest, but he ignored the pain to push himself into a sitting position and looked around. Someone had applied first aid to his wounded leg. It was sore but functional.

He decided that he was in the hold of the *Orgulon*. Around him were dozens of others—passengers and crew—seated or lying on a utilitarian surface. Raina Haj and Guth Bandar sat nearby.

"Where is Luff Imbry?" Baro said.

"Arboghast left him on the Monument," said the historian. "Said he was too injured to be useful."

"He will die."

"As will we all, one way or another," Bandar said.

"What about Kosmir?"

"Arboghast told him to stand still but he ran. That excited the Dree. When they are newly made their brains are undeveloped. They remain feral, creatures of instinct. They caught Kosmir and indulged their appetites on him before they could be shocked into immobility."

"Much the same as happened to the white-haired woman we found below the Monument, we surmise," said Haj.

"I do not understand," said Baro.

"We are still working it out ourselves," said Bandar. "Gebbling, bring him up-to-date."

"Wait," said Baro. "Is there any water? My mouth feels as if it has been left out in the sun to dry."

"There is a barrel with a dipper over there," Bandar said. "Walk slowly. The guards will shoot without warning."

Baro looked where the small man indicated and saw the barrel sitting alone in the middle of the vast floor, a dipper chained to its rim. Beyond was a wide stretch of emptiness, then two staircases leading up to the top of the hold. Halfway up each staircase stood an armed Rover.

"Those are pulse rifles," he said.

"Some of the 'mining machinery' in the *Orgulon*'s cargo," said Gebbling. "There were also heavy weapons and armor plating to convert the landship's gig and the scroot aircar into warcraft."

Baro limped to the barrel and drank. As he dipped a second time a door at the top of one of the staircases opened and two more armed Rovers brought in a man who wore the uniform of a windman. The prisoner seemed dazed and would have stumbled down the steps if he had not been held up by his escorts' grips on his arms.

They brought him down and laid him on the floor where the man lay moaning. The Rovers chose another from the crowd—Baro saw it was the plump steward he had questioned about Haj and Kosmir, it seemed a thousands years ago—and led her trembling up the stairs. The door slammed after them.

Baro walked carefully back to where his companions sat. "What is happening?" he said.

"They take them for testing," Gebbling said. "The few who fail are brought back. The many who pass are sent to the crèches."

"What kind of test? What are these crèches?" Baro could feel a dozen more questions bubbling up.

"Another revelation," sighed the historian. "Again, we have been privileged to discover something new, something that even our distant ancestors did not know when they fought the Dree and expunged them.

"The noösphere's flaw is that it retains only what everybody knows, but sometimes what everybody knows to be true is actually false. Thus it was believed that because the Dree resembled hive insects they must have bred like them, with a hive mother laying eggs and helpers rearing the young. Of course, no one who had ever seen the inside of a Dree hive ever came out to say different.

"Instead, it turns out that Dree reproduction was unique. They used captured members of other hives, not for breeding but for genetic restructuring. The captor's hive mind could reach into the captives' very gene plasm and compel it to become identical to that of the captors. They were aided in this work by a symbiotic plant that when ingested by the victim infiltrated the cells and prepared the genes for change."

Baro saw it. "The truffles of the Swept," he said.

"Exactly," said Bandar. "The stuff is harmless on its own. Its gene-altering effects can be triggered only by Dree mental energies."

"So those who eat the truffles and come within range of a Dree are remade? They lapse into the lassitude and end by becoming Dree themselves." Baro said.

"Not all," said Gebbling. "Some are more resistant than others, even when force-fed. The Rovers, for example, simply die. On the other hand, the Rover mental defenses are easily overwhelmed. They have all been enslaved."

"So some of us will become Dree," Baro said, "and the rest will be slaves?"

"Except," said Bandar, "for a small minority who go mad."

"I think I would prefer to die attacking the guards," said Baro.

"They refuse to cooperate," said Gebbling. "They do not shoot to kill."

"But the Dree were exterminated eons ago," Baro said. "How could they still be with us?"

"Better if I begin at the beginning," Gebbling said. "A few months ago I took a lease on some played-out tunnels at the far edge of the Fundament brillion mine property. I rented machinery and dug a new length of tunnel which I seeded with certain variants of blue and red brillion, the kind said to be associated with deposits of black brillion."

"There is no such thing as black brillion," Baro said.

"Of course not," said Gebbling. "If there were it would surely be nowhere near as beguiling a substance as that which exists only in the imagination of the gullible and greedy. And nowhere near as valuable."

He resumed his narrative. "I drove the tunnel down and at an angle from a used-up red brillion gallery and when I thought it deep enough, I began gouging out the niches where my 'investors' would find the red and blue variants. I then began installing the subsonic equipment which, when surreptitiously operated, would cause their skins to pebble and their hair to rise—sure signs that they were in the presence of the true black."

Gebbling had been lying on the tunnel floor, drilling tiny holes at the base of the wall when he had suddenly lost control

of his limbs. It was as if different parts of his body were assuming unusual sizes and weights, the effects constantly shifting and fluctuating. He became dizzy, then nauseated, lost all
sense of whether he was upright or prone, and clung to the
rock beneath him as if it were the face of a cliff.

"A gravitational cyst was working its way slowly to the
surface. Its rise through the rock had intersected my tunnel.
I could not tell its dimensions but I knew I should try to put
myself out of its reach lest it suddenly assign some crucial part
of me a greater weight than bones and tissues can bear. I
might have had my ribs snapped by a backbone that suddenly
assumed the weight of a tree.

"As I crept along the tunnel I looked up and there was Ardmander Arboghast coming toward me. I knew he had been
pursuing me, but I thought I had eluded him. I experienced
both disappointment and relief: the former that he had finally
caught me, and the latter that I was saved. He was aiming a
pistol and gesturing for me to rise. I could do no such thing
and tried to tell him so, but my jaw was too heavy to lift."

It was then that a further strangeness began, Gebbling said.
One moment he was looking at Arboghast in fear that the
scroot would shoot, the next he was looking at both himself
and the scroot with outrageous alterations in his organs of
perception. His vision did not encompass shapes, but ripples
and splashes of colored light, shifting and brightening and
dimming, with occasional sparks of intense illumination that
he soon realized were associated with motion.

Arboghast took a step toward him and came into the field
of the gravitational cysts. He overbalanced and tumbled to the
tunnel floor.

Meanwhile Gebbling had been coming to grips with the
new modes of perception. "I deduced that my consciousness

had been penetrated by some other entity. I must be in the ambit of a telepathic ultraterrene, a strong one, though why it would be down in a brillion mine or where it could hide in this narrow tunnel I could not guess."

Bandar took over and said, "Of course it was not a Dree. They were all long dead. It was the Dree equivalent of a noösphere, whose elements can apparently cohere to form a unified persona. Or perhaps the Dree Commons never had more than a single archetype. In either case, it had been captured within a gravitational cyst that had slowly journeyed to the core of the planet and now was finding its way after eons to the surface again."

"Is that possible?" Baro asked.

"It must be, because it happened," said Bandar.

Gebbling took up his tale again. "No sooner did I become aware of the Dree than I felt the force of its will. I was commanded to continue crawling out of the range of the bubble and so, clearly, was Arboghast. Fortunately, the anomaly, though powerful, was small in size. A few moments and we were clear of the effects."

But they were not clear of the ultraterrene's mental grip. Gebbling suffered the deeply unsettling experience of feeling a coldly powerful intelligence rummage through the contents of his mind. He made an effort to oppose the interference, but his resistance was brushed aside.

"Somewhere during this, I became linked to Arboghast," he said, "a more unpleasant sensation in some regard than having the Dree ransack my passageways and storerooms. I saw that he fought the pressure as I had, but with better results. The thing could not clamp hold of him; it was as if some essential part of Arboghast was polished too hard and smooth to allow the Dree a steady grip. His core was too self-contained, too *selfish*, for the entity to hook and hold him.

"I felt it withdraw—from him, that is, not from me. My mind made a picture of the two of them, Arboghast sitting with his arms crossed, staring down this darkness that wanted to envelop him. It withdrew from him then, and I felt its fierce, cold thoughts as it weighed him up.

"And then it used my voice to bargain with him."

Only days before, if a criminal had told Baro that a senior officer of the Bureau would haggle with an inimical alien intelligence the young man would have sneered in disbelief. Now he asked only, "What did Arboghast want?"

"What those like him always want," said Gebbling. "Power. The chance to rule over a multitude."

"And the Dree granted him his wish?"

"It did. And now they work hand in claw to bring the world into their grasp. The Dree entity had been instinctively reaching out and seeking those who might be suitable for transformation. But without the truffles the change could not happen."

"The first lassitude victims," Baro said. "They all died."

"Yes, but then came Arboghast," said Gebbling. "He linked his mind with the Dree's. They reached out together, mentally trolling for 'candidates' who lived near enough to the Swept that they could be introduced to the truffles."

Baro remembered Kosmir saying, *They don't travel well.*

One of the candidates was Erisme Helvic. Once she was afflicted, Arboghast arrested her father and brought him within range of the Dree entity.

"I know what happened to him," Gebbling said. "I was forced to endure the same treatment. Like me, Helvic believed all that Arboghast wanted him to believe, even while a part of him beat on the sealed door of his memory and cried out horrid truths he could not hear."

"But the best Arboghast will win from all of this is to be a slave to the Dree," Baro said.

"He does not see it that way," Guth Bandar said. "I believe he is a natural, that he has been absorbed by the grim archetype known as the Tyrant. His only desire is to stand atop a heap of humanity. To him the Dree are just another natural force, like a storm or a flood, that can sweep him onto a throne. Why should he care what transpires in the sky above so long as his feet are planted firmly on a thick carpet of his fellow creatures?"

"Now Helvic, like me, has served his purpose," said Gebbling. "They have already taken him away. Soon it will be my turn."

"We are all scheduled to suffer the same fate," said Haj, "if not a worse one."

"What are our choices?" Baro said.

"We have none," said Gebbling. "Some of us will be mindshackled and put to work. The majority are suitable for transformation and will become Dree. A few go mad and are set aside. Bandar believes they will be tortured for the Dree's satiation, once the hive mind has come into its own."

"The hive mind has not yet coalesced?" Baro asked the historian.

"Not judging by the way they went after Kosmir on the Monument," Bandar said. "I suspect there may need to be a critical mass, a minimum number of living Dree brains that must intermesh before the hive rises above instinctive behavior and becomes conscious."

"I think that's right," Gebbling said. "At the 'inculcation,' I could feel the Dree archetype trying to merge with the new-made ones, but they kept reacting instinctively to the screaming and running. Finally it had the Rovers subdue them with shockers."

He had more to say but at that moment the door at the top

of the stairs opened and a pair of Rovers began to descend the steps.

"They have not brought back the woman they took," Haj said. "She must have passed the testing and is either now toiling in the truffle beds or on her way to a new life as a Dree."

"How is the testing done?" Baro said.

"They bring you to the gravitational anomaly and into the presence of the Dree," said Gebbling. "In seconds it ransacks your being and makes its decision."

"I will fight it," said Baro.

"You cannot fight what is not there," said Gebbling.

Baro was framing his next question when the Rovers came for him. Their thick nailed fingers seized his arms and he was hauled to his feet.

"Wait!" he cried, but they did not.

———◆———

Dusk had fallen on the Swept, coloring the western sky with bands of vermilion, lemon, and magenta and the east with deep indigo. The guards took Baro toward the Fundament mine head, a tall structure of winches and girders above a huddle of rudimentary buildings that housed the mine's offices and maintenance facilities. Cold air welled up from the main shaft and Baro expected to be taken to an elevator and down into the chill darkness. Instead he was marched toward a small building set on a foundation of used mine timbers. Yellow light spilled from small windows on either side of the door.

One of the guards pulled open the portal and the other thrust Baro inside. He stumbled on the threshold but managed to maintain his balance and therefore his dignity as he came face-to-face again with Ardmander Arboghast. The section chief sat behind a battered desk reading from a sheaf of documents. The fact that he wore his Bureau green and black sparked a surge of outrage in Baro Harkless.

Arboghast continued to examine the papers and did not look up. Baro was reminded of the last time they had met, when he had stood rigid, eyes fixed on a point in the air above his superior's head, his mind a whirl of mingled fear and hope. That Baro was now long gone, that innocent fool who thought the world was drawn in smooth lines and clean-sawn edges. Now he knew it was all rough and jagged surfaces, a marketplace for half-truths and comforting lies where betrayal was the common currency.

Arboghast looked up and a smile spread across his meaty face. "Well," he said, "isn't it pleasant, meeting like this?"

Baro felt contempt for the man, but no fear of what he would do. What he wanted most was to strike back, to puncture his grinning pomposity. *The Hero is rising in me again,* he thought, a surmise that was confirmed when he heard the words that came out of his mouth. "You won't get away with it," he said.

"Yes, I will," said Arboghast.

"You forget that the Archon himself selected me for this assignment. Questions will be asked."

Arboghast's smile grew wider though his eyes showed a cold glint. "You're as vain as your father was," he said and his chuckle sounded to Baro like the satisfied grunt a fand might make biting into the warm flesh of living prey.

"The Archon has never heard of you. *I* chose you for this assignment, just as I pulled levers to get you assigned to Investigations for your probationary period when old Hamel would have sent you straight to the Research Branch, where you so clearly belonged."

The news came as a shock to Baro. "Why?" he said. "What am I to you?"

"The next best thing to your father," said Arboghast, "though a poor second, it must be admitted." He sighed. "How I would enjoy having him here today, to rub that proud nose in his complete failure, to tuck him into his niche and watch him first be torn down to a mindless husk, then rebuilt as a Dree."

Arboghast's eyes unfocused as he gazed into memories. "Unfortunately, he became aware that I had been acquiring certain knickknacks in the course of my duties."

"Bribes?" said Baro

"You have his voice exactly," Arboghast said. "He told me if I did not report myself to the Provost he would do so."

He smiled again. "But the high and mighty Captain Harkless didn't reckon on the third alternative—a few adjustments to the controls of his aircar and the melody of Ardmander Arboghast's life resumed its tranquil lilt."

"You killed my father," Baro said. A voice in the back of his head—a child's voice—added, *He did it, not me.*

"Yes, I did," said Arboghast. He rubbed the groove beneath his nose with an index finger and looked up at Baro. "And now I'm going to kill you. At least, I think so. It's a debatable point, is it not: where does the essential part of a human being go when the body that houses it is converted cell by cell into a Dree?"

Baro let the Hero take him. He launched himself across the desk, hands positioned as the Academy trainers had instructed, aiming for the trigger points in Arboghast's neck that would render the traitor helpless. But the older man had had the same training and was expecting the attack. He threw himself backward, simultaneously chopping down on Baro's wrists, sending bolts of pain up Baro's arms. Then he struck with a heavy fist at the spot where Baro's jaw was hinged, snapping the young man's head around and leaving him sprawled on the desk, half dazed.

The next thing Baro knew, his wrists were restrained and the Rovers had him by the arms. He was frogmarched out of the mine office and toward the pitch-black of the mine shaft. Arboghast strode jauntily ahead to lead the way.

The elevator's cage carried them down into darkness and cold. They dropped so fast that the chill upwell of air became a steady wind and the glaring lumens at the mine head were soon pinpoints of brightness as distant as the stars. As they sank the only light in the elevator was a dim glow from the control panel. It turned the creases in Arboghast's face into a mask of self-indulgent cruelty. The two Rovers stood impassively, but their grips on Baro's arms never weakened.

He looked down and saw through the mesh floor a small, illuminated square that gradually grew larger. It took a few moments for Baro to realize that he was looking at the base of the shaft, so far down beneath the surface that even their rapid descent still ate up minute after minute. Finally, the glow reached up to envelop them and the cage slowed and thudded against cushioning bumpers.

Three tunnels led away from the shaft, each higher than a man and illuminated at long intervals by lumens attached to the rock walls. A stubby vehicle with small tires was parked near one tunnel's mouth and Arboghast climbed into the seat behind its controls while the Rovers manhandled Baro into the cargo hopper. The engine hummed to life and they set off down the passageway. Behind them the elevator rose back into the darkness.

"Thinking about an escape?" Arboghast said after a moment. "You'd have a long walk and an even longer climb."

In fact, Baro had not been thinking of anything. His mind had become an empty echo chamber, surrounded by the red rage of the Hero. He was still slightly dazed from Arboghast's heavy punch, but more powerful was the traitor's casually delivered revelation that he had killed Captain Baro Harkless.

It ought to have been a relief to young Baro, final proof that his father's death was none of his doing. Instead the news had thrust him back into the helplessness of childhood. A part of his mind worked it out for him: his father had been the strongest force in his life, the irresistible force in the circumscribed universe of his boyhood; Ardmander Arboghast had overthrown and destroyed that power; therefore Arboghast must be invincible. Inside his head, Baro was a child sitting in a lonely room. No one would ever come for him and he would always lack the strength to set himself free.

The tunnel ended in a wide, low-ceilinged space held up by thick pillars of native rock left in place when the chamber had been hollowed out. Around its perimeter scores of round holes had been bored into the wet stone of the outer wall, each cavity wide and deep enough to hold a recumbent human being.

Directly across from the tunnel that brought Baro into the open space he saw a crew of human workers, miners by the look of their clothing, lifting something wrapped in a glistening shroud into a niche that was waist high from the floor. The bundle twitched and tried to bend, but the workers shoved it into the dark space. As the vehicle carried Baro toward the scene he saw one of the miners produce a long, flexible tube and lean down to the mouth of the cavity. The shrouded figure in the niche again tried to resist but the worker proceeded with practiced efficiency and by the time Baro's vehicle arrived the hose was in place and its other end was being attached to a pipe that ran along the ceiling.

"Dinnertime," said Arboghast. He turned and gave Baro a leering wink. "Don't worry, there's plenty for you."

The workers had lifted another wrapped form from a line of them laid at the base of the wall. Baro saw that they were passengers and crew from the landship, wrapped in a translucent material that bound their limbs to their bodies.

"Insulation," said Arboghast. "They need to be kept warm while the transformation proceeds. And it's best to restrain the young Dree until they are inculcated into the hive mind. Of course, the untransformed feedstock also requires a little constraint."

He approached the workers and spoke to them. "Wrap this one and situate him next."

The workers dropped their next victim and turned their dull eyes toward Baro. With skilled efficiency they swathed him in the insulating fabric until he was tightly cocooned from his feet to the top of his head. When the stuff covered his nose and mouth, Baro felt the panic of imminent suffocation until one of the workers slashed holes to let him breathe. But his eyes remained covered and he could see nothing but a filmy blur of light as they upended him and slid him on his back into a niche at floor level.

"Well, that wraps things up nicely," he heard Arboghast say with a chuckle that became almost a giggle.

Hard fingers dug into Baro's cheeks and his mouth was forced open. An acrid taste accompanied the scrape of a tube across his tongue. He gagged when it touched the back of his throat but in a moment the reflex was past and he felt the chill of the pipe sliding down his esophagus. Moments later the tube pulsed and more coldness passed into him.

"Liquefied truffles," came Arboghast's voice from above. "It won't be long before you meet your new self. I'll have them keep an eye on you. I want to be here for your unwrapping. I may keep your skin for a souvenir."

Baro heard his footsteps moving off, then the sound of the vehicle rolling away. The tube gave another pulse and pushed more of the liquid alien nutrients into him. The diffuse light visible through his wrappings darkened as the workers placed another swaddled form in the niche above him and connected the victim's feeding tube, then the light came back as the crew moved along the wall. He heard the rustle and crackle of the next victim's wrappings and a strangled moan of protest that was cut off as the tube went in.

Soon the workers had placed all of the wrapped prisoners who had been lined against the wall when Baro was brought down to the crèche. He heard a vehicle start up and move away and guessed that they had gone for another batch. The hum of the engine faded in the distance. The chamber became silent. Baro heard nothing but the sound of his own blood pounding in his ears and the suffle of his own breathing.

His detachment lingered. The Hero urged him to struggle against the tightness that bound him, scream around the blockage in his mouth, make an effort—any effort—to free himself. But Baro was now ruled by a coolly analytical facet of his composite self that heard the advice yet felt no inclination to follow it. *The Wise Man,* he thought, and understood that that archetype had always been strong in him. *Well, I hope you've got more ideas than I do.*

I may, said a voice within him.

Well? said Baro, but nothing more came.

He found that he was surprised that Arboghast had gone off and left him. In the stories he had read as a youth, villains always loved to gloat over captured heroes, teasing them with detailed descriptions of their cunning plans. Often, these interludes afforded the paladin an opportunity to catch the malefactor out and effect a last-minute turn of the tables, or at least to make a daring escape.

But Arboghast had not bothered to explain himself. He had simply taken time out of his activities to see that Baro was tucked securely away and left to be transmogrified into a Dree.

Perhaps he did not confide in me because he does not consider me a worthy opponent, his analytical function commented. *Perhaps I am just a loose end to be tucked in.*

It was not a cheering thought. He did not welcome death, but to go out as a hero was preferable to dying as an afterthought.

The tube sent another pulse of alienness into his body and as the sensation faded Baro felt a tickle in his mind—*No, not a tickle,* he thought, *more like a twitch of something hard and dry, like a sharp seed stuck in the soft tissues at the back of the mouth.*

It moved again, a little stronger, and he felt a tingling in his lips and fingertips, the onset of the lassitude. But now he knew what the sensations portended. *It is the Dree,* he thought. *It is quieting me, stilling me, before it begins the change.*

With the thought came understanding, bursting into his consciousness in a detailed image. He didn't need Arboghast to explain it to him. The answers were all there, slipped into his mind by the Wise Man.

The Dree had indeed been expunged, crushed into slime by the gravitational aggregator that had collapsed their tunnels and burrows. But there had been a side effect. Bandar was right: the gravity weapon had somehow captured the Dree's version of a Commons and thrust it down into the core of the planet, from which it had eventually begun a eons-long return to the surface, trapped in a slow-rising cyst.

As the Dree archetypical entity neared the surface it reflexively reached out for compatible minds. First it sought for those it could enslave. The Rovers with their pack instincts were easiest; once they were mentally seized and harnessed they carried on as if programmed. Armed with weapons shipped in on the *Orgulon,* they overthrew the mayor and police of Victor and herded the inhabitants into the mines where they were brought to the entity for testing.

As a posthumous dishonoring of his old enemy, Arboghast had arranged for the son of Captain Baro Harkless to be one of the first to be converted or destroyed. He would have chuckled as he worked his schemes, picturing the young fool prancing toward his undoing while dreaming of medals and honors from the Archon.

Now the first generation of new Dree were already walking Old Earth, or at least the tunnels beneath its surface. As more and more Dree were created, the entity would have actual Dree brains in which to install itself, ultimately tying together enough feral Dree to create a hive consciousness. When that happened, the reborn Dree would have the benefit of knowing what had happened in the first invasion, a knowledge that was forgotten by all but a few eccentrics like Guth Bandar. The Dree would organize and spread surreptitiously, establishing nests beneath major cities, enslaving some and converting others, while making hideous bargains with the likes of Ardmander Arboghast.

At some point, the Dree would emerge in overwhelming numbers to cow and rule a defenseless populace whose police force would have already been infiltrated and disarmed. There were very few military establishments in Old Earth's penultimate age, and no stores of heavy weaponry such as had contained and crushed the first Dree incursion.

They will use us for their cruel pleasures, Baro thought. *The Arboghasts will be the overseers, delivering fresh victims to the crèches and the torture arenas.*

Again, Baro felt his consciousness to be divided. One piece of him was horrified by the vision that the cool intellectual facet had splashed across the inner screen of his awareness. He remembered Imbry, left to die on the Monument, and felt a pang of guilt.

Why are you doing this to me? he said, to himself and to the other that he sensed had come into his mind. There was no response.

I know you are there, he said. *All of this* thinking, *this* analyzing *of the Dree and the Rovers and the plans, that is yours, not mine. Why do you throw it at me now, when I am bound and helpless, waiting to be devoured?*

What must be done must be done, came the answer in the dry, cool tone of the Wise Man.

What can I do? said Baro. He attempted to wriggle against his wrappings and found that his limbs would not respond, though he did not know whether that was the work of the Dree entity, disconnecting his brain from his body, or just the effect on nerve and muscle of being tightly bound.

You can do what you can do.

If he could have thrown his hands into the air and pulled at his hair in frustration, Baro would have done so. He had to be content with a silent, inner scream. Then the answer came: the Wise Man was not a person who could be queried or engaged in direct debate. It could only come to him as a component of his own psyche that could not function on its own. If he isolated it and probed it with direct questions, its only responses would be vague pronouncements; if he allowed it to think *with* him, to use his brain as an instrument, he would know what it wanted him to know.

Go ahead, he told it. *Show me.*

An image appeared in his mind: Yaffak the Rover, curled up asleep beneath his cart somewhere out on the Swept. Next came a memory of Yaffak in the Rover Commons, bound by the invisible harness. Then Baro saw himself step forward and sever the tie that went off into nowhere.

Of course, he said. *The Rovers can be freed. They are the weak point. Turn them on Arboghast and the Dree and the invasion dies in the egg.*

Now he saw another image: the room under the eaves, the old desk, the worn Agrajani rug, and the wardrobe. Then the path down to the green waters. *I must go back.*

He tried his voice. Even with the tube in his mouth and the rigor affecting his lips and tongue, he could still sound the tones that Guth Bandar had taught him. He sang the sequence that brought the door into being, rimmed with golden light. As he reached for the handle, the song brought a flash of another memory—he was a little boy on his father's knee and they were singing the song about the old man and giving a dog a bone—then he pulled the door open and stepped into the brilliance.

The light faded and he was in his boyhood room crossing to the wardrobe and seeing the mirror at its back with its lurker. His Shadow sneered, then put both hands to its throat in a throttling gesture, letting its tongue protrude and eyes roll. Baro ignored it, stepping through the image and emerging on the steep path. Moments later, he plunged into the dark tarn and swam into its light-filled depths.

He stood on the white road between the gray stone walls. From the edge of his vision he saw motes of light flickering and evanescing all around him, dreamers passing into and out of the noösphere. *Do the Dree dream?* he wondered. *If they absorb us all will they inherit this, to wander about and poke through our collective past? Or will all that was once ours fall into darkness when Old Earth's last human psyche is swallowed?*

It was a sad thought. Although only a handful of adepts

still bothered to master the tones and continued to visit the Commons, it was one of the enduring creations of humankind's long sojourn on the planet. It should not be lost.

We will win this, he told himself. *It must be done.*

He felt a welling tide of confidence and recognized the Hero filling him. He looked down at himself and saw the familiar chain mail and rough cloth, and felt the sword heavy in his hand. But though he felt ready to take action, he lacked a direction in which to move. The last time he had come to the noösphere, he had been led to the wall by the Hero, but now the barbarian was nowhere to be seen. He guessed that the entity could not simultaneously be present in its pure form while it was at work within him.

He wished that Guth Bandar was with him. He did not know enough to be on the loose in the Commons. He remembered the historian's warning, that once off the road he could easily step into an unseen hole that would deposit him in some Location where he would be impressed into the action and never be able to win free.

I need Bandar, he thought. *The Hero always needs the Helper.*

He looked at the winks and twinkles of light in the air around him, wondering if the little man might be one of them, dreaming his way into the Commons. As soon as he posed the question the answer came. He vaulted over the wall and crossed the field to the trees. He remembered the way—or perhaps he was led—to the spot where he and Bandar had passed into the hemming of the Dree. He sang the twelve notes and the vertical ripple appeared before him; he sang the next twelve as he stepped through and emerged onto the slope that overlooked the farmhouse.

Above the sound of his own voice, he heard again a chittering noise and knew it for what it was: the rubbing together of chitinous Dree limbs as they crouched in a tunnel mouth and directed an energy weapon toward the armored vehicles rumbling toward them across the flats.

Baro went down the slope and out onto the plain. He knew, without knowing how he knew, where the historian would be and soon found him crouched in the bottom of the trench, poking at the dead Dree while droning the thran that kept him invisible from the entities that populated the Event.

The young man knelt by the edge of the trench and touched Bandar's shoulder with the flat of his sword. The little man leaped up with a shriek, spun around, then tripped over a corpse. Baro raised his voice, chanting the thran louder to cover both of them.

"What are you doing here?" Bandar asked, then had to take over the chant while Baro replied.

"I've come for you."

They switched roles again so that Bandar could say, "It's too late. I am wrapped and deposited in a crèche with a tube in my belly and a Dree tickling my brain's innards. The woman security officer is in the same plight."

"Yet here you are poking at a dead Dree."

"I hoped there would be something I could use, some knowledge that would let me fight and survive." Bandar sighed. "But there is nothing."

Baro was finding it difficult to carry on a conversation while trading the thran back and forth. "Is there somewhere we could go to talk?" he said. "I have an idea."

Bandar produced his globe and traced a path. "Come," he said, taking Baro's arm and chanting eight descending tones. A fissure appeared and they stepped through it into a howl of wind and horizontal, face-tearing sleet. Baro was yanked to the left, heard another sequence of tones, and emerged into an emptiness of rock and sand that stretched in all directions.

A pile of wind-scoured bones lay at his feet. The sun was a yellow-white glare high above, brighter than the young man had ever seen. Baro felt the dry heat seize him like a hot fist.

"We need no thran here," said the noönaut. "It is the Desert."

Baro heard him emphasize the capitalization of the word. "No one will murder or enslave us?" he said.

Bandar said, "It is uninhabited. That is what desert means." He wiped his sweating brow. "Although we are here, so it is temporarily peopled by us, but if we stayed this heat and aridity would soon kill us and then it would be uninhabited again. But for a few minutes it is a place where we can talk without the insulation of a thran. You said you had an idea?"

Baro told him about the Wise Man and the proposal to free the Rovers before the Dree mind could consolidate.

Bandar sat on the ground and picked at the pile of bones. He lifted one and it fell away to dust. "It does not seem practical to me," he said. "Yaffak was far out of reach of the Dree entity, and thus when he was freed he could not easily be reshackled. The entity is in its cyst in a tunnel below Victor and Rovertown. Why can it not easily reestablish control over any Rover that we free?"

"I had hoped you would be more encouraging," Baro said. The Hero's garb he wore was intended for a colder climate. Sweat was running down his back and chest and his scalp itched under the winged helmet.

"You are under the influence of the Hero," Bandar said. "It tends to make you see me as the Helper. Whereas, to myself, I am still just me."

Baro felt a rush of irritation. *Why can't the man be more helpful?* Then a cooler current passed through his mind. "I am also under the influence of the Wise Man," he said. "And he believes we can do it."

"It does not do to listen to one or two archetypes," Bandar said. "They are *always* sure of themselves, even when they are rushing pell-mell to destruction. The sensible man consults a wide range of influences and draws a consensus."

"The sensible man does not allow himself to be trussed from head to toe and popped into a niche to await transmogrification into a mindless Dree."

"True," Bandar said, "but what is your point?"

"Even if what the Hero and the Wise Man counsel us to is useless," Baro said, "it is at least action. And if there is merely the tiniest chance of success, that is still better odds than we are offered by the Dree."

Bandar looked off into the haze of the distance. "My plans were different. If my examination of the hemming of the Dree produced no useful prospects I thought I would visit a few of my favorite Locations before I cease to exist. Some of the Heavens are quite wonderful. You're welcome to accompany me. We might decide to cease chanting and be impressed into one of them. At least that would mean going out on our own terms, not the Dree's."

Baro was almost tempted, but the Hero was not. "If I must die," he said, "I would prefer to fall while striving to defeat the enemy."

"I fear it is a lost cause," Bandar said.

"Those are the best ones."

"Spoken like a Hero," said the historian. "A full-bore, muscle-headed, sword-swinging, bound-for-glory, once-more-unto-the-breach, soon-to-be-chopped-into-pieces Hero."

"You are not convinced," Baro said.

"I am not," said Bandar. "Would you care to loose the Wise Man on me?"

Baro felt a shifting inside him. "There is one reason you will help," he said.

"And what is that?"

"This," said Baro and gestured to the waste around them.

"The Desert?" said Bandar.

"The Commons."

Bandar said nothing. He wiped sweat from his brow to his chin and as his hand descended it was as if it painted a new expression over the skepticism that had been there. The small man's face became a mask of regret.

Baro knew that the archetype was speaking through him as he said, "Even if there is but the smallest chance of preserving the noösphere, of saving this great construct to which you have devoted your life, will you not forgo Heaven and try?"

Bandar heaved a long sigh. "Damn you," he said, then he stood up and summoned the globular map of the Commons into existence. "At least I will lead you to the Wall."

———◆———

How do I know that the Rover Commons waits on the other side?" Baro said.

"I suppose you don't," said Bandar. "I was not here when you crossed before, and part of me still does not want to believe it ever happened."

But they found the place where Baro had swum beneath the Wall. A faint, pale scratch in the ground showed where the sword had cut a way to the Old Sea. Baro thought about the Worm, its great circle of a mouth ringed with serrated teeth. He shuddered.

"Could you find a cord to tie around my ankle? Then you could pull me back faster than I could swim."

"There is no cord here."

"Then fetch one from somewhere else."

"There is a rule against moving objects from one Location to another," the historian said.

Baro felt the Wise Man stir in him. "That is to protect the integrity of Locations," he said. "How better to protect their integrity than by preventing them from being forever obliterated?"

Bandar conceded the argument but said, "I am not sure that anything from here can survive down there. It might just dissolve."

This time, the Hero dominated. "Can you find a rope or not?"

The small man said, "Wait," and consulted his globe. He sang a short thran, turned to his left, and disappeared. Almost instantly he was back, a coil of thin rope over his shoulder. "From an ancient sea battle," he said, handing it to Baro. "I took it from the deck of a sinking galley. I doubt it will be missed."

Baro knelt and tied it around his ankle. He stood and set the sword point into the ground at the end of the old scar and pressed down. Again, the ground resisted like flesh, then yielded to the sword's thrust. He sliced along the line and beyond, almost to the Wall itself.

"This may take longer," he told Bandar, "so I've made a bigger cut. Will you try to prevent it from healing over?"

"I will try."

"Then here we go." Baro dove into the slit and again felt the nothingness of the Old Sea close around him. He did not bother to kick or flail this time, but oriented himself along the axis of the incision in the human Commons and willed himself up and forward. His extended sword point met the ceiling and broke through. He widened the hole and pulled himself once more into the Rover Commons.

He recognized the colorless place with the thorn hedge and

its amazing richness of odor. But this time there was no strong scent trail to lead him to where he needed to go. *I am not in a dreamscape,* he reasoned. *This is the Commons itself. To free a Rover I must find one dreaming and enter the dream.*

He untied the cord from his ankle and pulled a few lengths of it through the slit in the ground, then hung the coil on the thorns to guide him back to the exit. He looked about him, but there were no glints and twinks of light at the edge of his vision. *Why do I see no dreamers?* he wondered and even as he posed the question the answer came: because in this place seeing was a minor sense.

Baro flared his nostrils, cast his head from side to side, and in a moment he found what he was seeking. He followed the scent, deduced its direction, then sped forward to get in front of it. The odor burst upon him full strength then, the musky, sharp scent of a young female Rover, and with no sense of transition he was in her dream.

They were in a dark forest and she was struggling to free her forelimbs from a noose that descended from a canopy of wet black limbs and dripping, leathery leaves. Her teeth made no mark on the rope but she had gashed her own flesh. Blood dripped onto the dank and rotting carpet that was the forest floor.

Baro stepped forward, and her eyes swung toward him in fresh terror. "I am the Good Man," he said. "When I cut the cord, you must wake and run far."

She said something he could not understand—it might not even have been words—and he moved closer and swung the sword. It sliced through the tether and the noose dropped away. The Rover regarded her freed hands with wonder, then a shudder went through her and she dropped to all fours and ran.

Baro watched her go and saw that she followed a trail that led out of the darkness under the trees and toward a meadow bathed in sunlight. She was almost clear of the forest, the light glinting on her raised ruff when a looped cord snaked down from above and snugged itself about her neck. She was yanked to her hind feet and hung there, dangling and dancing almost on her toes, as the rope was cruelly jerked and tugged. Beyond her, the bright meadow was occluded by shadow, as if a curtain of rain had swept across it.

Baro ran to her and cut with the sword again but this time the tether was of thick, braided rawhide. The weapon's edge had sliced only halfway through the rope and even as he drew it back for a second cut he saw that the severed ends of the thongs moved like blind snakes, reweaving themselves and thickening.

A noise came from above, a clicking, scraping sound as of sticks rubbing against dried leather. Baro looked up into a rain of droplets shaken loose from the high branches and saw a shape moving in the darkness. A chitinous claw slid out of the leaves and down the rope, then the Dree's blind head followed, its feathery tendrils turning this way and that.

Baro set himself and took a two-handed grip on the sword, but the wise one's voice within him spoke. *It is the Dree archetype and in the Rover Commons it is all-powerful. We cannot fight it here. Lead it back beyond the Wall where our strength lies.*

He felt a struggle inside him as the two archetypes contended, then the Hero gave way and Baro backed down the trail to where he had entered the Rover's dream. The Dree continued its measured descent down the braided rope. When it reached the strangling female it climbed down her as if she were inanimate. Baro felt a shiver of revulsion at the thing's bland disregard of its captive's suffering. It was like watching a spider methodically wrap its struggling prey.

He backed farther down the trail. He knew when he reached

the spot where he had cut the first cord because he saw the sev- ered loop lying on the leaf mold. Even as he looked at it, the length of rope faded and disappeared, then the black mulch of leaves and twigs beneath it lost its darkness, becoming pale and wan.

He looked up and saw the Dree advancing stolidly toward him, its long, jointed digits opening and closing, its tendrils curling and uncurling at him, pulling his scent from the air. It moved in an unnatural way, its legs and torso bending and flexing at angles that were *wrong,* its smooth, ovoid head bob- bing on a segmented neck.

Around and behind it the forest and the struggling Rover faded and disappeared. Baro found himself back on the scent track where he had encountered the dreaming victim, and there was the blackthorn hedge, not far.

The Dree clicked and chittered at him, and now he caught its scent—acrid and sharp, prickling and tearing at his nostrils the way a shriek would pain his ears. Clear of the trees, he saw that the entity was larger than the new-made specimens he had seen on the Monument, its limbs thickly ridged and spiked with chitin, its claws like wedges that tapered to needlepoints when the digits clicked together.

It came faster now. Walking backward, Baro could not keep ahead of it. Though the Hero in him hated to do it, he turned and ran for the hedge, to the pale circle of coiled rope that marked the way back to his own noösphere. He heard it come after him, its hoof-hard feet clacking the ground, its bit- ter stench running before it.

It will always pursue fleeing prey, said the Wise Man.

The slit in the ground was smaller but it was still wide enough. He dove into it, grasped the rope that led back to Ban- dar and the human noösphere, and willed himself along it.

He looked out into the gray abyss of the Old Sea and caught the same distant motion he had seen before, the great Worm undulating toward him.

Again, he felt his energy fading, the emptiness of the uto-posphere leaching consciousness from him. That was death, he knew, because in this no-place Baro Harkless had no flesh, no blood, no bone. Consciousness was all that he was and if it went, he would be gone with it.

He looked back the way he had come. The Dree had not hesitated. It had plunged into the gray void after him and was now pulling itself along the rope the way it had descended the tether that strangled the dreaming Rover.

Baro felt a tug on the rope from the other direction. Bandar was pulling him toward the rent that led back into the human Commons. Baro willed himself to help his helper, and this time the trip back was much shorter, the Worm still a small and distant movement when he emerged from the Old Sea and stood again on the red fleshlike soil beside the Wall. He left the rope descending into the rip in the ground, positioning himself to strike with the sword when the Dree's head came up.

"Stand back," he told the historian. "It is coming after me. I do not know if I can kill it, but if I can keep it from emerging from the hole the Worm will take it. I do not think it can overcome the Worm."

"I would have said surely not," said Bandar, backing away from the tear in the ground. "But I would have said the same about your having traversed the Old Sea and survived, and here you have done it twice."

"Pull on the rope," Baro said. "Bring it to me." He took the sword in a two-handed grip and raised it over his head.

Bandar pulled and a length of the rope came out of the hole. "Again," Baro said. The sword's weight above his head became as nothing and he knew the Hero's strength was flowing through him.

Bandar pulled, and pulled once more. More rope slid through the tear, but the Dree did not appear. Bandar yanked hard and the end of the rope emerged from the void.

"What do you see?" the historian asked.

Baro looked into the shrinking rent at his feet. "Nothing. It seems the Worm took it."

"Then we are saved," Bandar sighed. "At this moment, the Rovers will be turning on Arboghast. I will not be surprised if they kill him." He blinked and his face opened in a smile like that of a man who, lost in perilous surroundings, suddenly discovers a safe way home. He brought out the globe and said, "Come, I will take us from here. Let us visit the Heavens until they come to pull us from our niches and unwrap us."

The hole into the Old Sea was almost completely healed. He turned and went to join the historian. Bandar opened his mouth to sing a thran, but from his lips emerged not a song but a gasp of pain and fright.

The Dree came out of the ground, through a rent it had torn in the base of the noösphere, setting its hooked limbs into Bandar and climbing him as it had descended the female Rover. When its rear limbs were clear of the rent it stood erect, the small man clutched in its forelimbs like a doll. Then its head rotated toward Baro and it threw the noönaut aside. Bandar struck the great Wall and lay inert, blinking and stunned. The globe fell to the ground and rolled away.

The Dree's sightless head turned toward the motion. It opened one claw into digits and scooped up the globe, brought the sphere up to where its face would have been. The tendrils atop its head flexed and a mat of tiny bristles appeared where a mouth might have been. Eyeless, it examined the map of the human Commons and Baro would have sworn it smiled.

"No!" he said and swept the sword in a sidewise arc that struck the globe from the thing's grasp and sent it bouncing toward the Wall. The Dree made a sound like fire crackling through dry twigs and thrust a limb toward him, the digits cohering to create a spike.

Baro felt the Hero guide his hand as he parried with the sword, but the shock of iron against Dree armor sent a chill up his arm. He saw that the claw was not even scratched.

Baro transferred his weight to his back foot. He extended the sword, then lunged at the creature's head. The Dree knocked the thrust aside with ease. Again it made a sound and Baro did not need to know Dree speech to recognize its contempt.

"How am I to defeat this?" he asked the forces within him. "You said we would be stronger here."

The answer came, not in words but in awareness. He saw the shape of things, not just the here and now of this collective realm where neither word had true meaning, but in an instant of epiphany he knew the flow of his entire life, every moment, every choice he had made since the day his father had walked down the garden path and through the gate. It had all been meant to lead to what he had to do.

"You fooled me," he said.

We did as we had to do, came the answer. *We chose you. We guided you, all of your life.*

It was not the voice of the Wise Man. It was somehow deeper, richer in understanding. Again, awareness came: it was all of the human noösphere, all of the collective Commons of Old Earth, all the archetypes and entities, speaking within him as one entity, making itself known to him.

"I am not the Hero," Baro said. "I am only the Fool. Why have you led me here to be destroyed?"

You are the Fool, the voice said, *but you are also the Hero.*

You are the Wise One, the Father and the Mother. You are all of us, if you will let yourself be.

The Dree considered the map where it lay against the Wall. Then its faceless head turned back toward him. He saw that it was larger now than when he had faced it in the dream forest.

"It is growing," he said.

The brains of the first new Dree are beginning to mesh with the entity. Soon there will be enough of them.

The thing made up its mind. It advanced on him, digits clicking into claws.

"It will kill me," Baro said.

It will do what it will do. You will do what you will do.

He looked at the sword in his hand. "This is useless."

It is not useless if you use it.

"I do not understand."

Look.

Baro looked again at the flow of his life, saw the strange, broken boy he had been, saw how he had narrowed himself, driven himself, shaped himself to a single end. To the Commons, every life was a story. Now Baro saw his story laid out before him. It was not a story about a boy and his father, nor about an agent mismatched with his partner, nor about a man beguiled by a woman's eyes.

The Dree was close. It jabbed a claw at him. Again he parried and again a shock ran up his arm. His hand went numb and he almost dropped the sword.

"I cannot kill it."

It is not about killing.

He saw now. "Yet it is about dying. But can that thing die?"

It is not about living or dying. It is about choosing. The choice is yours, has always been yours.

"It is about sacrifice," he said.

Yes, said the voice.

He accepted. "So I am the Hero, after all," he said.

Say that for this purpose the Hero is first among equals.

"Look after Bandar," he said. "He did not ask to be the Helper."

We will.

"And what about Luff Imbry?"

No time.

The Dree came on. Baro lowered the sword. The needle-tipped claw thrust at him and he stepped to meet it. It entered his side and sliced upward to where his heart would have been if he had been flesh and blood.

The Dree's spiked limb was like glowing ice inside him. He felt a chill radiate from it that was perversely like heat from molten metal. It brought weakness and a sudden flood of despair.

I have failed, he thought.

The noösphere's voice spoke within him. *No,* it said, *you can do it.* But now the voice was different, familiar though he had not heard it in so many years. A face appeared in his mind, his father's, wearing that expression he knew from his childhood, the one that said, *Get in there. I have faith in you, my son.*

The Dree's coldness was spreading through him. He understood that it was willing despair upon him, seeking to steal the last of his strength.

"No!" Baro said. Still impaled on its claw, he clamped an arm around the creature's segmented neck and embraced it. He drew it toward him, lifting his feet from the ground and letting his weight pull them down and forward.

He knew now what the sword was for. He struck with it at the red earth of the Commons, once, twice, three times, tearing open a gash that was as long as he was tall.

The tendrils on the Dree's head jerked and twitched. It tried to rear up and now Baro smelled the thing's fear like a sweet odor of corruption.

He yanked down on its neck, at the same time sweeping the sword against the lower joints of its legs, where they were thinnest. The Dree made a noise like steam escaping from a kettle and the reek of putrefaction became a cloying stench.

Baro slashed again and felt the iron bite. The Dree tried to spin, but the wounded limb gave way beneath it and together man and invader toppled into the Old Sea.

The Worm was waiting, not far below, its open mouth like a dark planet. They fell toward it. The Dree spasmed, then yanked its claw out of Baro's chest. It kicked away from him, struggling to reach for the rip in the face of the gray waters.

Baro grasped after its legs, let their spikes pierce the palms of his hands, closed his fingers about its armored skin, and pulled it, willed it, down.

The immensity of the Worm rose and took them. Baro saw its teeth pass him, then become a circle above him, framing the gray light as he sank into the blackness at its heart. He saw the great wedge-shaped fangs close upon the Dree entity and snap it like a child's cracker. Then the Worm opened its maw again and sucked the severed halves of the Dree into its darkness. Baro saw them fall past him, the pieces already dissolving.

Baro drifted slowly down toward the lightless belly of the Worm. It was silent here. Nothing moved. He saw a flicker from the corner of his eye and rotated his head to look. His memories were rippling about him like leaves on a wind-ruffled tree. He saw faces, places, moments; heard sounds and voices, was touched and embraced. There was music. He was being carried on his father's shoulders at a fair and they were singing the song about the old man and giving a dog a bone.

The darkness comforted him, swaddled him like a warm blanket, and Baro thought, *Now what?*

Something thudded into his chest. He reached out and felt a pair of small hands that immediately gripped his wrists. No sooner did they take hold than he was yanked up and through the mosaic of his own memories, out of the darkness and into the gray light that filled the Worm's gaping throat.

Guth Bandar's face bore a peculiar expression of mingled terror and determination. He showed his teeth to Baro, but the young man could not tell if he was seeing a smile or a rictus of fear. Above and beyond the noönaut the thin rope led up and out of the Worm's tooth-ringed mouth to the rent in the firmament of the Commons. Its end was knotted around Bandar's ankle.

But the Worm's mouth was closing. The circle of teeth was now a crescent growing thinner with each moment. The taut rope pulled Bandar and Bandar pulled Baro and together they scraped through the dwindling gap. Serrated triangles closed upon the heels of Baro's buskins, tearing them from his feet, then the two men were rising through the pearly luminescence of the Old Sea to be hauled through the rip above and returned to the human Commons.

The red-lipped rent closed. They lay on the non-earth of the noösphere. For a long moment Baro remained lost in the moment of stillness when he had accepted his own death. Then Bandar shook him back to awareness.

"We must leave here," the small man said. "Already the characteristic entities are returning to type."

Baro sat up and looked about him. The Hero and the Helper, the Father and the Fool, were letting fall the rope with which they had pulled the two men from the Old Sea. Their eyes turned to Bandar and Baro and the young man saw the madness of monomania in their gaze. Unbidden, he sang the thran that had insulated them on the stone bridge. The entities lost their alertness and began to drift away from the Wall.

Bandar had retrieved his map. "We will go back," he said. He chanted the thran that created an emergency gate and motioned Baro to step through.

"Wait," said Baro. "How did you enlist their help?"

"I called them and they came."

"But any one of them might have absorbed you."

"They did not come for me," Bandar said. "They came for you."

━━◆━━

MORE time had passed in the waking world than in the noö-sphere. Baro came into his body to find that it was not wrapped and hidden in a cold niche but reposing beneath clean, warm covers in Victor's infirmary. Bandar was sitting up blinking in the next bed.

In a bed on the other side of the room Luff Imbry rested against a ruck of pillows, a bowl of fruit balanced on the mound of his abdomen. His head was swathed in bandages but he was making short work of a honeyberry. He spat out a seed and said, "You're back."

"And you're alive," said Baro.

"They're both awake," said a woman's voice. Baro turned to see Raina Haj in the doorway. She stepped aside to admit a physician who wanted to poke and prod, but Baro shook him off. He sat up and looked about for his clothes.

"Where is Arboghast?" he said. His mouth was gummy and his throat raw from the feeding tube.

"Fled," said Imbry. "He had a Bureau pursuit speeder and ran for it the moment things went against him."

"The Rovers?" Bandar asked.

Haj said, "They suddenly ceased to follow his orders. Instead they began killing the aliens and freeing the captives. An investigatory team is on its way to determine what happened here."

There was a glass and a carafe of water on the table beside Baro's bed. He poured and drank, then told Haj, "I want a uniform and a weapon. I'm going after Arboghast."

"Unlikely," said Haj. "The inquiry will be particularly interested in your testimony."

"He killed my father."

Haj's face registered first surprise, then an expression that offered no accommodation. "I am sorry. Larger questions must be answered."

"I'm going after him."

"You are under orders to remain here at the inquiry's pleasure."

Baro rose from the bed, drew his simple gown around himself, and said, "I resign from the Bureau."

"Then you are under arrest as a material witness," said Haj. "Either way, you stay."

"Let the boy go," Imbry said. "You owe him that, at least."

"I will do my duty," said Haj.

"You will protect your career."

In a chest beside his bed Baro found the clothes he had been wearing when he had been captured. He dressed quickly. But when he turned to leave he saw the shocker in Raina Haj's hand. She stood before the room's only exit.

"Get out of my way."

"I will shoot."

He took a step toward her and she aimed the weapon.

"Wait," said Bandar. "I have a proposal."

——◆——

They loitered on the white road between the gray walls. Motes of light flickered and evanesced past them.

"What will you do?" said Bandar.

"Perhaps I will study with you and become a historian," said Baro. He sensed that having lived the story of his life to its completion, the Commons was a fitter place for him than the waking world.

Bandar sighed. "I have grown to like you, though you still terrify me," he said. "But you have opened up new fields for research. We might find a way."

"I would be . . ." began Baro, but now a motion caught his eye. He pointed up the road. "There," he said.

A mote of light floated toward them. Bandar put out a hand and intoned a complex thran. As he sang the last note, Ardmander Arboghast appeared, his semitransparent face all fright and bewilderment.

"Here," said Bandar, "hold him."

Baro seized the traitor's diaphanous arms and pulled them behind him. Arboghast struggled, but weakly.

"He has no strength yet," Bandar said. "But hold tight while I pull him deeper."

The prisoner grew more difficult to restrain as Bandar intoned a new thran. Now Arboghast became more substantial under Baro's grip and his efforts to resist were harder to contain. The young man shifted to the Bureau's most effective come-along hold, and the struggles were replaced by dedicated cursing.

"I have imported as much of him as can be safely drawn without killing his sleeping body," Bandar said. "Is your grip secure?"

"It is."

"Then we go."

He consulted his map, then led them a few paces down the

road. They climbed over the wall. Baro had to wrestle the swearing Arboghast over the barrier but he was far stronger here than his prisoner.

Bandar sang open a gate and they passed through. On the other side was Heaven, a place of lush green lawns dotted with flowers and copses of exquisitely blossoming trees, the air as sweet as an angel's breath.

"Come," said Bandar. He began a new thran and marched off.

Baro came after, dragging Arboghast. "We knew," he said, "that wherever you hid, you would have to sleep. And to sleep is to dream."

"Where are we?"

"Why, this is Heaven," said Baro.

"What are you going to do with me?"

At that, Baro only smiled.

They came to a downslope and followed it to where the grass ended and there was nothing but sky beyond. Baro brought Arboghast to the lip and showed him the view below.

A great granite tower rose from the earth, tier upon tier, through clouds and empty air, to end in a flat roof of flagstones not far beneath where Heaven floated. From the platform rose scaling ladders and climbing the rungs were demonic figures clad in armor of black chitin bearing hooked swords and jagged halberds. They swarmed up into Heaven, only to be met by a phalanx of angels, the air above their heads incandescent with their commingled haloes. Shields met shields, flaming swords sang and hooked spears thrust.

Bandar, intoning the thran that kept them safe from the combatants' perceptions, led them away from the battle. They reached a quieter part of the rim and Baro had Arboghast look over again.

"What are you going to do with me?" Arboghast said again.

"Throw you over," Baro answered.

"I will die!"

"No, here you cannot die. Whatever happens to you, it will not kill you. You will live on eternally."

Arboghast looked into the young man's face and clearly did not relish what he saw there.

"Please," he said.

Baro pointed with his chin. "Do you see that creature circling below," he said, "the one with the leathery wings and talons on its feet?"

"It has the head of a beast."

"Would you believe that that creature and I are engaged in a contest?"

Arboghast began to moan.

"It is a contest to see which of us hates you more." He shifted his grip.

"No! Don't!"

Baro flung the man who killed his father out of Heaven. Ardmander Arboghast fell screaming, arms flailing as if he hoped to fly.

Once beyond the ambit of Bandar's thran, he was noticed by the flying demon. It lazily flapped its wings, then flipped onto its back and caught him with its hind feet. Baro saw the dark claws sink into the flesh of its unexpected catch and the high-pitched scream told him that Bandar had brought over enough of Arboghast to make his endless sentence in Hell a true torment.

Baro watched the fiend spiral down toward the lake of fire. "And I have won," he said.